ABBY FINCH doesnt RELAX

RITA HARTE

Copyright © Rita Harte, 2023

First published 2023

Email: ritaharteauthor@gmail.com

All rights reserved. Without limiting the rights under copyright reserved above, no part of this publication may be reproduced, stored in or introduced into a database and retrieval system or transmitted in any form or any means (electronic, mechanical, photocopying, recording or otherwise) without the prior written permission of both the owner of copyright and the above publishers.

Cover by Cover Ever After

ISBN: 9798396810341

Imprint: Independently published

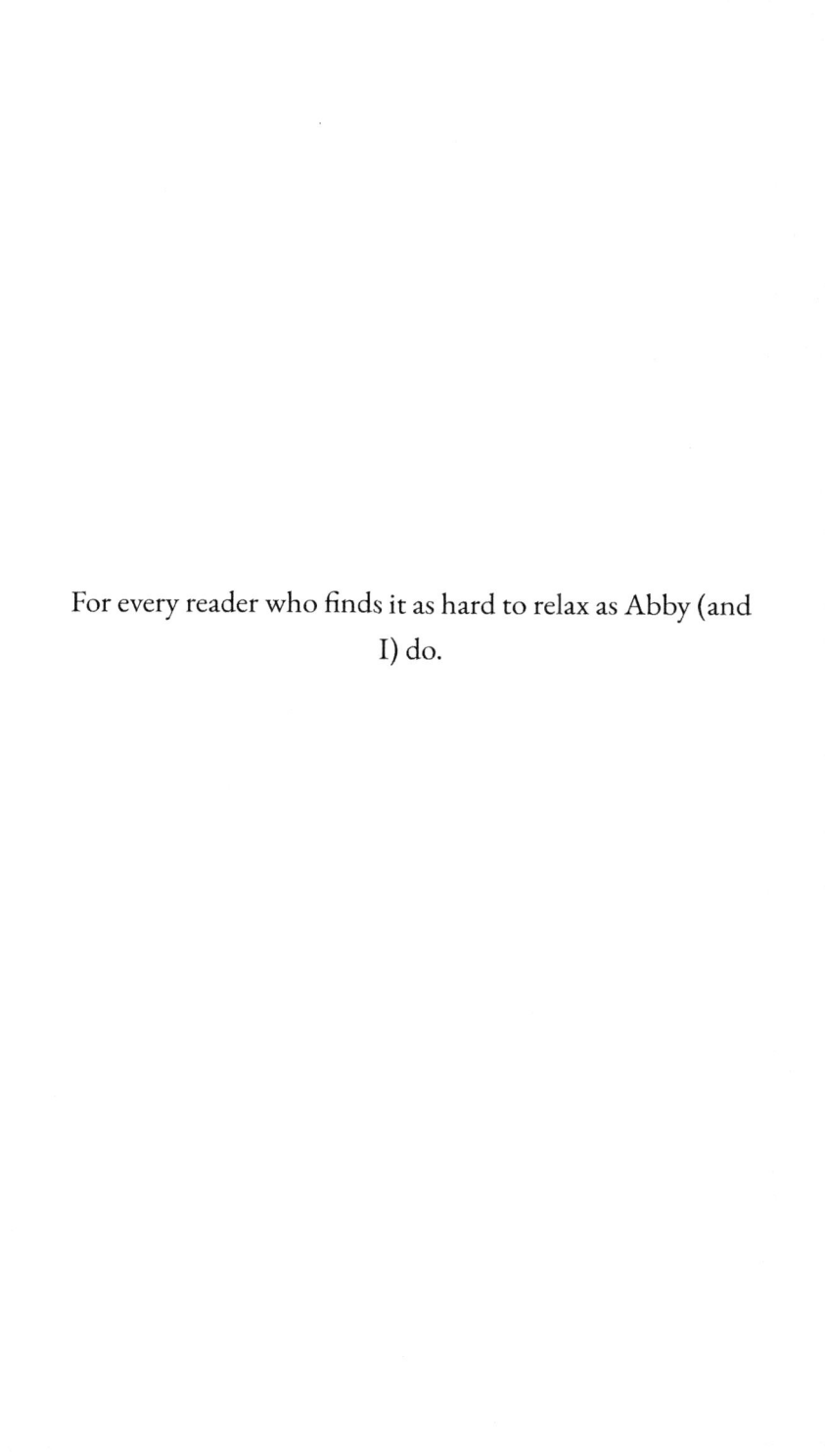

For every reader who finds it as hard to relax as Abby (and I) do.

Abby Finch Doesn't Relax

An Australian romantic comedy

Rita Harte

1 Abby

"You get a bubbles, you get a bubbles, and I get a bubbles!"

A bottle of sparkling wine in a scuffed silver ice bucket appeared before me, accompanied by three glasses.

"What's the occasion, Oprah?" I looked up at my grinning sister, who spread her arms wide like the benevolent talk-show goddess herself.

"The occasion," Michelle announced with a flick of her shiny brown hair, "is that it's a beautiful night, and I'm here with my lovely sisters. Isn't that enough of a reason to celebrate?"

"It's a pretty good reason," I agreed, trying to see the label on the bottle. The Brekkie Beach Hotel stocked four kinds of sparkling wine (ranging from cheap and vomit-inducing to reasonably priced and delightful) and one genuine champagne. My bank balance was very much hoping she hadn't chosen the actual champagne. "What do I owe you?" I pulled out my wallet, preparing for the worst.

"Don't be ridiculous!" Michelle pushed my wallet away. "It's my treat. We deserve to have nice things!"

And while that might have been true on a self-love and girl power level, affording nice things was a different story.

Michelle gave a little nod of satisfaction as she began to pour the sparkling wine that might or might not be champagne. The three of us – Tessa had not entered into the champagne debate – were seated on the balcony of the Brekkie Beach Hotel, an unpretentious pub with seriously drool-worthy views of the beach it was named for. The sun had begun to set, its dying light spilling over the gently undulating waters and almost-pristine sand. The view of the beach always made me think of how glad I was that I had left England for the great southern land, but it didn't distract me from the matter of the champagne.

"I'll transfer you some cash." Even now that we were all adults, I didn't like my little sister to pay for anything for me.

"You do that, and I'll transfer it right back." Michelle wagged a finger at me as she returned the half-empty bottle to the bucket. "With compounded daily interest. I might even index it to inflation."

"She's not kidding," Tessa said in a stage whisper. "She did it to me after dinner at that seafood place."

"Abby, you might be our big sister, but don't fight me when it comes to treating you." Michelle handed me a glass. "Drink up, shut up, and enjoy it."

I took a greedy gulp. And I did enjoy it, but shutting up? Not likely. "I'll get the next round, then."

"Actually, I'm pretty sure it's my turn," Tessa said. "Besides, you said your budget was kind of tight while you're doing this whole business expansion thing."

"I can still afford to treat my sisters!" My bank balance probably disagreed, but I had zero intention of admitting it. "But I might have to wait for next time. I've got to drive to Byron Bay tonight, so I should only stay for one or two more. If I leave soon, I can get a few hours of sleep before the job starts."

"You're driving to Byron? And sleeping in your van?" Michelle scoffed. "Abby, that's completely insane. You shouldn't be doing stuff like that over thirty."

"It's for a job!" I was slightly hurt by the 'over thirty' comment. "A big job. It's worth it. And I've packed snacks."

"Let me guess." Tessa wrinkled her nose. "Protein bars and those weird vegetable chips you like? I really need to teach you how to cook."

"Cooking is too time-consuming," I disagreed. "I like food. Food is good. But cooking sucks."

"That's what I used to say," Michelle said, tilting her head. "And now Patrick and I cook together. Maybe you should find a dude who can cook."

"I need a dude like a fish needs a bicycle." I snorted indignantly at the idea.

"Thanks for that, Gloria Steinem," Tessa said wryly. "But seriously, why are you driving to Byron? It's a one-hour flight! The client should be covering your travel costs!"

"I have to bring my product with me! Shelf dividers, acrylic storage trays, glass jars for the pantry, cord concealers, wicker baskets—" I counted off on my fingers. "I can't put that stuff in a suitcase or even three suitcases. Besides, the client's covering my travel time, so it's totally worth it."

"Will you be safe driving alone?" Tessa put a hand on my arm, her features – both like and unlike my own – contorting into a concerned expression. "Someone should go with you. I could—"

"Don't be ridiculous," I told my sister. "I'll be in my van. Nothing bad can happen to me if I'm the one driving the creepy white van."

"Fair call," Michelle chuckled. "Still, that's a hell of a trip."

"I like driving." I shrugged. "And I'm getting paid to listen to my audiobooks. That's a pretty sweet deal."

"What is it this time? *Extreme Hardcore Maximum Productivity*, written by a former Navy SEAL?" Tessa teased.

"You should try fiction sometime," Michelle suggested. "I just listened to this great book with this American chick and a sexy highlander. Well, multiple sexy highlanders actually. Why choose?"

"You and your sexy highlanders! I'm surprised you haven't made Patrick wear a kilt."

"Who says I haven't?" Michelle gave me a guileless look, and all three of us laughed at the mental picture. Patrick, Michelle's boyfriend, was blonde, tanned, and looked like a stock photo for 'Handsome Australian'. A kilt definitely wouldn't suit him, even if he did have the muscular calves a kilt demanded.

"I thought your new housemate was moving in this weekend," Tessa said with a slight frown. "Don't you want to be there to supervise him? What if he messes with your system in the pantry?"

"I'm perfectly capable of disembowelling him when I get back if he does," I said. "Honestly, it's best if I'm not there when he moves in. I couldn't stand seeing him putting his t-shirts in the drawers out of colour order."

Tessa huffed out a laugh, but she still looked concerned. "You're not worried about living with a complete stranger?"

"I have to be okay with it," I said. "It's not my house; I don't get to choose who the landlord moves in. Besides, he can't be any worse than some of the housemates I did choose myself. Remember Sandy, who didn't tell me that she had three cats?"

"And they were all black, so she kept trying to tell you it was the same cat, and you were imagining that there was more than one?" Tessa laughed at the memory.

"And what about Phil, who had two boyfriends who didn't know about each other?" Michelle said eagerly. "He made you cover for him all the time!"

"Phil was even worse than Sandy. He washed his underwear in the bath and dried it on the towel rack." I pretended to gag at the memory, though it didn't take all that much pretending. Having to brush my teeth with someone else's tighty whities right next to me had definitely been a low point in my housemate journey. "I'm sure this guy can't be any worse than Phil. Besides, I'm hardly ever at the house. It's not like I'll have to spend time with him."

"What if he's deliciously handsome, and you do want to spend time with him?" Michelle sounded excited. "We kind of have a history with neighbours and housemates." She wasn't wrong; Patrick had been her neighbour when she had rented an Air BnB in Brekkie Beach, and was the primary reason she had moved here permanently. Tessa's boyfriend, Dylan, was her former boss's son, and their romance had sparked when he had unexpectedly returned to his childhood home.

"I highly doubt he will be," I said. "Seriously, so long as he maintains basic hygiene and doesn't try to talk to me too much, I'll cope."

"He'll need better than basic hygiene to meet your standards," Tessa said. "If he tries to leave pots in the sink to soak, I dread to think what you'll do to him."

"Oh, he won't do that," I said, tilting my head to one side. "Not more than once, anyway."

"You don't take any shit, do you?" Michelle gave me a fond look.

"I try not to," I said, looking down at my phone. Surreptitiously, I opened my internet banking app, hoping my sisters wouldn't notice. The number was much smaller than I'd like but not less than I had predicted. So long as nothing unexpected happened before I got paid for the Byron Bay job, everything would be—

"Oi, why are you checking your phone?" Michelle made a grab for it. "You always tell me off about that!"

I swore and shoved it into my bag. "Just making sure everything's ready for the job," I lied. "No last-minute changes. This client's already changed the dates on me twice."

"What a pain in the arse." Tessa wrinkled her nose in commiseration. "How's work going, anyway? Is Josie as good as you hoped?"

"Even better than I hoped," I said. "In a couple of weeks, I think she'll be ready to take jobs on her own."

"Reckon you'll be able to let her?" Michelle raised her eyebrows. "I mean, you're kind of a control freak. I say that with love!"

"Josie's sixty-two years old!" I protested. "Of course I'll be able to let her work on her own." If I was honest, the thought of letting someone carry out projects under the Organised Home Co banner without me was unsettling. But I wasn't going to admit that, either.

"And then you've got your online shop opening soon, too." Michelle refilled her glass with raised eyebrows. "You've always got to do everything all at once, don't you?"

"I'm expanding the business." I held my hands wide, as though my sisters needed a demonstration of what expansion meant. "I reached the ceiling on how much I can make on my own. But with a team and selling product too, who knows how big this baby could get?"

"So long as it doesn't tear you open while you're delivering it." Michelle took a gulp of wine.

"Gross, Michelle." Tessa looked vaguely disgusted. "Let's keep the midwifery metaphors to a minimum."

"Nothing is going to tear, metaphorically or otherwise," I said, tapping my notebook. "I've got a plan. This week, we're doing sneak peeks of my product samples on social media. Monday is the shelf dividers, Tuesday we're doing cord concealers, Wednesday it's those little labels in rose gold, and—"

"I'm not saying you don't have a plan," Michelle cut me off. "Just that you've taken on a lot all at once. Hiring an employee, investing all that money in your product line. It's a big risk."

"I know that," I said irritably. "If it all goes wrong, I can always live in a shack made of drawer dividers and t-shirt folders. I bet it would get tons of likes on Insta. Maybe even a Buzzfeed article."

"Oh, Abby." Tessa looked worried, biting her plump lower lip with her teeth. I had always envied her lips, while she had always complained about missing out on our dad's olive skin. It was a shame you didn't get to choose your genetic makeup. "I know you've put a ton of your savings into this thing. If you need a loan, I can—"

"Or I can help out," Michelle cut in. "Don't call it a loan; call it an investment. We could set it up so I was buying shares in Organised Home Co, so you—"

"I don't need a loan!" I said, a little too fiercely. "I told you both! I can finance this expansion myself. I'm just on a tight budget for a few months. I'm not going to starve."

And it was true. I wouldn't starve. I could survive a long time on potatoes and ramen; it would be a character-building experience.

Michelle rolled her eyes. "You'd never let us help even if you were."

"If I was actually starving, I promise I'd tell you," I said. "But I'm nowhere near that. I'm at the level of doing my own nails at home and only buying coffee every second day. I'm just being fiscally responsible. Come on, do you really think I would have gone into this if I didn't have it all worked out?"

"That's true," Tessa agreed reluctantly. "You've probably got a whole cash flow chart in coloured pens."

"I do," I said, displaying my notebook for a moment. Not long enough for my sisters to examine the figures but enough for them to catch a glimpse of the green, purple, and orange rows of numbers. "Seriously, don't worry about me. If you want to be supportive, just like and share my Facebook posts."

"Of course we will," Michelle said. "But if you did need a loan, I can—"

"Don't make me throw this at you," I said warningly, taking a piece of ice from the bucket and sliding it between my fingers.

Michelle ducked her head in surrender. "Fine!" she said. "But at least let me give you a top-up. She held up the bottle of what might be champagne (it wasn't like I could taste the difference) and waved it back and forth enticingly.

"I can't," I said, shaking my head. "Gotta drive, remember?"

"Crazy," Michelle proclaimed.

"Like you've never worked through the night!"

"And that was crazy too, and part of the reason I quit that job," Michelle said, topping up her own glass. "I just don't want you to push yourself too hard."

"It's the good kind of pushing," I insisted. "I'm a small business owner. I'll never expand if I don't push out of my comfort zone."

"There's a lot to be said for leaving your comfort zone." Tessa held out her own glass for a refill. "Just take care of yourself, okay? We love you, you know."

"I do." I felt a fierce surge of affection for my sisters but pushed it down so I didn't tear up. "Okay, maybe just another half glass before I head off."

"Good girl," Michelle said approvingly, as though all I had to do to be successful in her eyes was finish my glass of bubbles. If only it was that easy.

· ♥ · ♥ · ♥ · ♥ · ♥ ·

Three hours later, I was driving past Newcastle, was halfway through my second no-name energy drink (it claimed to be 'tropical' flavoured, which could only be true if the tropics in question happened to contain a hazardous chemical factory) and had reached the part of my audiobook where a former marine was describing how his experience in Afghanistan was vital to forming a no-excuses mindset.

"Making good time," I said to myself, nodding in satisfaction. The GPS claimed it would take me another five and a half hours to reach my destination, but I was confident I could do better than that. Then all I'd have to do was find somewhere to park the van, grab a few hours of sleep, and I'd be fresh (or at least able to present the illusion of being fresh) and ready to meet my client. Everything was right on track.

"I've got this." I gave my reflection a glance in the rear-view mirror, and then scowled. Was I getting a pimple on my chin? I hadn't brought an extensive range of skincare with me, and those pimple patches Tessa swore by were in a neat acrylic dividing tray in my bathroom drawer back in Brekkie Beach.

I was debating pulling over to examine my chin more closely when the audiobook suddenly paused, just as the author's SUV had come under attack from enemy militants. That meant my phone was ringing.

"Hello, this is Abby Finch," I answered, trying to sound perky, professional, and not like I was hyped up on dangerous amounts of caffeine and war stories.

"Abby?" The voice was a familiar drawl. "This is Amanda Perkins. I'm sorry, but I've just realised someone is scheduled to re-turf the tennis court tomorrow. So, it won't be convenient for you to come."

My stomach dropped, flipped, and complained at the amount of carbonated caffeine inside it. I swallowed hard.

"Oh," I said, fighting to keep my voice even. "I see. It's just that I'm already on my way."

"You are?" Amanda sounded surprised. "What a shame. But I do think next weekend might be better. I'll call you when I've checked my calendar."

"I can't do next weekend," I said, feeling anger rise up. "This was my last available weekend slot for the next two months. Maybe you could reschedule the tennis court people."

"Oh no!" Amanda sounded aghast at the very idea. "I couldn't possibly do that. I'm sure we'll find a time one of these days. Or I'll find someone local. That could be best, you know."

My stomach lurched, and I fought back the urge to tell Amanda to go and do something to herself that a woman in her position probably hadn't heard since high school. "I guess you will," I said finally through gritted teeth.

"Such a shame." Amanda let out a long sigh. "Well, buh-bye!" The call ended, and I resisted the urge to repeatedly bang my head against the steering wheel like they did in movies.

Instead, I pulled into a petrol station and turned off the van.

"Buh-bye?!" I repeated, my face in my hands. "She cancels a massive job at the last minute, and all she has to say is buh-bye?!"

I let out a sound that was somewhere between a shriek and a wail, and two young men coming through the automatic doors shot my van a concerned look. I didn't care. I pressed the heels of my palms into my eyes and tried very hard to force back the angry tears that threatened to burst forth.

It wasn't very effective.

I let myself cry for exactly ten minutes in the petrol station car park and earned three more concerned looks. Then I rubbed my face vigorously, swallowed the last of my Tropical Trip energy drink, and started the engine.

The stern voice of the former marine started up again, but I shut him off. I was in no mood to hear about how I could be the master of my own feelings right now. All I could do was turn around and calculate, in my head, just how I'd rearrange my finances to avoid a negative bank balance until the next client invoice hit my account.

· ♥ · ♥ · ♥ · ♥ · ♥ ·

I could see the evidence of my new housemate as soon as I opened the door. There were a few cardboard moving boxes in the living room and an assortment of unfamiliar pots, pans, and knives on the kitchen counter in a haphazard arrangement that made my fingers itch impatiently.

But it was the clothes that made me raise my eyebrows. At the bottom of the stairs was a pair of shoes. Which, while being irritating, was understandable. What was less understandable was the pair of jeans, t-shirt, black mini skirt, tube top, and thong that littered the stairs in a path towards the bedroom.

I rolled my eyes and swore quietly. I wasn't a prude, but bringing someone home on your first night in a new house? Surely that was pushing the boundaries of housemate relations.

But I was too tired to care, so I made my way up the stairs, stepping over the abandoned clothes and raising my eyebrows at the bra slung over the banister. Actually...

I grabbed my phone, and took a quick photo, sending it to the group chat I shared with my sisters.

Abby: <image of bra on stairs>

Abby: It seems like my new housemate is entertaining guests already...

I let out a soft snort of laughter and made my way into my own bedroom. While I had zero control over who my landlord moved into the house, this place did have one huge bonus – each of the two bedrooms was fitted with an ensuite. At least I knew I wouldn't be bumping into any naked strangers if I needed to pee in the night.

The sight of my bedroom, at least, was soothing. I had taken enormous care to create a sanctuary for myself, with a rattan bedhead, soft grey sheets in what claimed to be a blend of linen and bamboo, a big (fake, because I couldn't keep a real one alive) fiddle leaf fig plant in a copper pot in one corner, and my chest of drawers painted in what was now called 'millennial pink'. A floor lamp bathed the room in soft light, illuminating the framed photos that hung from the picture rail, while my double-lined curtains would ensure the sunrise didn't wake me.

Every surface was free from clutter or even a hint of dust, but the room did lack one critical feature.

Soundproofing.

It sounded like an ill-tempered sheep was bleating in the next room, and I couldn't help rolling my eyes again as I went into the bathroom to wash off my makeup. I was tempted to use a cleansing wipe and call it a day, but the bottle of squalene cleanser seemed to be giving me a judgemental look. So, I lathered up my face and finished my skincare ritual with a serum that promised to prevent the seven signs of aging and which I wouldn't be buying again until my finances were in a very different position. After slipping off my clothes and putting them directly into the laundry hamper, I found my earplugs just where I knew they'd be in an acrylic tray divider in my bedside drawer.

Earplugs in place, I switched off the lamp and got into bed, trying to find a comfortable position under my heavy duvet and ignoring the tension in my shoulders. I was still uncomfortable about the Amanda situation. Well, uncomfortable was an understatement. Pissed off was more accurate. Very pissed off, in fact.

"I should put something in my contract about cancellation fees," I mumbled. "And make them sign it in advance."

I closed my eyes again, but even with my earplugs, the bleating was still audible. Worse still, it was getting louder.

"Oh god, do me just like that! Such a naughty daddy, give it to me hard!" A woman's shrill giggle followed that outburst, and I let out a sound of disdain. Was 'naughty daddy' the best she could come up with?

Another burst of bleats, more cries to god, and then—

My bedhead began to shake as a fist pounded on the wall. "Yes, daddy! Don't stop!

And that was too much. Sex noise was part of living in shared accommodation; I knew that. But a reverberating wall was definitely a step too far.

I banged my fist against the wall, hoping my new housemate and his guest would get the message. There was a brief pause and then an indignant sound.

"Don't stop! Give it to me like you mean it!" A rhythmic thumping began, knocking my bedhead against the top of my head.

That was *it*. I swore, switched on the light, and got to my hands and knees.

"Oh daddy, spank me like a disobedient avocado!" I shouted, pounding my fists against the wall in the one-two motion I had learned in a boxing class. "Pound my pussy into guacamole! Devour me like a bowl of organic corn chips!"

There was a pause. And then the unmistakable sound of a man's laughter, which quickly turned into a cough. Hissed whispers I couldn't make out, and then—

Well, it wasn't quite silence, but their activities must have resumed in a different part of the bedroom, and at a lower volume.

Satisfied, I switched out the light.

At least I could fail to fall asleep and worry about just how I would deal with the loss of my Byron Bay project in peace.

2 Wyatt

"Tequila," I groaned as soon as my brain became conscious. I could taste tequila in my dry mouth, and the previous night flashed into my mind in a succession of jagged images. Yep, definitely tequila. I had been at the restaurant, and we had been... Working on the cocktail list. Somehow, that had turned into a staggering walk to the pub, and then... A woman. A woman in a tight black skirt had been *very* insistent on coming home with me. And I had been pretty pliable at that point. There had been fumbled, not particularly satisfying sex, though the woman had been very vocal about what a good time she was having. And then...

...banging on the wall from the other side, something about guacamole, and the sudden realisation that my new roommate was *not* away for the weekend like I had been advised.

I winced and forced myself to open my eyes. To my eternal relief, my bed – though far less comfortable than I was used to – was empty. The woman and her tight black skirt were long gone. At least now I didn't have to try to remember her name.

"Missy?" I wondered out loud. "Milly?" I snorted. "No one's called Milly anymore; it can't have been Milly."

Groaning, I reached for my phone, flicking the screen to life and sending a message to someone who I knew would understand my situation.

Wyatt: i've already made a bad impression on my new housemate

My phone buzzed immediately in response.

Danni: not surprised, given the drunk texts i got from you last night. did you vomit on her shoes or what? i thought she was meant to be away

Wyatt: i brought someone home from the pub with me, and she was kind of loud...

Danni: <eye roll emoji> i doubt you did anything to warrant that. men who've been drinking generally aren't capable of making a woman scream

Wyatt: ouch

Wyatt: turns out my housemate was in the next room the whole time. she must have been pissed off about the noise because she banged on the wall and yelled something about getting spanked like a disobedient avocado. who even says that?

Danni: <laughing emoji> i like her already!

Danni: just apologise and laugh it off. no big deal

Wyatt: why should i apologise? i thought the house was empty!

Danni: do you want to be right or do you want to get along with your new housemate? i swear, your whole 'never apologise' thing drives me nuts

Wyatt: it's the principle of the thing

Sighing, I set my phone down and pushed myself out of bed, passionately wishing I hadn't been so enthusiastic about trying every contender for a spot on Beach Garage's cocktail list. I hadn't been this hungover since Danni's twenty-first birthday party, where I had tried to drink enough to forget that the party was being held in a stable that smelled all too strongly of horses. And horse shit.

But thinking about Danni's twenty-first made me remember my own twenty-first birthday. It had been held on a yacht, and my dad had made a whole speech about how proud he was that I was taking my place in the family business and—

I wasn't in the mood to think about my parents right now.

As I entered the bathroom, my own face and bare torso greeted me in the mirror. I scowled and then let out a reluctant chuckle. Had my hair looked like that when the woman in the black skirt had been here? It was sticking up on one side like I had gelled it there on purpose, while the other was plastered against my skull. I took a quick shower, enjoying the warm water on my gritty-feeling face and soaping up my body to ensure that the smell of last night's mistakes didn't linger on my skin.

After cleaning my teeth, my breath smelled less like the contents of a tequila distillery, and I was feeling closer to human. I still looked a little worse for wear, but the thought of the coffee machine I had spotted the day before in the kitchen made me decide that I was presentable enough.

If only I could find my jeans...

"Shit," I said aloud, wincing as I remembered that my jeans – along with my shirt and probably jocks – had been wrenched from my body to decorate the stairs. I bet my housemate had enjoyed a good laugh at that, as well.

"She was supposed to be away," I muttered, opening my suitcase for fresh clothes and pulling them on roughly. "The house was *meant* to be empty."

And that was true, but it didn't change the fact that my new housemate had definitely been very much present to witness my adventures the night before.

Maybe, I thought, if I was very lucky, my housemate would have left for the day already. But as I made my way down the stairs, I could already smell coffee, and hear the faint sound of laptop keys clicking.

No such luck.

I turned the corner into the kitchen and stopped abruptly. Sitting at the laminated wood table, a rose gold MacBook in front of her, was my new housemate. But her face wasn't new to me at all. We had met before. Seventeen years earlier, in fact.

She looked up at the sound of my footsteps, raising her eyebrows. Yep, it was definitely her. The last time we had met, she had been a teenager, but there was no mistaking her face, or those bright blue eyes, though they were no longer rimmed by thick black eyeliner. Her hair was different, too. Back then, it had been ironed into poker-straight submission but now it hung in soft waves around her face.

"Good morning," she said finally, in that Birmingham accent I still remembered. "You must be Wyatt. I'm Abby."

She didn't remember me. And I wasn't sure why that felt like such a disappointment.

I didn't trust myself to speak, not right away. When the silence grew too intense, I carefully tested my voice. "Uh, hi," I said. Thankfully, the words came out as intended. "Nice to meet you, Abby."

"Nice to put a face to a voice," Abby said, her eyes bright with mischief. "Although technically speaking, I didn't hear much of your voice. Just your friend's.

I paused mid-step as I made my way into the kitchen. "The real estate agent said you'd be away this weekend, so I didn't think you'd be here last night, when I was..." I coughed slightly.

Abby smirked into her coffee. "Last minute change of plans," she said with a shrug. "Your friend left early, by the way."

"Right," I said, nodding and looking around for something to say. "So, Abby," I began, inventing on the spot. "Is that short for Abigail?"

"No, it's short for Abomination," Abby deadpanned. "The sun turned black and it rained blood when I was born."

"Sounds messy," I said, huffing out a breath of laughter. Abby was still funny, I thought with a jolt. That hadn't changed in the last seventeen years. But she had no idea who I was. That could be for the best, given the unfortunate impression I had made last night.

"It is short for Abigail," Abby clarified after a pause. "But no one calls me that. If you're hoping to get on my good side, you won't, either."

"That's definitely the plan," I said. "So, is the coffee machine yours or part of the deal with the house?"

"It's mine." Abby tilted her head. "But you're welcome to use it. If you buy your own pods and remember to clean the milk frother when you use it."

"Pods," I repeated. "I'll have to get some." I looked at the glass jar of shiny aluminium coffee pods next to the machine, and my poor, hungover, caffeine-deprived brain suggested that I should cause some kind of diversion in order to steal one. So much for making a better impression.

"You can use one of mine this morning," Abby said, still sounding like she was trying not to laugh. "You look like you need it. Must be tiring, having friends over late."

"You could say that," I said. "And thank you," I added, picking up one of the pods and looking helplessly around for a mug. The kitchen, I noticed, was spotless. Apart from the coffee machine – and my own pots and pans – not a single item littered the countertops. Abby must be a very tidy person, I thought.

"Cupboard next to the pantry," Abby said, as though reading my thoughts. I really hoped she couldn't; the last thing I needed was a clairvoyant housemate. "My last housemate left those stripey ones here, so I guess they're yours now."

I opened the cupboard to find a row of soft pastel-coloured mugs with gold handles. They were arranged so precisely that I could have sworn Abby had used a ruler to measure the gaps between them, every handle facing three o'clock. Behind them, I found the aforementioned stripey mugs and selected one in an unappealing combination of mustard yellow and orange. I didn't have to ask who the much nicer mugs belonged to; I was pretty sure that using one of those would be a declaration of war.

I slid the pod into the machine and watched as it sent frothy dark liquid into my extraordinarily ugly mug.

"The kitchen's very tidy," I said, hoping to start a more friendly conversation. "You have very neat mugs."

Abby looked at me for a moment. "Thanks," she said, almost begrudgingly. "Goes with the territory. I'm a professional organiser." She paused again. "I mean, I've got a professional organising business."

"Really?" My eyebrows shot up in surprise. "Like Marie Kondo?"

Abby rolled her eyes, clearly having heard that comparison too many times. "Not exactly," she said. "I don't ask my clients if things spark joy. It's not up to me whether or not they want to keep stuff or chuck it; I just make it possible for them to actually find the stuff they do want to keep. And I make it look Instagram-worthy. All part of the service."

I opened the pantry expectantly and was greeted with glass jars of pasta, acrylic baskets of tinned legumes, and a Lazy Susan of condiments, each labelled in shiny rose gold lettering.

"That's definitely Instagram-worthy," I said. I'd have to be careful not to borrow so much as a teabag because I had the distinct sense I'd piss her off if I were to put anything back out of place. "I've never seen anything like it."

"There are some shelves and cupboards clear for you," Abby said, almost defensively. "You can organise those however you want. Or, you know, not organise them. It's your house too."

"Very gracious of you." I gave Abby a grin, which she reluctantly returned. "But I won't be around much. I'll be practically living at the restaurant for the next few months."

"What restaurant? There aren't any restaurants in Brekkie Beach."

"That's why I'm opening one."

"You're opening a restaurant?" Abby looked interested. "Are you a chef? I can organise food and I can eat food, but I kind of suck at the cooking part."

"I'm not a chef," I said. "I mean, I can cook, but I've hired a proper professional chef. I'm just the owner. I've always wanted to do this, and now...well, I'm trying to make it happen."

"Huh," Abby chewed that over. "So you're a small business owner too. I guess that makes this house one of those obnoxious start-up hubs I've read about online. If you bring in a ping-pong table, I'm complaining to the landlord."

"I would never."

"I'm not in the house all that much either," Abby said after a moment. "Running a business is...well, busy. So, if you want to have more guests over, you'll definitely get the place to yourself sometimes."

I coughed. "Last night was..." I searched for a word and came up empty. "I don't do that kind of thing a lot, but we were testing the cocktail menu last night at the restaurant, then we went to the pub, and things got out of hand." I winced slightly. "Usually, I'm very responsible."

"I see." Abby sounded dubious on that point, but she was still smiling. "So, I shouldn't expect any more guests who drape their underwear on the stairs?"

"Not without express prior notice." I hadn't been lying when I had told her that one-night stands weren't my usual style, but I was hardly a monk and didn't want to make promises I couldn't keep.

"So long as they don't use my mugs, and you keep the noise down next time, you can have as many guests over as you like." Abby made it sound like it didn't matter much to her. Once again, it bothered me that she clearly didn't have a clue who I was. Yes, it was seventeen years ago, but I didn't like to think I hadn't been as memorable to Abby as she had been to me.

"I'll be sure to do just that," I said. "I'd hate to invite the wrath of a disobedient avocado."

At that, Abby laughed out loud. "Good call," she said, turning back to her laptop. "I hear they can be ferocious."

I looked at her profile as she scowled at the computer one last time before turning to leave. How was it that the person who had made such an impression on my teenage self didn't even remember me?

A garage with whitewashed bricks and a tin roof wasn't the most obvious choice for a restaurant venue. It wasn't like I didn't know that. But something about the old garage, which had served Brekkie Beach until the mid-eighties, had called to me. There was a spark of possibility in the high-ceilinged, vaulted roof, the paint and oil-speckled concrete floor (now sealed under a layer of thick, clear gloss), and even in the rolling doors. The building had already lived one life, serving its intended purpose. Now it was time for it to become something new. Maybe I found that relatable.

Or maybe it was just every other beach-adjacent commercial space of a reasonable size I had inspected would have cost more in rent than a fledgling restaurant could possibly hope to cover.

"How are we all feeling this morning?" I called out as I entered the space we were attempting to turn into a functional commercial kitchen.

"Utterly disgusting," Mindy said, scowling at me from behind an enormous takeaway coffee cup. "And that's coming from someone who's slept in alleyways with a needle sticking out of my arm." She wrinkled her nose. "Pretty sure I woke up feeling better after those nights."

"Sorry to hear that." Mindy was in her late thirties but looked older; her face showed the effects of time spent living on the street. She made no secret of her past and her struggles with addiction. Actually, I thought she rather enjoyed saying things she thought might shock those of us with more suburban sensibilities.

David, the professional chef I had told Abby about, clicked his tongue sympathetically. "I woke up wishing for death," he signed, slumping his shoulders.

At least, that's what I thought he said. I was still learning Auslan, so it was possible that David had actually thought he was already dead.

David and Mindy were precisely the sorts of people who my parents would never have employed at Parsons Property Inc. But I didn't regret either of my hiring decisions. Even if the tequila had been David's idea.

"Cocktails are lethal," I said, making sure I was facing David as I spoke and trying my best to sign along with my words. I didn't know the sign for "lethal" and spelled it out slowly with my fingers.

David nodded emphatically, clearly in agreement.

"We'll take it easy today," I said, but Mindy shook her head.

"Nope. The crockery was delivered last night; we'll have to unload it," she said, her hands almost a blur as she signed along far more fluently than I could.

David pretended to collapse over the stainless-steel workbench he and I had chosen the week before. "I'm a chef, not a labourer!" He looked up at me from his horizontal position with an expression of disgust.

"I know," I said, shaking my head sympathetically. "But won't it be worth it to have some decent serving ware when you're plating up?"

David rolled his eyes but nodded, easing himself off the bench.

"I could go and get coffee before we start," I suggested, taking pity on my employees. And myself. One coffee definitely wouldn't cut it this morning, even if Abby had been kind enough to spare me a pod.

David signed his agreement while Mindy let out a needy groan that reminded me uncomfortably of last night. "Oh god, *please*."

"You've already got one," I pointed out, looking at the cup beside her.

"One," Mindy said, "is not enough. I didn't live under a bridge for a month because I was the queen of moderation, did I?"

"Fair point," I said. "I'll be back soon, okay?"

I left my restaurant manager and head chef wilting on the countertops like hothouse flowers exposed to sudden frost and made my way towards the nearby coffee shop.

Nick and Nikki's served genuinely excellent coffee and an array of baked goods that could only be described as an acquired taste. Given that Beach Garage's dessert menu didn't include any hemp powder, carob nibs, or spirulina, I didn't think they counted as competitors.

Squinting in the bright sunshine, I wished, once again, that I remembered where my sunglasses were and shaded my eyes against the assault of light with my hand. And then my pocket began to vibrate violently. Somehow, I knew even without looking, who was calling. I checked just the same. There was always the possibility it was something to do with the restaurant or perhaps Mindy calling to ask if Nick and Nikki could provide her with an entire bucket of coffee.

But when I pulled it out, I saw exactly what I expected.

'Dad' was calling. I grimaced and swiped my thumb to silence the call, shoving my phone back into my pocket. I had a carton of crockery to unpack, a hangover to manage, and the unexpected reappearance of Abby to deal with. There was no way I could handle a call from my parents expressing their great disappointment in my life choices now. I wasn't in the mood to defend my decision to leave the family business and pour everything I had into Beach Garage, and I sincerely doubted my father was calling to apologise. I certainly wasn't going to apologise for what I had said to him.

I quickened my pace, letting out a sigh. I really needed that second coffee.

3 Abby

I was almost late to meet Tessa at the coffee shop. Almost, but not quite. My morning had certainly been distracting, but I was a stickler for being on time. Annoyingly so if you asked my sisters. So, if I had to jog down there to ensure I met Tessa at precisely eleven, well, that was worth it to avoid her teasing.

"A large flat white with an extra shot?" Nick grinned at me, his straggly greying curls pushed back from his face with a black headband. I always got the impression that Nick drank more espresso than was wise, medically speaking.

"You know me," I said, smiling ruefully. I had to wonder whether spending $6.50 on coffee was wise after Amanda's last-minute cancellation. But it wasn't like I could just sit there and sip the free water. Things weren't that dire. Yet.

"Hey, you." Tessa gave me a hug as she came up behind me. "I can't believe your big job got cancelled last minute!"

I groaned. "Please, let's not talk about that."

"I won't," Tessa promised. "But at least you don't have to do all that driving. I know you too well to think you'll take some time off this weekend but promise me you'll at least try to rest a bit."

"What do I need to rest for?" I wrinkled my nose. "I'll rest plenty when I'm dead."

"You worry me," Tessa said with a sigh, paying for her coffee and sitting on one of the upturned milk crates that served as chairs.

"Don't worry about me," I told her. "I'm fine! Anyway, we have more exciting things to talk about. I met my new housemate this morning."

"Yeah?" Tessa looked up at me. "What's he like?"

"You're not going to believe this," I said, still shaking my head in disbelief. "But I know him. Well, kind of."

"You do? Who is he?"

"You remember how we used to stay with Dad's parents in Adelaide, and there was that one trip where we spent almost the whole time watching those skater boys in the park?"

"I do." Tessa looked a little wistful at the memory. "And on our last day, you spoke to the cute one and snuck out to kiss him that night. I was absolutely in awe of you." She paused. "Wait, it's him? No way!"

"I couldn't believe it either," I said, not wanting to mention that my stomach had flipped, my skin had grown hot, and I had struggled to breathe at the sight of the person who had given me my very first kiss, standing right there in the kitchen. "But it's definitely him. Wyatt, the skater boy, is all grown up. And living in my house!"

"That's amazing!" Tessa's eyes lit up. "I can't believe it! So, what happened? Did you talk about it? Is he still cute? Does he still have that hair?"

"He didn't recognise me," I said, shaking my head. And that had hurt. "Which is probably a good thing. Remember how I looked at fifteen, with the chubby cheeks and all that eyeliner? He probably doesn't even remember kissing me."

"I don't believe he wouldn't remember you." Tessa shook her head. "He kept looking over at you all week, even before the kiss!"

"Well, he definitely didn't recognise me," I said, shrugging. "But it's a crazy coincidence, huh?"

"Definitely!" Tessa agreed. "Michelle would say it's fated. Second chance romance, now that you're all grown up, ready to make your romantic history come alive once more—"

"Michelle reads too many romance novels," I declared. "And one clumsy pash in the park isn't exactly a romantic history."

"It was your first kiss!" Tessa nudged me. "You were pretty excited at the time."

"I was fifteen! Everything was exciting."

"So, is he still cute? Does he still have that spiky hair?"

I chuckled at that, remembering the gelled spikes that a teenage Wyatt had once sported. "He does not," I confirmed. "I guess he's...reasonably attractive."

And that was a giant understatement. Teenage Wyatt had been gangly, all long limbs in his baggy shorts and chunky sneakers, with a sweet smile that showed his braces. The adult Wyatt, however, was something else. He was still tall, but now his body showed the distinctive muscle definition of someone who spent hours in the gym. His smile, no longer sporting braces, had gone from sweet to smirking, and I got the feeling he was the kind of dude who smirked a lot. With high cheekbones and bright hazel eyes, Wyatt definitely had the type of face that made women do a double take when they passed him on the street. His guest last night had proved that.

"Reasonably attractive," Tessa repeated. "I'm going to take it that he's hot, then. What's he doing now?"

"Actually, that part's pretty cool," I conceded. "He's opening a restaurant right here in Brekkie Beach."

"Seriously?" Tessa looked excited. "We need one; I hope he's a decent chef!"

"Oh, he's not the chef," I explained. "Just the owner."

"Well, that's a shame." Tessa sighed. "Having a housemate who was a professional chef would be amazing. Think of the leftovers!"

"True."

"So, there's definitely no sparks flying?" Tessa pressed. "Come on, I need to live vicariously through you now that I'm all happy and settled with Dylan. No sparks? No butterflies? No electric tension in the air when his steely gaze meets yours?"

I snorted. "Absolutely not," I said. "What do I want with sparks? I've got a business to run, and I'm seriously under the gun. He's not my type, anyway. He brought some woman home last night, and I heard them through the wall. Who brings someone home with them the first night they move into a new place?"

Tessa tilted her head. "Someone who hasn't met their gorgeous housemate yet, and doesn't realise she's their teenage crush?"

"I doubt that would have made a difference," I said drily. "Besides, I saw his friend leave this morning. And if that's the type of woman he's into, I can guarantee there will be zero sparks on his side. She had certain assets I lack." I gestured at my chest, which wasn't completely flat, but certainly wouldn't get me a job at Hooters if my business collapsed.

"Boobs aren't the only thing that attracts a man," Tessa said, sipping her coffee.

"Says the woman with double Ds." I nodded pointedly at Tessa's tight t-shirt, which showed exactly what genetics had given her, and denied me. "And who says I want to attract him? I'm just pointing out that I'm not his type, so we don't have to worry about any weird vibes."

"No weird vibes," Tessa repeated. "If you say so."

"Anyway, I'd better head off. I'm going to the lock-up to meet Josie and start sorting out that product delivery that came in yesterday. I thought I'd have to wait until I was back from Byron, so at least I've got the chance to get a jump on it."

"Seriously?" Tessa gave me a pained look. "Shouldn't your schedule be wide open after that client cancelling last minute?"

"It was, and I filled it," I said, resisting the urge to pull out my notebook and show her how many to-do items were listed in magenta under today's date.

"I bet you did." Tessa puckered her mouth. "You know, it's okay to take a break sometimes. To just...I don't know, chill or something. Watch TV, read a book. And not one about social media marketing strategy."

"No rest for the wicked," I said, drinking the very last drops of my coffee. After all, I had paid $6.50 for it, and I was going to get my money's worth because café coffee would be cut from my budget for the foreseeable future.

"But you're not wicked," Tessa said, squeezing my shoulder. "You're wonderful, kind, generous, and thoughtful. Take care of yourself, okay?"

"I always do!" I stood up, arching my back to stretch it. I had slept in a strange position, probably to escape the noise of Wyatt's guest. "I'll see you soon, okay?"

"Sure," Tessa said. "And I'm allowed to tell Michelle about Wyatt, right?"

At that, I snorted with laughter. "I'd expect nothing less. No secrets between sisters!"

・♥・♥・♥・♥・♥・

When I parked my van in front of the storage locker that housed my life savings in product form, Josie was already waiting for me.

"I can't believe Amanda cancelled on you again!" Josie said heatedly, by way of greeting. "Do you have a blacklist we can put her on or something?"

"I should," I grimaced. "But at least it gives us the chance to go through these boxes right away." I bent to fit the key in the lock, wincing as metal on metal made an unpleasant screeching sound as I pushed up the roller door. "Thanks for being available at such short notice."

"What else am I going to do? Go to The Coffee Club and camp out with a Senior's Special coffee and raisin toast for three hours? I don't think so!"

I laughed. "Not your style, huh?"

"Absolutely not." Josie was adamant. With her grey hair cut into a tousled bob, no-nonsense faded sneakers, and square jaw set with fierce determination, Josie gave the impression she could handle anything, up to and including a nuclear apocalypse. Josie would just scowl at the mushroom cloud, roll up her sleeves and start sweeping the fallout dust.

"So, what've we got?" Josie asked, flicking on the dusty bulb hanging from the ceiling. "Bloody hell, that's a lot of boxes!"

She wasn't wrong. Cardboard boxes filled the storage locker, crammed up to the ceiling.

"Yep!" I gritted my teeth. "It all arrived earlier than I expected. No clue what's in them." I paused. "I think it's the shelf dividers and acrylic drawer organisers, but my Cantonese isn't great." I tapped one box, which bore Chinese lettering that might describe the box's contents, the name of the factory where the box had been made, or give a recipe for dipping sauce.

"And I'm the wrong type of Asian to help you," Josie told me, squinting at the lettering. "Not that my Vietnamese is up to much these days, either."

"Not exactly," Wyatt said, taking a seat opposite me. "According to David, we're serving modern Australian with a Mediterranean influence. I'm letting him take the lead on the menu; he knows his stuff."

"That's smart," I said, nodding. "Recognising when someone has more experience than you, I mean. And listening to them." I took a mouthful of pasta and swore loudly.

"I know," Wyatt said, clearly in agreement. "See? This is why I'm letting him decide the menu."

"You are so right to do that," I said once I had swallowed and recovered. "That is seriously amazing. I haven't had pasta like that since..." I thought about it. "Well, I did have some pretty amazing pasta when I went to Florence for a week with friends from uni. But nothing since then has come close."

"I'll tell David," Wyatt said. "He'll be pleased."

"So, this whole restaurant thing," I said, once I had swallowed another mouthful. "Have you got a business partner? Or is it just you?"

"Well, I've got David and Mindy – she's the Restaurant Manager," Wyatt said. "And we're hiring more kitchen staff and waiters. It's not like I'm one guy in a food truck."

"But it's just you who's actually responsible for the whole thing, right? It's your money on the line?"

"Oh, that's definitely all me," Wyatt said. "And yes, it is vaguely terrifying. But I spent my twenties doing what my nostrils, I didn't care that the tray was sitting on the table without so much as a placemat to protect against the heat. "The pasta roller came today, and David – he's my Head Chef – got very excited."

"I can see why," I walked over, bending down to examine the source of that exquisite smell. My stomach gave an almighty rumble, reminding me that so far today, I had eaten only coffee, protein bars, and breath mints. "But you don't have to bring me food. I don't know if I'd share this."

"You said you like to eat, but you don't cook," Wyatt reminded me, and my stomach gave a brief flutter; he had remembered. "Besides, I thought I needed to make a better second impression. I thought of asking David to make guacamole, but I figured that might be a bit on the nose."

"Probably. But a good guacamole is amazing. Even if the avocados are being disobedient."

"So, do I have permission to use your bowls and forks if I share this with you?" Wyatt asked. "Because this is the part where I admit I've got hundreds for the restaurant and zero for myself."

"With pasta like that, I'd almost let you use one of my mugs."

"Oh, I'd never presume to do that," Wyatt said mildly, taking two bowls from the cupboard and spooning heavenly-smelling ravioli into each one.

"So, is your restaurant Italian, then?" I asked, taking the bowl and sitting down at the table.

family expected, but now it's time to do something I'm passionate about. Even if I do fail. Publicly and epically."

"I get that," I said, wrinkling my nose. "My business has been going well for a few years, with me as a sole trader. But I always wanted to expand and see if I could make it something bigger. So, I've just hired my first employee, and I'm bringing out a product line through an online store next month." I quirked my mouth. "I've done my research, and everything's planned out, but it's still a gamble."

"That's a lot, all at once," Wyatt said, setting down his fork. "You must be nervous."

"No," I shook my head vehemently. "It's fine. Like I said, I've got it all planned out. It's just that I'm on a very tight budget for the next two months. I didn't want to take out any loans, so my savings are currently sitting in a storage locker or allocated to paying Josie. I want to do this myself, without anyone's help."

"I get that," Wyatt said, though his face was oddly stiff. "The restaurant is...well, I guess I'm on my own with that too."

"At least it's a restaurant, so you won't starve any time soon," I said, trying to make a joke. "It's not like I can eat my shelf dividers if things get really bad."

Wyatt laughed out loud. "True. No instant ramen for me."

"Instant ramen is a valuable food source for those of us without the cooking gene," I said, looking up at him through my lashes and then immediately hoping he didn't think I was flirting. Especially since I, clearly on some subconscious level, absolutely had been. "Although, after this pasta, I don't know if I could enjoy it."

"I've ruined ramen for you, then?" Wyatt's eyes were twinkling. "I can't say I'm sorry."

"I bet you're not." I returned his gaze, not letting my eyes drop. "But even if I am risking instant ramen and living in my van, I've got to do this. Follow the plan, keep my chin up, and hope for the best."

"You're braver than me." Wyatt raised those almost-too-perfect eyebrows. "I've been having nightmares about terrible reviews, an empty restaurant, and my staff turning on me and beating me to death with a cast iron skillet."

"It's hard doing this alone," I conceded. "No one to fall back on, throwing all your savings into your dream. But what's the point of life if you don't try to do the things you really want, even if they scare you?"

"Very wise," Wyatt said, looking away from my gaze. "You know, if your organising business does fall flat, you could always move into life coaching."

I rolled my eyes even as I smiled. Picking up my bowl and fork, I made my way to the dishwasher to set a good example of how it ought to be loaded. "Thanks for the pasta," I said, looking up at him again. "You've definitely appeased the goddess of housemates."

Broken nails, stubbed toes, impossible-to-explain scratches... I'm not the most graceful of humans."

"That's a surprise," Wyatt said, raising those dark, elegant eyebrows.

"Why?" I frowned. "Because women are meant to be ethereal, graceful beings?"

"Nope," Wyatt said, shaking his head. "Just, you seem to..." He trailed off. "Well, I guess, the way you carry yourself, I wouldn't have pegged you as clumsy."

"Nice save," I said, raising my eyebrows. "But the jury's still out on whether you're harbouring unconscious sexist attitudes."

"I should have known you wouldn't let me off that easy." He paused. "But I have an offering that might make you change your mind."

I raised my eyebrows at that. "An offering? You make me sound like some kind of vengeful goddess that has to be appeased, or I'll rain terror down upon you."

"Isn't that what all housemates are like?" Wyatt gave me a smirk, and yep, I had called it. He was absolutely a smirker, and what's more, he looked disgustingly handsome when he did so. And if my insides fluttered just a little, I wouldn't admit it to anyone.

"You might be right," I said. "So, what's this offering?"

"Handmade ravioli filled with beef ragout, in a reduction of King Island cream and shaved black truffle," Wyatt pulled back the foil on a tray. When the smell hit my boy had been the one laughing, but the sound was just the same. What had teenage Abby said that had been so funny? I couldn't remember that, but I couldn't forget the hot rush of pleasure that had come from making him laugh.

"It's just a few boxes," he said. "And it looks like you've done enough manual labour." He pointed at my arm. "That's a hell of a bruise."

I turned my arm over and peered at it. Sure enough, an enormous bruise, blue and purple, was just above my elbow. "Huh," I said. "I don't even know how I got that."

"Do you have any dangerous hobbies I should be aware of?" Wyatt raised his eyebrows. "Or is asking that toxic masculinity again?"

I laughed ruefully. "I must have done it at work. Occupational hazard."

"It looks painful," Wyatt was still staring at the bruise, and I could see something like concern in his eyes. Why did he give a shit if I had a bruise, anyway? I was just his housemate. "You sure it's from work?"

I let out an incredulous sound. "You think someone did this to me? I'd like to see them try!"

"Fair point," Wyatt said mildly. "But I'd be an arsehole not to ask the question. And I do try not to be."

"I probably would have asked, too," I admitted, grimacing and looking at the bruise again. "But it looks worse than it is. Honestly, there's always something from work.

"I'll help you," Wyatt said, walking past me and ignoring my dismissal. I dumped the boxes on the floor and went after him.

"I really don't need any help. I can lift my own boxes. Seriously, this is my workout."

"I don't mind helping," Wyatt said, reaching the van before me. "Those ones as well, yeah?" He pointed at where six more boxes were piled behind the driver's seat.

"I can do it," I said, slightly annoyed. "I don't need the patriarchy in my own home! I can carry a box."

"It's not patriarchy!" Wyatt said, scoffing as though the very idea was ridiculous. "Trust me, if you were a dude, I'd help you too."

I rolled my eyes, unconvinced. "Fine," I said. "If you could grab those two, I'll get the others and—"

Before I could finish, Wyatt lifted all six boxes like they contained nothing but air and possibly a few loose feathers.

"It's no trouble," Wyatt said over his shoulder as he strode away with my boxes, leaving me empty-handed. "We were unpacking the crockery today at the restaurant; these are nothing compared to that load."

I locked the van and followed him into the house. "I still think this might be toxic masculinity," I said, though my tone was teasing. "I'm going to reserve judgement."

But Wyatt just laughed, and, with a jolt, I remembered that laugh from so long ago. Back then, a gangly teenage

"You're not old!" I said, frowning. "You definitely deserve a stick. I could get one too, to threaten irritating clients."

Josie laughed, looking pleased to hear I didn't think she was old.

"Anyway," I went on, pulling out my phone to show Josie the pictures our client had sent through. "This is what we'll be dealing with."

Josie looked over my shoulder at the photos and winced. "Gees, her wardrobe is bigger than my bedroom! But what a mess. Are those Louboutins all over the floor?"

"I know," I said, rolling my eyes. "Rich people are something else, huh?"

"They certainly are!"

· ♥ · ♥ · ♥ · ♥ · ♥ ·

I had an armful of boxes under one arm, held steady by my chin, and was fumbling for my keys with the other hand when the door suddenly flung open. For a moment, I was terrified, and then I remembered I had a housemate.

And just who that housemate was.

"Need a hand?" Wyatt asked, trying to take the boxes from me before I could reply.

"I'm fine! Just got a few more loads to grab from the van—"

made her cry, but then she carried on bravely. "I had to step up after Bill left, anyway. I'm just lucky you gave me a chance."

"Luck had nothing to do with it," I said firmly. "You were the best applicant, by far." And that was true. When I had advertised for a trainee, I had received endless resumés from women who followed me on Instagram but couldn't organise their way out of a paper bag. But Josie had been different. Her cover letter had included photos of her pantry, her fridge, and her fabulously organised toy room that was routinely demolished by her troop of adorable grandchildren. As soon as we had met for coffee at Nick and Nikki's, I had known she was the right woman for the job.

Now all I had to do was ensure that Organised Home Co stayed solvent.

"Anyway, what's on the agenda this week?" Josie asked, brushing off my compliment as she examined the contents of another box. "A wardrobe job, wasn't it?"

"Yep," I said. "And she's very excited she's going to be the first client to get access to our exclusive product line. She sent through pictures of what we're working with, and we'll need a ton of dividers and more acrylic boxes than you could shake a stick at."

"I'd rather like a stick to shake at people." Josie sounded wistful. "But I worry it would make me look old.

"I thought millennials were supposed to be the experts on social media," I said, grinning at her. "But you really know your stuff."

"I like Instagram," Josie said, looking thoughtful. "Lots of nice dogs and empowering messages about how you don't need a man to make your life worthwhile. Besides, Instagram was how I found you, and look where that's got me!"

"Well, amen to that!" But I was glad Josie liked the empowering messages, too. Her story was a sad one, despite the brave face she put on it. For forty years, she had cooked, cleaned, cared for children and grandchildren, while her husband put his feet up. And then, just as Josie had looked forward to spending quality time with him in retirement, he had left her for a woman half his age and found the sort of arsehole lawyer who left her with very little after their divorce. "You definitely don't need a man to make you happy."

"I'm certainly happier without Bill now," Josie said with a defiant nod. "But at first... Well, you know about that. I didn't know how I could build a life on my own. I thought I'd be working at that supermarket forever, with all the young ones laughing at me. Until you saw fit to hire me."

"I'm glad I did," I said warmly. "There's no way I could manage the client schedule and the launch without you."

Josie looked away. "Thank you, Abby." There was an awkward moment in which I was terrified I might have

But now was not the time for fear, or at least not the time to show it. Instead, I lifted my head to the camera. "I'm about to open the very first batch of products for the Organised Home Co online store. Let's see what they look like!"

My box cutter slid easily through the tape, and I opened it to find a mass of plastic wrap, and then...

"They're perfect!" I said, relief flooding through me as I held up three sleek, matte pink shelf dividers. "I might actually be in love!" I held the dividers to my chest, fluttering my eyelashes like I was overcome with emotion. My followers loved it when I got emotional about organisational equipment, and I wasn't above hamming it up.

Josie stepped towards me, zooming in on the dividers for a final product shot, and then she put down her phone. "They look good," she said, taking one from me and examining it. "Better than those prototypes you showed me, I reckon." She stuck a finger in to test the mechanism that made the divider adjust to different shelf widths. "Seems like that works, too."

"We're going to put them through rigorous testing," I said. "But they look good, at least."

"I'll send you the video to upload." Josie was pulling out her phone. "You look lovely, but I'll filter it to Summer Breeze, and then you can chuck Valencia over the top when you upload it."

"We'll just have to open them," I said, taking two box cutters from my bag. "I was hoping we could do something for Instagram, but this isn't a great place for a flat lay."

"We could do an unboxing instead," Josie suggested, pulling out her phone. "My grandkids are obsessed with unboxing videos. I don't get why they want to watch other kids open toys, but they insist on showing me, and I've got to feign interest like a nice Grandma." Josie gave me a rueful smile. "Bring that big one out into the light, and I'll film you."

"I wasn't planning on being filmed today," I said, putting a hand to my hair. It was pulled up into a messy bun on top of my head, and I was certain it had flopped to one side. "I'm not wearing proper makeup."

Josie gave a dismissive snort. "Don't be ridiculous; you're young and lovely! Besides, I know all about filters. Now start unboxing."

"Thanks," I said with a laugh, but her words did make me feel better. At least Josie thought I was young, even though I was officially over thirty. Kneeling on the ground, I felt a twist in my stomach that had nothing to do with getting older. I had sunk an enormous amount of my savings into the contents of these boxes, and I couldn't help worrying that something had gone horribly wrong. The prototypes from the factory had looked perfect, but what if my shelf dividers were all khaki and mustard yellow instead of greyish-beige and millennial pink?

"Glad to hear it." Wyatt's hazel eyes were crinkling. "I was going to open a bottle of wine if you wanted to join me. It's for the restaurant, so I have to test it to make sure it's worth the obscene mark-up we'll be charging."

And for a moment, I considered saying yes. I *wanted* to spend more time with Wyatt. As it turned out, the adult version of him was every bit as fascinating as the teenage version had been, despite the lack of chains hanging from his baggy shorts, backwards baseball cap, and chunky skate shoes.

"I can't." It was the right thing to do, and I could resist temptation. "I've got a ton to do tomorrow; I should probably get an early night. And before that, I've got to..." I pulled out my notebook. "Update my social media accounts, order a birthday present for my sister, do my Pilates workout, and test the payment gateway for my product website. Plus, the kitchen could do with a good wipe-down."

"That's a lot." Wyatt let out a slow breath. "Good thing you're so organised; I'd never be able to keep track of all that."

"I like to stay organised," I said, closing my notebook and hugging it to my chest. "And keep busy."

"It's already nearly seven." Wyatt looked at his watch, and when I looked at his wrist, my eyes widened in surprise. "Will you have time for everything?"

"Of course," I said dismissively, my eyes still fixed on his wrist. "Is that a Rolex? Your old job must have paid you a shit-ton!" I had seen watches like his before, but only on the wrists of my most well-heeled clients.

Wyatt's face froze, and he looked at the watch like he had never seen it before. "It's a knock-off," he said after a moment. "Guess it must be a good one?"

"Right," I said, still looking at the watch. "I don't have to kick you out of the broke business owner's club after all."

Wyatt laughed, but his eyes didn't quite meet my own. Perhaps he didn't like talking about money. Most people didn't, especially if they didn't have much. "Are you sure I can't tempt you with the wine? I've heard wine and Pilates go well together."

"Really?" I gave him an incredulous look.

"No, I made that up." Wyatt gave me another of those smirks. "Another time, maybe." He shrugged like it wasn't important.

"Yeah," I said. "Maybe another time."

But as I made my way up the stairs, I told myself very firmly that drinking wine with my teenage crush – who didn't even remember me – was *not* something I should be doing any time soon. Not when I had a business expansion to focus on.

I need to think about my social media advertising budget, product photography, and when Josie could start working independently, and not about my unexpectedly tempting housemate.

4 Wyatt

"Is this it?" Danni gave my restaurant the look she usually reserved for poorly maintained horse floats. "Seriously, dude, I know you said it was an old garage, but I figured it wouldn't still look so much like one."

"Rude," I said, flicking the brim of Danni's baseball cap. She swore and flipped me off. I probably deserved it. "I'm going for, like, a rustic industrial kind of vibe."

"It's definitely industrial," Danni said, scuffing her riding boot against the cracking concrete. "Are you going to do something about this? People will trip and fall before they even get into this joint."

"Yes, I am doing something about the concrete," I said, rather petulantly. "I've got someone coming in to pull it up and lay down a fresh slab this week."

"And the opening is the fifteenth?" Danni raised her eyebrows. "You're cutting it kind of fine."

"I've got a timeline," I told her, with more confidence than I felt. "Besides, it's not like I can just pay rent on this place indefinitely without it bringing in any income."

"You totally could, actually."

"I want to run this as an actual profitable business," I said. "Not a trust fund kid hobby."

Danni let out a snort worthy of a prize stallion. "But you *are* a trust fund kid. We both are! Trust fund kids unite!"

I winced. "Just don't say that in front of my housemate."

"Abby?" Danni wrinkled her nose again. "Why not?"

"It's complicated," I said, opening the side door and letting Danni into the kitchen. I hoped that would impress her more than the exterior. "The thing is, Abby's got her own business, and she's working on a big expansion. She's put all her savings into it, and she was joking about living off ramen if it doesn't work out, and she just kind of assumed that I was in the same boat."

"You mean you let her assume!" Danni pointed a finger at me. "Wyatt, you bloody liar! I mean, I could understand not telling some random housemate that our family's loaded, but Abby was the great love of your teenage life? Why didn't you tell her the truth?"

"She doesn't remember me!" I shot back. "Look, if I told her about my parents, about the trust, she'd look at me differently. She'd think I was just some rich arsehole using his parents' money to run a business for fun. And that's not what I'm doing. I don't want this to have anything to do with my parents. You know why."

"I do know," Danni softened slightly, running her hand over one of the gleaming stainless-steel benches. "But it still seems shitty to make her think you're struggling when you're not."

"But I am struggling," I countered. "Leaving the family business was a total shitstorm, you know that. And there's so much to do to get this place up and running in time, all these staff counting on me to make it work. And it's my own money on the line; I'm using my savings. I haven't taken anything from the trust. Plus, it's my reputation I'm risking. I'm just not struggling in quite the way she thinks I am."

Danni shook her head. "I guess," she said, giving me a dubious look from underneath the cap. "I mean, I don't always tell women about my stables right away. Don't want them to think I'm one of those horsey rich bitches."

"You *are* one of those horsey rich bitches," I teased, turning her own words back on her. "Bet they can smell the horses, anyway."

At that, Danni swiped a saucepan at me, and I ducked, laughing.

"I scrub up very well when I'm on the pull!" she said, still brandishing the saucepan. "Zero horse smell!"

"You do!" I conceded, taking the saucepan from her. "You probably have better luck with the ladies than me."

"Let's not get carried away."

"So, you won't say anything to Abby if you meet her?"

"When I meet her," Danni corrected. "There's no way I'm not going to meet the famous Abby. She was your first-ever kiss! And your first heartbreak."

"It wasn't much of a heartbreak," I protested. "I was going back to Sydney; she was going back to Birmingham. We didn't even know each other's last names. We just held hands in the park and snogged one night."

"Heartbreak," Danni insisted. "I won't say anything. But I don't have to approve."

"Deal," I said. "But can you please tell me you approve of this kitchen?"

"Look, I know nothing about commercial kitchens," Danni said, hands in her pockets. "But this looks like a good one. You've got lots of big shiny knives and saucepans. That cooktop is massive; you could flame grill a small human on that thing."

"We've chosen not to take menu advice from Hannibal Lecter, but thanks," I said drily. "Come on, I want you to see the dining area. You can tell me everything that's wrong with my plans for the décor."

Danni rubbed her hands together. "That's an offer I can't refuse," she said, swinging her jodhpur-clad legs from the kitchen counter and eagerly pushing through the saloon-style doors.

I followed my cousin, relieved she wasn't about to spill my secret any time soon.

♥ · ♥ · ♥ · ♥ · ♥

"Is this it?" Danni asked, stopping in front of the modest two-story brick house that was now my home. "That was, like, a two-minute walk."

"Why do you think I chose this place?"

"Well, I did wonder why the hell you were in a share house," Danni said, giving me a look. "Given you could have just bought a house here."

"I told you, I'm not using any trust money for this," I said. "And I'll practically live at the restaurant these next few months. Why would I want to pay for a house I'll barely use?"

"I guess that makes sense. But I couldn't stand having housemates. You're a brave man, Wyatt Parsons."

"You do have housemates," I said. "Enormous, stinky housemates with bulging eyes and a tendency to shit on the floor."

"I don't actually live in the stables!" Danni turned on me. "You know that!"

"You've definitely slept there," I countered.

"Only when one of my babies isn't feeling well," Danni said. "As any responsible mother should."

"I don't know how you can stand it." I felt my shoulders move in an involuntary shudder at the idea of sleeping in a horse stall. "I'd rather sleep in a public toilet than beside a horse."

"And you still claim you're not afraid of them."

"I'm not! I just don't like them," I said, unwilling to concede. "They make me uncomfortable. It's the eyes. And maybe the teeth."

"Maybe it's that horses can tell a lot about a person, and you don't want them judging you."

"I think I can face the judgement of a horse," I said, letting out a breath. "I'm not that much of an arsehole."

"No, you're not. You just sometimes cosplay as one."

"Thanks."

"You're welcome," Danni said, and then she poked me. "So, am I going to see inside this place, or what?"

"Just remember not to say anything to Abby," I said. "I don't think she's home, but just in case."

"I won't reveal your big secret." Danni rolled her eyes. "Even if I think you should tell your teenage dream the truth before your chemistry heats up like that frigging massive stove in your restaurant."

"It's not like that," I said. "Abby doesn't even remember me; it was seventeen years ago! There's nothing between us now. We barely know each other!"

"Chemistry never dies," Danni objected. "Remember when I saw my ex after ten years at the National Rodeo Finals? She looked completely different, but I was still a mess when I saw her."

"I thought that was because she broke your heart by sleeping with half of Sydney."

"Well, yeah, she did." Danni's mouth was screwed up thoughtfully. "But I still wanted her to sit on my face."

I let out a snort as I opened the door, unwilling to have that particular image of my cousin enter my brain space. "Well, this is it."

"It's a lot nicer than your garage," Danni said, patting a knitted throw arranged artfully over the sofa. "But I'm guessing that's Abby's doing."

"True," I admitted. "The whole place was furnished; I just had to move my crap in."

"I bet it's a total mess." Danni shook her head despairingly. "You were always a slob, Wyatt."

Then she made her way into the kitchen, opening the fridge. "Holy shit! This thing looks like a photo shoot!"

"Don't touch anything!" I warned, coming up behind her. "It's all Abby's; I haven't been grocery shopping yet."

"This is insanely well-organised," Danni said, her eyebrows disappearing into the baseball cap. "Does this chick have OCD or something?"

"This chick does not have OCD," a voice said from behind us, and Danni jumped, shutting the fridge guiltily.

I turned to see Abby herself. And okay, maybe Danni had a point about chemistry never truly dying. Or maybe it was just that grown-up Abby was gorgeous, regardless of whether or not my teenage self had been in puppy love with her. Dressed in sleek leggings, a loose tank top that whispered over her body, and with her dark hair loose around her face, it was all too easy to feel a tug of *something* when I looked at Abby.

"Obsessive Compulsive Disorder is a serious condition characterised by intrusive thoughts and repetitive behaviours, not a synonym for being well organised," Abby said, raising her eyebrows, her clear blue eyes sparkling with amusement – or maybe mischief. "But as organising's my job, I'll take it as a compliment."

"I meant it as one." Danni was cringing while scowling at me as though her faux pas was somehow my fault. "Sorry, I didn't mean to—"

"It's not a big deal." Abby shook her head. "Or the first time I've heard it. I'm not offended or anything, but I've got to speak up about what OCD really is. It gets thrown around like a joke, which sucks for people who actually have it."

"Well, now I feel like a total arsehole." Danni sighed. "If anyone should be sensitive to words getting thrown around as a joke, it's definitely me. Don't report me to the LGBTQ+ Board of Directors; they'll revoke my lesbian license. And that would be devastating. Possibly fatal."

At that, Abby laughed. "Don't worry about it," she said. "It's no big deal. I won't let you get cancelled."

Danni let out an exaggerated sigh of relief. "I'm Danni, by the way. Wyatt's cousin by chance and best friend by choice." She nudged me, grinning. "Well, mostly choice, anyway. I'm just here to check out his new digs. And the restaurant. Digs are definitely more impressive than the restaurant."

"Hey!" I interjected. "The restaurant's coming along! Once I've got the new concrete, the signage, the greenery, and the outdoor tables, it'll look way less like a garage."

"Oh, is that where you're opening?" Abby looked interested. "I wondered if anyone would ever lease that place. I'm glad you're doing something with it; it's kind of an eyesore."

"It still is," Danni confided, winking at Abby. "But Wyatt reckons it will look amazing by the time they open."

"It will!" I'd make sure of that. "I showed you the concept drawings; you liked them!"

"I did like them," Danni said. "But it still looks like a garage."

"You've got, what, a month? You can do a lot in a month."

"Thanks," I said, looking at Abby in surprise. I hadn't expected her to back me up.

"It's tough, though, doing something like this on your own, with no backup and a tight budget," Abby continued, giving me a sympathetic look that made me wince, and Danni roll her eyes from behind Abby's head.

"Well, I've got everything mapped out," I said awkwardly. "It should be fine, financially, once we're up and running."

"Maybe you should hire Abby to organise your kitchen," Danni suggested, giving me a wicked look. "I bet she could get it sorted out."

"There's nothing wrong with how the kitchen is organised!" I felt a little defensive. "David's putting everything where he wants it. I'm not going to mess with the chef's orders."

"Good call," Abby said. "Besides, there's no way you could afford me."

"You're probably right." That earned me another eye roll from Danni.

"But if you have any rich friends or fancy aunties, feel free to pass my details on," Abby added.

"Oh, he's got tons," Danni said, her eyes mischievous.

I scowled at Danni from behind Abby, but she just smirked.

"Good to know," Abby said mildly. "Anyway, I've got to get going. Nice to meet you, Danni." I watched as she took an energy drink from the fridge and a protein bar from the bamboo basket in the pantry before leaving.

"So that's Abby," Danni said after the door closed.

"Yep," I agreed, rather pointlessly.

"And you're still telling me there's no chemistry? Because dude, you couldn't take your eyes off her."

"Lies," I said dismissively, even though it wasn't. "Do you want to grab a coffee, or do you have to get back to the farm?"

"Stables, not farm." Danni punched me lightly in the arm. "And you can definitely buy me coffee while you explain to me how the hell you're going to transform that garage into a functional restaurant in a month."

So long as she didn't ask any more questions about Abby, I could deal with that.

· ♥ · ♥ · ♥ · ♥ · ♥ ·

"So, I'm interested in a membership," I said, my eyes almost watering from the abundance of aggressively cheerful yellow plexiglass that decorated the gym.

"My brother, that's freaking awesome!" A man with a nametag reading 'Matt' pinned to his very tight tank top looked like I had just proposed to him. "We can't wait to welcome you to the Muscle Land family! You're going to love it here!"

"Sounds good," I said, unable to match Matt's enthusiasm. "Just looking to lift a few weights, maybe a few runs on the treadmill."

"You've never seen anything like our weights zone," Matt promised me, his hands clasped together as though thanking some unknown god for the miracle of weights. "You'll think you've died and gone to lifting heaven!"

"Sounds good," I said again. "So, how much is it per week? Do you want a credit card, or do you do direct—"

"Let me give you the tour first, dude," Matt said, clapping me on the shoulder in an overly familiar gesture. "And we'll develop a membership plan tailored just for you."

Bemused, I followed Matt up a narrow set of stairs to the gym floor. With every step we took, the thumping music became louder until I could feel the floor reverberating with the bass.

"This is where the magic happens!" Matt said as he reached the top of the stairs, turning in a circle with his arms outstretched like an unusually beefy Disney princess. "Are you a free weights kind of guy, or more into the machines?"

"Both are good," I said with a shrug. I'd never admit it, but I had never been to a commercial gym before. Back at the enormous penthouse that my father referred to as 'somewhere to crash when we're in the city', there was a private gym just for residents of the building, complete with a full-time personal trainer who claimed to have won medals at the 1964 Olympics and could definitely still bench press more than me.

But here in Brekkie Beach, there was no private gym or personal trainer. I'd have to learn how to stay in some sort of shape all on my own. Yet another challenge for a spoiled trust fund kid; I still needed to face trying to do my own laundry.

"We've got eight squat racks," Matt told me proudly. "Come and take a look; these bad boys are up to competition standards. What's your one rep max?"

"I've never really tested it," I said. At least I knew what a one-rep max was, thanks to my former personal trainer. "I usually just go for volume."

"Nothing stops the gains train, my brother!"

Dutifully, I inspected the bright blue, green, and red plates and the various barbells and listened to Matt's explanation of why using a foam protector was necessary to avoid bruising one's trapezius muscles. And then a vaguely familiar voice interrupted us.

"Wyatt? Oh my god, it is you! Hi!"

I looked up to see... What the hell was her name? The last time I had seen her, she was wearing a tight black skirt, and then nothing at all. Now, she was wearing a unitard so tight I couldn't imagine how she got in or out of it. With her bleached blonde hair in a tight ponytail, the woman whose name I didn't remember was delicately dabbing at her collarbone with a towel and looking up at me with a smile as wide as a crocodile's.

"Hi," I said, hoping it wouldn't be completely obvious that I had forgotten her name. Under normal circumstances, I was no longer the kind of guy to sleep with a woman without even knowing her name. But testing David's cocktail menu had sent me right back to my hedonistic youth and obliterated my over-thirty short term memory. "How are you going?"

"I'm going great! Are you signing up here too?" She looked keenly at Matt's clipboard. "We could work out together some time."

"Maybe," I said, not wanting to make any kind of commitment. "But I'm probably going to be working out at weird times of the day. You know, with my restaurant to run."

Black Skirt's face crumpled in dismay. "Oh, what a shame," she said, her nose wrinkling up like a rabbit's. "I was hoping we could hang out again. Maybe at my place this time."

I fought the urge to laugh as I thought of Abby banging on the wall and shouting about disobedient avocados, though I could tell Black Skirt hadn't found the experience anywhere near as funny as I did.

Black Skirt was still staring at me as my mouth twitched, and Matt had paused in his enthusiastic praise of the quality of the barbells to watch our exchange, bouncing on the balls of his feet.

"I'm going to be really busy with the restaurant for the next few months," I said when the silence became awkward. "So, I don't know if I'll have any free time to...hang out."

That earned a glare from Black Skirt, which I possibly deserved. "Huh," she said and tossed her ponytail. "No, that's totally fine; I get it. Guess I'll see you around."

With that, she set herself up at the rack right in front of us, sticking her bottom right out as though that might convince me I had been wrong to turn down her offer of a 'hang out'. It wasn't very effective.

"Let's check out the machines," Matt said cheerfully, showing more tact than I would have expected from a man in neon green shorts.

When we moved away from Black Skirt, Matt lowered his voice. "Friend of yours?"

"Not exactly," I admitted. "I just moved here, and we met at the pub, and..." I trailed off and hoped he didn't expect me to explain the rest.

"Ah, I understand, dude." Matt gave me another hearty clap on the back, his hand striking me hard enough that it could have counted as an attempted Heimlich Manoeuvre. "It was fun, but you've got more important things to focus on, right?"

And that was true. But even I had been surprised by how quickly I had shut down the possibility of any future rendezvous with Black Skirt. She was reasonably attractive, and the possibility of no strings attached sex should have been appealing.

So why had I shut her down?

"I guess so."

"I get it." Matt nodded again. "Nothing can distract you from your gains, am I right?" I decided not to disabuse him of the notion that increasing my muscle mass was my only focus in life.

"Yeah," I said, not wanting to discuss the matter further. But Matt had other ideas.

"Or maybe it's not just the gains." Matt looked thoughtful. Or at least, he looked as thoughtful as someone in a tight singlet could look. "Maybe, you've only got eyes for someone else."

Someone else? That was ridiculous. And yet...

High cheekbones and wavy dark hair swam into my mind, clear blue eyes giving me a thoroughly unimpressed look. I tried to push the image away, but the imaginary Abby was surprisingly persistent, just like the real Abby.

"I don't know about that," I said. But that wasn't entirely true.

5 Abby

"Oh, I haven't worn that in years! It won't go over my hips!" Melissa, our client, was stretched out on her bed and greedily sucking from a travel mug that I suspected contained wine. "Put it in the trash pile, I suppose."

I nodded approvingly as Josie took the dress (it looked like silk, shot through with silver threads) off the hanger and folded it neatly into one of the hessian bags we had provided. "Well, that's all your hanging garments sorted," I said, dusting off my hands. "We can get started on your folded clothes now."

Folded was perhaps an inaccurate description. Though Melissa's walk-in wardrobe was larger than the bedsit I had lived in during university and contained enough rails, drawers, and shelves to outfit a boutique, there was a mass of sweaters, leggings, hats, gloves, scarves, and what looked like lacy lingerie piled haphazardly on the floor.

"Oh, really?" Melissa's face fell. "This is just so exhausting; I need a break. Why don't you two make a start while I grab a bite to eat and take some time for myself?"

"We can do that," I said, raising my chin. "Josie, we'll start by—"

"Separating by type and then by colour," Josie finished. "All over it, boss."

I smiled at that as Melissa wafted from the room, sighing deeply as though she had been the one on her feet, bending and lifting all morning, instead of us.

"Imagine having such nice stuff and just leaving it on the floor like this," Josie whispered in an undertone. "I mean—" She held up a jumper that looked like cashmere and made a face.

"Well, it keeps us in business."

"Yeah," Josie said with a little sigh. "Rich people are different from us, I guess."

"Oh, they're a whole different species. Homo Wealthius, their brains have evolved to ignore the things that servants like us can do for them."

Josie snorted, but her eyes were fixed on her pile, and she was quickly turning it from a chaos of colour and texture into neatly folded stacks. I was starting to think she might actually be a faster folder than me. And that made me speed up, because apparently, I was stupidly competitive even with my own employee.

"At least she likes the dividers and tubs," Josie said as she shifted her position on the floor to attack a new pile. "She didn't even care about the price."

"Well, when you've got Gucci lying on the floor, I guess $29.95 for a pack of shelf dividers seems like nothing," I said, though I had been secretly glad Melissa had blithely agreed to add so much of my new product line to her invoice. I just hoped my other clients would feel the same way.

Josie snorted again. "Too right!"

Four hours later, my muscles were aching and I could have single-handedly consumed a Christmas turkey with all the trimmings. But it was done. And I couldn't deny the satisfaction that came from seeing Melissa's goblin lair of a wardrobe turned into something I was thankful she was willing to let me post on Instagram.

"I just can't believe it!" Melissa said, spinning slowly around in the wardrobe, her eyes wide. "I never thought everything would fit, but here we are!"

"I'm so pleased that you're happy with the results," I said in my best professional voice. "And it's been such a pleasure working with you."

"I think this will be so good for my stress levels." Melissa sighed happily, trailing her fingers through a neat row of tops arranged in colour order. "You don't know what it's like, starting the day and not being able to find anything to wear!"

It was true that I didn't know what that felt like, but I found it hard to believe that Melissa, who had never had anything resembling an actual job, was facing too much stress.

"It can be so beneficial, creating a sense of calm and order in your space," Josie said, nodding empathetically even though I was sure that her eyes were desperate to roll.

"Yes, I think so." Melissa made it sound like Josie had said something deeply profound. "Calm. Order. Peace!"

Then she looked down at the three hefty "donate" bags full of her rejected clothes. "Are you going to take those away?"

My heart leapt in my chest. Most of my clients asked me to donate their cast-offs to a worthy cause, but occasionally, they invited me to keep anything I liked. That was why I owned three pairs of designer sunglasses, a vintage Gucci belt, and a 2004 Louis Vuitton handbag. Melissa was a different size to me, and her style wasn't anything I'd choose, but I knew from the labels that her discarded clothes would fetch an excellent price on eBay, and I could do with all the extra cash I could get.

"We can take those away for you," I said. "Is there a particular charity you'd like them donated to?"

Melissa let out a loud sigh. "Honestly, I don't care what you do with them, so long as they're not here. Keep them, sell them, chuck them in the river!"

And that was all the invitation I needed.

"Not a problem!" Josie said eagerly, already picking up the bags and slinging them over her wiry forearms. "We'll get these out of your way."

"I'll add those shelf dividers and acrylic tubs to your invoice and send it over this evening," I said, still maintaining my professional persona. "Thank you so much for the opportunity to work with you. I do hope you enjoy your new wardrobe."

"Oh, I will," Melissa said, again collapsing onto her bed. "You know, I might just sit here and enjoy it for a while. You can see yourselves out?"

"Of course," I said, picking up the last bag. "Have a wonderful evening."

Josie turned to me as we made our way down an elegant marble staircase and out through the long hallway surfaced with tiles that Melissa had informed us were imported from Tuscany.

"So, are you going to donate all the clothes? Because she said she didn't care what happened to them, and some are my size, and..." Josie trailed off, looking embarrassed. "But if that's not what we do, I understand."

"Would you like to go through the bags for stuff you'd like to keep?" I said, knowing exactly what she was getting at. "Because that's totally fine. Go for gold!"

"Really?" Josie's eyes were wide as she opened the van door and carefully placed the bags between the boxes of product. "I always kept my kids well turned out, but Bill made me feel guilty for buying so much as a pair of slacks for myself. And since the divorce, well—" She plucked at her admittedly faded t-shirt. "Are you sure you don't want any of it?"

"Nah," I said, shaking my head. "You have it; it's not my size."

I plastered on an encouraging expression and was rewarded by Josie's grateful smile. "Thanks!" she said. "I really appreciate it."

"You don't have to thank me," I insisted. "It's all Melissa's stuff, and you worked your arse off today. Enjoy the perks!"

Josie smiled again, taking her seat in the front of the van.

But I stood outside for a moment longer and pulled out my phone. Frowning, I checked my bank balance. It was not good. It *really* wasn't good. I was still waiting for a big invoice to come through, and somehow, I didn't think Melissa would be the type to pay her own invoice without multiple reminders.

Sighing, I swallowed hard and transferred another lump sum from my dwindling savings. If only that Byron Bay job hadn't been cancelled, I thought. If only my clients paid their invoices as quickly as I paid mine. If only my online store was ready to go.

"It'll be fine," I told myself in a stern whisper. "Just have to keep going."

I pushed my phone back into my pocket, determined that Josie wouldn't guess that the Organised Home Co could have done with the cash injection Melissa's rejects would have fetched on eBay.

After all, I was the boss. Feeling the pressure was just part of the gig. Besides, now that I wouldn't be photographing and listing clothes on eBay tonight, I could sneak in an extra Pilates session, send out reminders for my outstanding invoices, bleach the shower, and tackle whatever else was listed in bright and demanding coloured pens in my notebook.

· ♥ · ♥ · ♥ · ♥ · ♥ ·

By the time I had made the long drive from Sydney's Eastern Suburbs (where Melissa lived in the sort of house that television production companies used to show someone was obscenely wealthy) and dropped Josie off, it was late in the evening. I was hungry, tired, and grumpy.

The knowledge that tonight's dinner plan featured plain pasta with chickpeas and frozen spinach didn't improve my mood, and I may have slammed the door behind me and let out a groan as I did so.

"Everything okay?" A cheerful voice called out, and I swore softly under my breath, having briefly forgotten that the house was no longer my sole dominion.

"All good," I replied, making my way into the kitchen. I'd better get started on my sad pasta. "Just a long day."

Wyatt was already at the bench, chopping a chicken thigh into small pieces. I could already see vegetables sliced into the thin, neat pieces that eluded my knife skills, and there was a jug of what must be sauce waiting next to them.

"Hey," he said, giving me a smile that might have brought plenty of women to their knees but I didn't think was capable of improving my mood. "Rough day?"

"No." I shook my head. "Not rough, just long. I was doing a wardrobe in Point Piper, and it went well, but damn, it was a big job. You should have seen the place; it belonged on *The Real Housewives*, or something. So much marble!"

"That does sound tiring." Wyatt paused. "I'm making a stir fry. I pilfered the ingredients from the restaurant, of course, but they were about to go off, so I didn't want to waste them."

"That makes sense," I said, quietly impressed by his thrift. "Will I get in your way if I boil some pasta?"

"Nope," Wyatt said. "But there's going to be heaps of this if you like stir fry."

I did like stir fry. I definitely liked it a whole lot more than I liked sad pasta. Especially with frozen spinach. But I didn't like people doing favours for me, especially not maddeningly handsome men who had popped up from my past and into my kitchen.

"It's not your job to feed me," I said, shaking my head and making for the pantry to decide which pasta shape would make my dinner the least unappealing. Not spirals, I thought. Spirals were too cheerful.

"Oh, I know that." Wyatt shrugged. "But like I said, the ingredients were about to go off. If this doesn't get eaten tonight, it's going in the bin. And that would be a minor tragedy."

My stomach rumbled, possibly audibly. "If you're sure..." I said hesitantly. "I was going to make chickpea pasta. With spinach."

"That sounds nutritious," Wyatt said, the corners of his eyes crinkling and his mouth twitching.

"Oh, it is," I said, sitting at the table and rubbing my temples. Was I getting a headache, or was I just tired and stressed? Was there even a difference? "But it's hard to get excited about chickpeas."

"I don't know." Wyatt seemed to be considering my statement. "Put those bad boys in a tagine with slow-cooked lamb, some cumin and turmeric, and they're delicious."

"That's way above my level," I said bluntly. "I was thinking salt. If I'm feeling fancy, mixed herbs from a jar."

Wyatt laughed. "I'm sure the jar is beautifully labelled, though."

"Labelling I can do," I said, strangely comforted by his easy laugh and warm smile. "But me and cooking? It's not a good match. One time, I tried to make rhubarb and apple crumble. The internet said it was easy. But how is handling rhubarb easy? All those stalks and leaves! My crumble looked like one of those kid's science experiments where you make a volcano. Except it didn't taste as good."

"Rhubarb crumble, huh?" Wyatt looked interested. "I've never had it."

"It's definitely more of a UK thing," I said. "Probably the only thing I miss about England, to be honest. My sister, Tessa, makes a great crumble, but she can't stand rhubarb so I'd never ask her to make it for me."

"Well, if rhubarb is the only thing you miss, then it sounds like it was a good decision to leave England," Wyatt said, tilting his head as though thinking about it.

"No regrets." And that was true. "Uh, how was your day?" I asked quickly, realising I had complained about mine, waxed lyrical about crumble, and had totally failed to return his polite curiosity.

"Also long," Wyatt said. "But not located in Point Piper, so there's that." He took a pan from the cupboard and held it aloft. "Don't worry, I'll wash up and put everything away when I'm done."

"No, you won't," I told him and continued before he could disagree. "You're cooking, so I'll clean up. It's only fair."

"And I'm going to let you because I was handwashing the new cutlery all day, and my hands are shrivelled up." Wyatt held up his hands to prove his point. "And then I was putting up decorations in the dining room. I got a bulk lot of vintage advertising signs at an auction, I reckon they'll look cool."

"Very trendy," I said, looking away when I realised I had been staring at his hands. He had broad palms and long fingers, and it was too easy to remember how it had felt to hold the teenage version of that hand in mine, our palms sweaty and shaking.

"My step count today was insane, just going back and forth in the restaurant," Wyatt said as he poured oil into the pan, swirling it around in a way that looked expert to my untrained eyes. "I need to get rollerblades or something."

"Wouldn't you prefer a skateboard? Or don't you do that anymore?" And then I realised what I had revealed. Crap. Double crap. Now I was going to look like a creep.

An awkward silence hung in the air, punctuated only by the sizzling sound of the oil in the pan.

"You do recognise me!" Wyatt sounded almost accusing.

"I..." For once, I was lost for words. I swallowed hard. "Well, yeah, of course I do. But I thought you didn't remember me, so I didn't want to make it weird."

Wyatt made a sound a bit like a scoff and shook his head. "I remember you," he said, adding the chicken to the pan and turning away. "I'm hardly going to forget my first kiss."

I let out a breath. "Your first? Seriously?"

"Seriously," Wyatt said, looking back over his shoulder. "You couldn't tell?"

"I thought you were super experienced with all that tongue action," I said. I didn't blush because I was not a blusher, but there was a certain heat in my face. "I was very impressed at the time."

Wyatt let out a groan. "I can only imagine how that was for you. I had a mate who told me that girls liked as much tongue as possible."

"Well, he might have been right," I said. "Just not about kissing." And crap, had I really said that? Now it sounded like I was flirting! Which was not what I should be doing right now.

"My skills have improved a lot since then," Wyatt said, looking back at me again. "Way less like being probed by an alien tentacle. Or so I've been told."

And that sounded a hell of a lot like he was flirting right back. Almost like he was daring me to ask him to prove it. Which was crazy, right? We had been teenagers, and that kiss had been a lifetime ago. He couldn't possibly want a repeat of that moment. And I couldn't possibly let myself get into any kind of situation with my housemate, no matter how handsome and charming he had grown up to be.

I barely knew the adult Wyatt; besides, I had a business to run. A business with a serious cashflow problem.

I squared my shoulders. "Uh, so do you still skate?"

Wyatt didn't turn back to me this time. "Nope," he said. "I was a total poser, only did it for that one summer."

"That's a shame," I said. "Your kickflip was decent. Some of the time."

Wyatt laughed, and this time he did turn to look at me. "I landed it right more often when you and your sisters weren't watching me."

"I gave you performance anxiety?" I had told myself I wouldn't flirt. But here I was, flirty banter spilling from my mouth like I had no control over it.

"I wouldn't say that," Wyatt chuckled, tipping the chicken onto a clean plate and then adding the mountain of vegetables into the still sizzling pan. "Just that a pretty girl watching me made me kind of nervous."

"Well, you didn't say much back then," I said, remembering. "Just let me run my mouth. I thought you were the strong, silent type. You didn't seem shy."

Wyatt stopped still, holding the wooden spoon aloft. I wondered what on earth I had said that had spooked him.

"I guess I was just nervous," he said finally, returning to his stir fry.

I let out a breath. "I should go and..." I looked around helplessly for inspiration. "Take a shower," I said. "I bet I stink after all day in a wardrobe. Then I need to review the audience targets for my new Instagram campaign. Or there's this webinar on social proof I wanted to catch. And I need to get in a Pilates session. Actually, maybe I should take my shower after I do that—"

"You really don't stop, do you?" Wyatt said, a tiny frown appearing between his brows. "If you've got stuff to do, I can just make you a plate."

I knew I was being rude, taking off when he had just cooked for me. Well, not for me. For himself. I just happened to be benefitting from his expertise in the kitchen. Expertise I so thoroughly lacked.

"If you don't mind," I said, knowing I was being cowardly to avoid him and wanting to punch myself for it. Or at least give myself a very firm talking to. "And I'll clean up just after I pack the van for tomorrow."

"Are you sure you can't relax for a minute?" Wyatt raised his eyebrows.

"No rest for the wicked," I said, as I so often did. "Uh, thanks for dinner."

"You can thank me after you taste it," Wyatt said a strange expression on his face. "I'll see you later, Abby."

Abby: so, it turns out that wyatt does remember me

Michelle: duh! of course he does! you were a teenage dream!

Abby: do you remember my eyeliner? i was a teenage nightmare

Tessa: oh god, your emo phase was hilarious

Tessa: and of course he remembers you! why didn't he say anything before?

Abby: he thought i didn't remember him. it was a whole thing

Michelle: that sounds like it would have been a chemistry-filled conversation <winky face emoji>

Tessa: definitely!

Abby: no chemistry, just banter

Abby: it's not like i have time for chemistry

Michelle: not even with your first love, who you thought was lost forever, but fate has reunited you?

Abby: ... i'm begging you to stop reading romance. begging

Michelle: then beg

Tessa: i know you're busy with your business and the product line coming out, but you have to make time for romance

Abby: i can't and won't

Tessa: how's it all going, anyway?

Michelle: is everything okay after that big job got cancelled? financially, i mean

Abby: everything's fine! just busy

Abby: how are you guys going?

Tessa: i'm on the second draft of what might be my last ever ghostwriting job. which is great. and terrifying

Abby: you should have stopped ghostwriting ages ago! your kids' books are freaking bestsellers!

Tessa: but that's not guaranteed, and ghost-writing is steady, and it's not like i hate it. we'll see

Michelle: i have to agree with abby, lean in! forget ghost-writing; you're worth so much more than that

Tessa: <heart emoji>

Michelle: work is good. had a tricky client today, but my boss actually backed me up when I pushed back. it's so weird having a supportive boss!

Abby: you stayed at your old job way too long. they treated you like crap

```
Michelle: well, i know that now!
```
Tessa: i'm just glad you quit when you did and that we get to have you here

Abby: definitely <heart emoji>

Tessa: so, are you both free for dinner at mine tomorrow? i'm making dublin coddle. with the soda bread!

```
Michelle: <gif of an overweight cat begging for food>
Michelle: i am so there
```

Abby: i can't make it; i've got a crap ton to do. reviewing the online store wireframe, photographing the product line, chasing up invoices...

Tessa: i told you dylan was happy to do the photography for you

Abby: he's a professional photographer. i'm not going to let him waste his time taking photos of shelf dividers on a white background when i can do it perfectly well myself

```
Michelle: you're going to burn out
if you don't take a break
Michelle: remember how you always
told me that?
```

Abby: it's fine! it's just a busy period. it's going to get better once the store launches and josie is ready to take jobs on her own

Tessa: but will you be okay until then?

Abby: of course i will!

Michelle: she's got wyatt to look after her

Abby: NO ONE is looking after me

Abby: <gif of Destiny's Child performing *Independent Woman, Part 1*>

Tessa: i wish you'd let someone look after you. it doesn't have to be him.

Abby: i can look after myself! you know that

Tessa: just showing sisterly concern <sad face emoji>

Abby: and it's appreciated, but i've got it all under control

6 Wyatt

Opening a cardboard box with a kitchen knife probably wasn't my best idea ever, but I was sure Abby would be unimpressed if I rifled through her desk for a pair of scissors.

Not that I had even considered going into her bedroom. Of course not.

I narrowly avoided cutting off one of my fingers as I wrestled with tape and cardboard, what seemed like enough plastic to doom the Pacific Ocean, until I retrieved...

"Nice!" I said, flicking the 'test' button on the smoke alarm. Immediately, a loud and insistent beeping filled the room while a bright light flashed along rhythmically.

"Are you having a rave?" I looked up to see Abby, clad once again in the leggings that made me completely unable to keep my eyes on her face and a white t-shirt that didn't entirely hide the outline of her bra.

I flicked the smoke alarm off. "I didn't realise you were home; I didn't mean to disturb you."

"I was just doing a quick yoga session before I head out," Abby said, plucking at her t-shirt. "It's meant to keep me grounded. Make me feel all peaceful and shit."

"Until I tested this thing." I gave her a rueful grin, tapping the smoke alarm.

"What is that?" Abby said, looking at it with interest and moving closer. Close enough that I could smell her shampoo, see the faint sheen of sweat on her collarbone and—

"Uh, it's a smoke alarm," I said. "The standard ones won't work for us, my head chef – David – is deaf, so I needed to get one that lit up too."

"Huh." That didn't give me much to go on. "That's..." She paused. "I guess I hadn't really heard of any chefs who are deaf before."

"Most people haven't," I said, shaking my head. "Which is why David was finding it impossible to get a decent job, even though he's freaking brilliant. Most restaurants think it's too hard, but it's really not. I'm pretty shit at signing, but I'm learning, and his lip reading is next level. We're making it work."

"You're learning sign language?" Abby had an expression on her face I couldn't quite read. "For your chef?"

"Well, yeah. With the restaurant, I..." I cleared my throat, trying to think of how to word it so I didn't sound like a conceited arsehole intent on performative philanthropy. "I wanted to hire people who might find it hard to get a job somewhere else. Because it's bullshit that talented, smart people can't get a job just because they've got a disability or maybe some trouble in their past."

Abby let out a breath. "Wow," she said. "I didn't know that was what you were doing."

"I don't want it to be a big deal," I said quickly. "I don't want that to be what Beach Garage is known for. I want people to come because we're good, not because they think they're doing us some kind of favour. Because that's bullshit too."

Abby nodded. "I get that," she said. "But am I allowed to be impressed? I mean, most people who are starting a business wouldn't want to take any unnecessary risks. It's already so easy to lose everything."

I shifted uncomfortably, trying to decide how much to share. "I guess..." I said, pausing again. "It's important to me. I have an uncle – well, I had an uncle. Uncle Byron. He used a wheelchair after an accident when he was young, but he never let anyone feel sorry for him. And he was brilliant, too. Had his master's in finance, and he always thought he'd be part of the family business—" I cut myself off, wishing I hadn't mentioned that. I didn't want to have to explain just what scale my family business operated on.

But Abby was too busy being outraged to notice.

"But they didn't let him?" Abby looked incensed. "Your family wouldn't let him work there just because he used a wheelchair?"

"It was my grandad who had the attitude about it," I said cautiously. "He just didn't see the point. Byron was well taken care of, so why would he want a job when it would be harder for him? But my dad never stood up to him about it, either. I don't know if he even cared all that much."

"That's bullshit." The blazing intensity in her eyes might have technically been frightening, but I couldn't help but think she looked more beautiful than ever, fierce with indignation on behalf of a man she had never met. "Couldn't you do anything?"

"I was just a worker ant," I shrugged, not wanting to explain that my title had been Director of Operations but that I hadn't had the power to hire Byron. "I should have fought harder, though. And when Byron was dying, he told me that he felt like he had wasted his life because no one would give him a chance. So, I always promised myself that one day, I'd have my own business where I could employ people who other companies – shitty companies – would see as too much of a risk."

"That's..." Abby shook her head, some of the fury leaving her face as she looked up at me. "That's pretty amazing, Wyatt."

"I should have done it sooner," I said, not wanting her to think I was some great humanitarian.

"You must have had to build up your savings to do something like this," Abby said, a gentle hand on my arm. "Don't be too hard on yourself. Launching a business takes a lot of money."

And that made me feel like an arsehole for lying to her, but I couldn't explain, not right now. "I guess I'm just glad I'm doing it now."

"And that's the important part," she said. "What was your family business, anyway?"

And there it was. "Uh, construction," I said lamely. "You know, houses and stuff." And that was technically not a total lie. Parsons Property Inc did build houses. Thousands of houses, on huge estates. Not to mention hotels, shopping centres, business parks, and the occasional airport.

"But they could have given him a desk job," Abby said, still angry.

"Oh, there was definitely room for a desk job," I said. "I mean, I certainly wasn't out there with a hammer and nails."

"Shame. You could totally rock the high vis gear."

"You think so?" That sounded almost like a compliment.

"Definitely." She was flirting with me; I was sure of it. "But you'd be wasted doing that when what you're doing now is so important."

"I don't want you thinking I'm some do-gooder type," I cautioned her. I couldn't let her think that. "It makes sense from a selfish capitalist perspective too. If I employ people that other restaurants wouldn't consider, and I'm good to them, then they won't leave me when a better offer comes along. See? Selfish."

Abby laughed, her face relaxing slightly. "Glad to see that you're a bourgeoise overlord after all. I don't know how I'd feel sharing a house with such a do-gooder."

"No one's ever accused me of that before," I said. "It's really not a big deal. With David, I only have to get a few extra bits and pieces in the kitchen that light up rather than just make noise. And I'll get the sous chef and kitchen hands to do an Auslan workshop. David says he'd be fine, even if I didn't – like I said, that dude is the master of lip reading – I just don't think he should always have to."

"I'm still impressed," Abby said, her voice unusually serious. "I did a kitchen reorganisation for a client who was blind a few months ago. It was awesome; I worked with her and her occupational therapist. Just little stuff like lighting and choosing high-contrast colours makes a big difference. We did get a talking oven, though; that was pretty cool."

"That sounds like a great project," I said. "See, you get it. It's not that hard to make a space accessible."

"No," Abby agreed. "But most people wouldn't bother."

"My restaurant manager already knows Auslan," I said. "And she's freaking amazing, but she was struggling to get a job too. She had some stuff in her past that made employers a little...edgy." I wasn't going to explain Mindy's history. It wasn't my story to tell.

Abby tilted her head in understanding. "But it didn't bother you?"

"I saw a damn good restaurant manager who had overcome some serious shit," I said, nodding to emphasise my point. "She was the best person for the job. But most people couldn't see that."

"Like with Josie."

"Josie? Is she your assistant?"

"My very first employee," Abby clarified. "Her official title is Organisational Executive. She's going to start solo jobs soon, but until then, I guess she's kind of like my assistant." Abby sighed. "She couldn't get a decent job either. She was a homemaker for forty years because her dirtbag husband didn't want her to work. Then he walked out the door, and all she could get was a job at a supermarket. And there's nothing wrong with supermarkets, but she's got so much more to offer!"

"But you hired her?"

"Because she's amazing!" Abby said, a little defensively. "You should have seen her cover letter and the photos of how she has her place organised. And yes, she's in her sixties, but she's super energetic and probably fitter than me."

"I don't doubt it," I said with a smile. "I can't imagine you hiring anyone who couldn't match your energy."

"Oh, she's way better than me."

"I'm not sure about that," I said, knowing I was coming close to saying something I shouldn't. "I won't tell anyone you're a big softie; it would totally ruin your rep. I haven't forgotten your whole tough girl thing, with the studded bracelet, the eyeliner..."

Abby let out a groan, covering her face. "I am not a softie!" she objected. "There's nothing soft about me!"

I decided not to mention that I had noticed a few hundred times just how deliciously soft and inviting her body was.

Abby stood up, shaking her head. "Anyway, if anyone's the softie, it's totally you. I hired one person who most businesses wouldn't take a chance on. You've got at least two."

"I told you that was an entirely selfish business decision!"

"And I told you I was impressed," Abby said, looking right into my eyes. Her blue eyes seemed somehow unguarded, and her lips were slightly parted like she needed to take an extra breath.

"I guess I should say thank you, then," I said, feeling my stomach tighten. "And that I'll clean up this mess." I waved a hand at the mass of plastic and cardboard littering the usually pristine kitchen table. "I promise."

"Oh, I'd expect nothing less," Abby said. "Seriously, if you leave crap around, you'll find out I'm not a softie real fast."

"Is that a challenge?" And damn, that sounded way too flirty. But I couldn't resist. Even after all these years, I wanted Abby's attention and was willing to do more than a kickflip to get it.

"Only if you're up to it," Abby said, and she bit her lip as she looked at me one final time before disappearing up the stairs.

· ♥ · ♥ · ♥ · ♥ · ♥ ·

"Don't fall off!" Mindy warned as I leaned up, trying to attach the smoke alarm to the ceiling while balanced on top of three stacked chairs. A step ladder was definitely on my list of things to buy.

"That's just what I was planning to do," I said, not looking down. "I'm trying to break my leg, so I'm stuck on crutches for weeks."

Mindy snorted. "Just trying to look out for you, boss."

With a grunt, I fixed in the final screw. "Okay, I'm going to test it," I said, turning back to look at Mindy and David and signing along as best I could.

David gave me a thumbs up, looking expectant.

I pressed the button, and immediately the kitchen was engulfed in flashing lights and obnoxiously loud beeping. I gave it a few seconds until Mindy swore and covered her ears.

"It works!" I said, triumphantly jumping down from the stack of chairs.

"It's like a rave!" David signed, spelling out the final word as though he knew I wouldn't understand the sign.

"That's what my housemate said. Will it work for you?"

"Definitely," David replied.

"This is the housemate you kissed in a park, right?"

"When we were teenagers!"

"But is there still something there?" David gave me a thoughtful look.

"I don't have time for something," I insisted, but my head chef gave me a look that needed no interpretation. "Is your sous chef coming later today?

David nodded. "We're going to test the chargrilled spatchcock."

"Then it's a good thing I installed the smoke alarm," I said with raised eyebrows. "I'm going to check out those tables I found online. You know, from the restaurant that's closing down. See if I like them."

"You'd better like them," Mindy warned me. "We're opening in a month, and I'm pretty sure diners prefer not to eat with their plates on their laps."

David laughed loudly. "Are you going home after that?"

"That's the plan."

David turned and made for the enormous fridge I had been fortunate enough to score for a reduced price due the scratches on the glass. "Take this for your housemate." He handed me a glass bowl of his spanner crab and saffron risotto.

"Don't you want it?" I asked. "This stuff is like heroin-coated crack."

David laughed again. "I've had too much already."

"I bet she'll like it," Mindy said. "And it's better than heroin-coated crack. I'd know, after all."

I gave a reluctant chuckle. "Abby told me it's not my job to feed her, but she loved the ravioli."

"An independent woman," Mindy said approvingly. "But keeping your housemate on your good side can't hurt. Even if you don't have any interest in her."

"Which I don't!" But I took the risotto anyway.

They were right. Abby *would* like it. And while it wasn't my job to feed her, I couldn't resist the thought of the sounds Abby might make when she tried it.

·❤·❤·♥·❤·❤·

"How many tables do you reckon I could fit in a horse float?"

That statement was met with an indignant snort worthy of the usual occupant of said float. "And hello to you too, Wyatt," Danni said, sounding bemused.

"Sorry," I said because that was a dickish thing to start a conversation with. "Is there any chance you might let me borrow a horse float to move some tables? So I don't have to rent a truck?"

"That depends," she said. "Are you going to give me some of that chargrilled spatchcock you sent me the photo of?"

"I think it's all gone," I admitted. "But I bet David could do another batch."

"Nah, I won't make him do that," Danni said. "I'm sure I can find another favour you can do for me?"

"Wingman at the next ladies' night at the club?" I suggested. "Even if I got my arse pinched last time. I swear, that bruise was purple!"

"Your arse will just have to cope," Danni said, chuckling. "Everything's going well with the restaurant, then? Does it look less like a garage yet?"

"Well, no," I admitted. "But it will."

"Your mum called me the other day," Danni said after a pause. "Asking how you are. And how the restaurant is going. You could call them, you know."

I groaned. "So they can tell me what a huge mistake I'm making? How selfish I'm being, walking away from the family business?"

"Well, you did kind of leave abruptly," Danni pointed out.

I groaned again. "I had to. There was never going to be a good time, and every time I tried to give my notice, Dad ignored me."

"I get that," she said. "But they're your parents, and you're their only freaking child! And I know they can be a bit much sometimes, but it's not like you're never going to speak to them again."

"Of course not. But I'm not ready to speak to them yet." Desperate to change the subject, I played a trump card. "How are the horses?"

"I know you're deflecting, but I'm worried about Kingston. When I took him out today, his canter was off. If he's not back to his usual self by tomorrow, I'm going to get the vet in."

"Maybe he's tired," I suggested. "Or he's having a midlife crisis. Have you noticed him trying to mount any of your younger female horses?"

"If he starts asking to have his mane braided, I'll let you know," she said. "I'm trying not to freak out. I mean, everyone's allowed an off day. But he's my baby."

"He is," I said, clicking my tongue sympathetically. "Even I like Kingston. Well, sort of. He's okay. For a horse."

"I don't know how we're friends with you being afraid of horses."

"I'm not afraid of them!" That wasn't strictly true. "They just make me uncomfortable. It's the bulging eyes. They look judgemental."

"Oh, they're definitely judgemental," Danni said appreciatively. "And extremely high maintenance."

"Your taste in animals is exactly the same as your taste in women. You know that, right?"

"Speaking of taste in women," she said slyly. "How's Abby?"

I coughed, clearing my throat. "Well, it turns out she does remember me," I said, recalling our conversation the night before.

"Of course she does!" Danni was pleased. "Are you going to admit that there are sparks yet, or are you still deep in that river in Egypt?"

"Look, it's not like I haven't noticed that she's attractive—"

Danni made a sound worthy of Kingston.

"Okay, very attractive," I deferred. "But that doesn't mean anything. Lots of women are attractive. I've got a restaurant to open in a month, and as you have so kindly pointed out, it still looks like an abandoned garage. And I have to live with her! What's the phrase you always so charmingly use? Don't shit where you eat."

"I do say that a lot," Danni admitted. "I don't know, dude, it's just... It seems like a thing, you know? A blast from the past returning just when you've changed everything in your life. It should mean something."

"It's just a coincidence," I said, shifting uneasily in my seat. "Yes, Abby's very attractive, and she's good company. I mean, we've got some great banter happening. But that's it. And that's all it should be."

"You just keep telling yourself that," Danni said. "Anyway, I've got to go. I reckon Kingston could do with an oat bath."

"Are you seriously going to give that creature an oat bath?"

"Absolutely!" Danni said indignantly. "He deserves it. Call me tomorrow, okay? You can tell me all about how absolutely nothing will happen with Abby because it's not like that."

"It isn't like that!" I said again, but Danni just laughed and ended the call.

And as I looked over at the bowl of risotto carefully strapped into the front seat beside me, I had to wonder if maybe, just maybe, it was a little bit like that after all.

7 Abby

"I just didn't realise there was so much stuff in here!" Jeremy, my client of the day, looked apologetic as he waved his arms and looked hopelessly around his overstuffed garage.

I privately wondered how he could possibly have failed to realise. The garage in question was a decent size, but you couldn't have parked a kick scooter in there, let alone a car.

"It's not a problem," I said airily, taking another unlabelled cardboard box from the shelf. The packaging said it was an air fryer, but the contents felt much heavier. "All we need to do is move everything out onto the driveway, then you can decide what to keep and what to get rid of, and then it's my job to get what's left in order." I lifted my chin as I looked at him. "I've seen much worse. This will be easy."

"Really?" Jeremey looked doubtful as he slid one hand over his thinning hair, as though wanting to check what was left was still intact. "I just want to be able to get my car in here. It's a Mercedes, you know. An E-class."

"It's a lovely car," I said, knowing it wouldn't be the last time I would be required to admire the Mercedes. Jeremy had brought it up approximately four hundred and thirty-six times already. "And we're definitely going to get it in here by the end of the day. Watch this space!"

Jeremy, seemingly buoyed by my words, nodded and grabbed another box, charging forward with it and—

"Ow, shit!" I swore, lurching unsteadily to one side before falling flat on my arse.

"I'm sorry!" Jeremy abandoned the box, looking mortified. "It slipped out of my hands! Did I hurt you?"

The box containing what felt like lead weights had indeed slipped from his hands and fallen directly onto my foot. I cursed myself for thinking sneakers were a good idea today. I should have worn the steel-toed Blundstone boots I reserved for the most perilous of jobs. But no, I had stupidly believed Jeremy when he had told me his garage was 'just a little cluttered'.

My foot throbbed painfully, and it was worse when I wiggled my toes inside my delightfully orange but insufficiently protective sneakers. "It's fine," I said, getting to my feet and hiding my wince. "Just a bruise. All part of the job!"

"I really am sorry," Jeremy said again, seeming to deflate. "Should I take you to get it checked out? We can take my Mercedes. Very fast, you know."

"No need!" I said, ignoring the pain and picking up the offending box. "Let's just crack on with it. I'll walk it off!"

"If you're sure..." He looked uncertain.

"Very sure." I wasn't sure. My foot was throbbing, and every step made me curse Jeremy and his bloody Mercedes. I wished Josie had been there, but when she had mentioned it was her grandson's school athletics carnival, I had insisted she attend. What was the point of a job like this if you didn't have the flexibility to see your nine-year-old grandson win the hurdles?

"Let's crack on," I said in a falsely cheerful tone. "Or we won't be able to get your car in here tonight. And that would be a tragedy."

· ♥ · ♥ · ♥ · ♥ · ♥ ·

Walking it off, it seemed, had been a bad idea. A very bad idea indeed if the excitingly purple, black, and blue shades currently covering my right foot were any indication. I yelped as I shifted the bag of frozen peas onto the suffering appendage. It helped, but it certainly didn't obliterate the pain.

Nor had the two paracetamol, two ibuprofen, or even the leftover prescription painkillers I had saved from my wisdom tooth removal years before. The good painkillers had given me a pleasantly mellow feeling, however, which had been heightened by the glass of wine I had felt more than entitled to indulge in. Not bad for a bargain bin cleanskin.

Speaking of which...

My wine glass was empty. While I tried not to drink on work nights, the current circumstances seemed to necessitate a second glass of wine. And maybe even a third. Shifting my laptop onto the coffee table, I staggered to my feet. Well, foot. There was no way I was putting any more weight on my bruised foot, so I hopped, wine glass in hand, back to the kitchen.

Topping it up with a pour that would have earned the censure of a Responsible Service of Alcohol Marshal, I took a greedy gulp to avoid spillage and gingerly began to limp back to the sofa, even the faintest pressure on my foot making me swear again. I was going to come up with some new and exciting curses, that was for sure.

"Son of an arsehole!" I swore, setting down my wine unsteadily and collapsing, unceremoniously, onto the sofa.

That was, of course, when the front door opened and Wyatt stepped in.

The bright grin he turned on me immediately faded, possibly because he might have thought I was calling him the son of an arsehole.

Quickly, I put the bag of peas over my black and blue foot and tried to smile. "Hi," I said. "Sorry about that. You're not the son of an arsehole. At least, I don't think you are."

"What happened to you?" Wyatt was at my side in an instant. "Did something happen to your foot?"

"It's no big deal," I told him. "I was doing a garage today, and a box got dropped on my foot. Well, my client dropped it, actually. While he was telling me about his car. Do all Mercedes owners feel the need to remind you that they own one every five minutes?"

"Most do." Wyatt quirked his mouth. "Let me see." He reached for the bag of peas, but my hands flew to my foot protectively. I didn't want him to see the bruise; I didn't need him making a big deal about it.

"It's fine!" I held my bag of peas in place. "Just a bruise. I'm doing the right stuff, icing it and resting!"

"Doesn't look like you're resting." Wyatt indicated my laptop with a tilt of his head.

"My brain's fine; it doesn't need rest." I waved a dismissive hand. "And I'm drinking wine! If that isn't restful, I don't know what is."

"Let me see," Wyatt said again. This time, his tone was resolute. It wasn't a request; it was a statement of fact. I wasn't used to anyone using that tone with me because it was exactly the tone I used on other people, especially my sisters.

"It's just a bruise," I said again, moving the peas very slightly to show the edge of the bruise.

Wyatt made an exasperated sound and grabbed the peas away with one big hand. "Jesus, Abby!"

"Give me back my peas!" I said, grabbing for them and trying to hide my foot. But the pain made me swear again and collapse back into the sofa.

"That looks really bad," Wyatt said, and before I could stop him, his strong, warm fingers had captured my throbbing foot. I gasped out at the warmth of his hands against my iced skin. With my injured foot in his hands, all I could do was sit there and...let him.

I bit my lip. "It looks worse than it is."

"I don't know about that," Wyatt said, tracing the outline of the bruise and then gently pressing the tip of his finger against the black centre. I flinched, letting out a hiss of pain. "Do you know how many bones there are in the foot? I think you've broken at least one of them."

"It's fine," I said, but my voice was weak, and I gritted my teeth against the pain. "I still finished the job. If I can walk on it, it's fine. Right?"

"You kept working on this foot?" Wyatt sounded both astonished and distinctly pissed off. "Abby, that's batshit crazy."

"I had a job to do," I mumbled. "I had to finish."

"I'm pretty sure you can postpone a job when the client causes you grievous bodily injury," Wyatt said, carefully replacing the bag of peas on my foot. "We need to take you to the emergency room; you can't just ignore a broken foot."

"It's not broken!" I protested. "And I'm not going to emergency. I don't have hours to waste sitting around just for some poor overworked doctor to tell me, yes, that is indeed a bad bruise."

"Or that it's broken," Wyatt said. "I'm not a doctor, but I've seen enough gnarly bruises to know this isn't normal. I really think we should get you to the ER."

"Absolutely not," I said flatly.

"Abby..." There was a dark warning in Wyatt's voice, and it made me shiver with something other than the throbbing pain of my foot. Since when did I shiver at men being insistent with me? I *hated* it when men told me what to do! I blamed the wine or the painkillers. Possibly both.

"Look, let me rest it tonight." I sensed that a compromise might be my best option given that my very tall and strong housemate was looking at me like he might just throw me over his shoulder like a caveman and carry me to the emergency room. "And if it's still bad in the morning, I'll go to the doctor. I promise. But let's give peas a chance."

"That might be the worst pun I've ever heard." Wyatt shook his head as though he couldn't quite believe I had said it. "But I'll allow it. So long as you actually rest tonight. No work." He picked up my laptop and closed it with a snap.

"But I've got things to finish! And don't tell me 'no'. I don't like it when men tell me what to do."

"And yet here I am, telling you what to do. For your own good, of course." Wyatt raised his eyebrows. "If you pick up that laptop again, I'll call an ambulance."

"I don't need an ambulance!"

"I'll still call one if I catch you working," Wyatt said. "Or I'll call your sisters. You did tell me they're local."

"Not my sisters!" I was genuinely alarmed at the prospect. "They'll make a huge fuss about nothing!"

"It's not nothing," Wyatt objected. "And I won't call them if you stay there." He picked up the TV remote, flicking it on. "Now, what's your poison? You're going to sit here and watch trashy TV."

"I've got work to do," I complained, but I knew it was hopeless. And the prospect of trashy TV was all kinds of appealing.

Wyatt shook his head and navigated into my Netflix profile. "Oh, you're a *Selling Sunset* fan too? Excellent, I haven't seen Season Three. What's that awful Christine up to?"

"You're seriously going to watch it with me?" I asked him, incredulous.

"I am," Wyatt said firmly. "And what's more, I'm going to feed you, bring you wine, and stop you from undertaking any unnecessary movement."

"Why would you do that?" I was genuinely confused. Was he seriously just that nice?

"Because someone's got to look after you, Abby," Wyatt said, his hazel eyes meeting mine for a moment. A smile played on his lips, but he sounded absolutely serious. "I know you're not going to do it yourself."

I was about to ask him why he thought it had to be him, but on second thought, I was in no fit state to hear his answer.

Instead, I took a sip of wine and let myself be drawn into the antics of competitive real estate agents selling comically enormous homes to obnoxiously wealthy people. But I was still very aware of Wyatt, sitting by my side.

· ♥ · ♥ · ♥ · ♥ · ♥ ·

Despite the wine and painkillers, my sleep was fitful, broken, and the exact opposite of restful. Taking a deep breath, I pulled the blanket back and swore.

"How the hell can it be *worse*?" I groaned, wiggling my toes ineffectually. A wave of pain shot through me, and I closed my eyes, gritting my teeth to avoid yelling out loud.

Hobbling to the bathroom, I scowled at my reflection. There were dark circles under my eyes, and my hair looked like I had stuck a finger in an electrical outlet. Even putting on a loose dress was a challenge; there was no way I could handle my usual leggings.

"Fine," I said as I staggered to the sofa, unwilling to let Wyatt know I had slid down the stairs on my bottom. "I think I do need to go to the doctor. You were right!"

"I'd be more pleased that I was right if you weren't so obviously in serious pain," Wyatt said, approaching me with a frown. He knelt in front of me in a move that made my breath hitch, even if I knew it was just to look at my foot.

"Bloody hell Abby, that looks painful." He reached out to cradle my foot in his long fingers for a moment, and I let out a hiss. He looked up at me, hazel eyes meeting mine and showing only tender concern.

I *really* wasn't used to anyone looking at me like that.

"It'll be okay," I said, swallowing back the unexpected – were they unexpected? – rush of feelings that threatened to swarm me. "I'm just going to make some coffee, and then I'll go. If the wait isn't too long, I should be able to get to the lock-up afterwards and—"

"I'll make the coffee," Wyatt said in that tone of his that made it clear he didn't expect to be questioned. "You stay right there." But then he quirked his mouth. "Permission to use one of your pods? And touch your nice mugs?"

I let out a breath. "Permission granted," I said, sighing. "Sorry if I was kind of territorial about them."

"Hey, it's your stuff. You're allowed to not want some random guy touching your stuff. Especially when you've got it so beautifully organised."

"You're not some random guy."

"Well, that's flattering," Wyatt said, flashing me a smile from over the coffee machine. "I've clearly been promoted in your estimation."

"I..." I swallowed again. The pain was clearly making me soft. "You've been a great housemate so far," I said instead of something I'd regret. "I mean, you've shared your amazing food with me, and there's been, like, zero disturbances since..."

"Since the first night," Wyatt finished, ducking his head slightly as though embarrassed. "You should know that I don't...I mean, I don't bring home strangers like that very often. There was a lot of tequila involved in that decision-making process. And I try not to let tequila make decisions for me, as a rule."

"It's none of my business who you bring home," I said, looking away. Why was Wyatt telling me this? "So long as your guests don't make the wall thump like that again."

"I know, but..." Wyatt sighed, and he brought over the cup of coffee. It smelled amazing, and I suspected it would taste better than the coffee I made for myself, even from the same machine. "Drink up," he said instead. "And then I'll drive you to the doctor."

"I can drive myself!" I shifted my position on the sofa to appear less fallen angel and more like an upright professional who could look after herself.

"Abby, even if I wasn't worried about you personally, I'd be an arsehole to let someone with a broken foot loose on the roads. I think it might technically count as criminal negligence. Your right foot is kind of critical when it comes to operating that van of yours, am I right?"

And shit, I hadn't thought of that. I took a gulp of my coffee and let out a grunt that I'd blame on the pain.

"And besides," Wyatt went on, sitting beside me and giving me another of those smirks. "If you don't let me, I'll call your sisters. Don't think I won't." He was smiling, but there was absolutely a threat behind his words.

I let out a theatrical sigh. "Fine," I said. "I surrender. On this one occasion!"

But Wyatt just laughed. "If that's a challenge, I'm definitely up for it."

And the way my insides squirmed and rearranged themselves as he looked at me had absolutely nothing to do with my throbbing, blackened foot.

· ♥ · ♥ · ♥ · ♥ · ♥ ·

"I can't believe I've got to wear this thing for a month!" I scowled at the sturdy grey 'walking boot' that the doctor had insisted was necessary for my recovery.

"I can't believe you talked them into that thing instead of a proper cast," Wyatt replied. "You've got a broken metatarsal! That's bad!"

"Fractured," I objected. "Just a fracture."

"Semantics," Wyatt said. "I bet they told you to take it easy, too?"

I frowned. "Maybe."

"Definitely," Wyatt said. "And I bet you've got zero intention of following medical advice."

"I've got a lot to do!" I said. "I told you, this is a critical time for my business! I don't have time to just be lying around taking it easy! I can't—" I cut myself off and sighed.

As we reached the car, Wyatt opened the passenger door for me, totally unnecessarily. I had noticed that Wyatt, like the box-dropping Jeremy, drove a Mercedes, but when I asked him about it, he told me a friend was letting him drive it while he was overseas. I wished I had friends like that.

"Then I guess I'll just have to be the enforcer," he said, taking my arm to help me into the passenger seat. And I didn't need help; I could do it perfectly well on my own.

But the feeling of his strong hand gripping my forearm, one arm snaked around my back was...

"You think you can stop me?" I asked, looking up at him and jutting out my chin.

"I don't know," Wyatt said, looking at me with a strange expression. "But I'm sure as hell going to try."

And that left me with a curious fluttering feeling in my chest, right under my ribcage, and for a long moment, I completely forgot about my throbbing, foam-clad foot. I was too busy examining my throbbing feelings.

8 Wyatt

"What do you mean, postponed until next month?" I ran a hand through my hair, getting perilously close to tugging some out. I refrained in deference to me looking nothing like Vin Diesel and thus unable to rock the bald look.

"The Fire Safety Inspection Officer assigned to your case number has gone on personal leave," a bored-sounding woman said. I could actually hear her cracking gum, which I found more than a little disgusting. Was it pink and sticky? Was she blowing bubbles while ruining my life? "The soonest we can reschedule is in ten weeks."

"But my grand opening is in four weeks!"

"You'll have to postpone," the woman said flatly. "You can't open without a safety certificate. There's a fine for every day that a business operates without a valid safety certificate."

"I get that I need the certificate," I said, trying to collect myself and put on the charm. "I really do, and I know this isn't your fault. But surely there's more than one Fire Safety Inspection Officer. Can't someone else come out before then?"

A long sigh. "They're all fully booked," she said. "You'll just have to wait, Mr Parsons. Will there be anything else?"

"No," I said. "Thank you," I added in a tone dripping with sarcasm. I let out a grunt and slammed the phone down on the table.

It wasn't even nine o'clock, and my day already felt like a disaster. My fingers twitched as I looked down at my phone. I could fix this. I knew I could fix this. One phone call to my family's 'government relations consultant' (which in truth meant 'fixer') and I'd find myself exempt from needing the damn certificate. It would be so easy. But I had sworn I would do this without any of the Parsons money – or muscle.

"That sounded like a bad one," Abby said, coming into the kitchen at a brisker pace than her walking boot would suggest was a good idea. "Let me guess. Council?"

"How did you know?"

"If someone with a small business has a shitty, stressful phone call, there's a ninety per cent chance that local government's involved." Abby gave me a wry smile. "What is it this time? Refusing to allow outdoor seating? Noise limit after six?"

"Worse," I said, groaning again. "The Fire Safety Inspection Officer was meant to come today to sign off on our certificate. But he's gone on leave. This woman swears they can't possibly send anyone else for at least ten weeks."

"But you open in four weeks."

"Exactly," I sighed. "But she said that wasn't her problem, and we'd just have to wait."

"But you can't wait!" Abby was aghast. "I mean, you've got all these staff about to start and you have to pay them. You've got your launch planned..."

"I know," I said. "But what am I supposed to do? I can't exactly bribe them."

"This is the problem with local government," Abby began, viciously pointing a finger. "If you were some big business or rich arsehole, you could totally bribe them. Or 'apply strategic pressure'. The big players never have to worry about this bullshit; it's only us little guys who get screwed!" She looked fierce, and once again, it just made her all the more attractive to me. Even if she was railing against rich arseholes and big business. Both of which I technically represented.

"You're right," I said. "Or a big business could just absorb the cost of a fine."

"Yes!" Abby nodded ferociously. "I see it all the time, shitty property developers not waiting for planning permission because the fine they have to pay is nothing compared to what they'll make in profit. But small fry like us just can't do it."

"Well, I appreciate you letting me rant," I said, picking up my phone. "And even being kind enough to agree with me. I'd better call Mindy first, see if we can push back the start dates for the floor staff and—"

"Wait a minute," Abby said, holding up a hand that made me pause. She was scrolling through her phone with distinct determination. "Ha! I knew I still had it!"

"Had what?"

"The phone number for one of the Councillors. He's the Deputy Mayor, actually. I did his whole house last year. It was a huge job, so I got to know him a bit. His wife cried once it was finished, and he reckons it saved their marriage. To be fair, I can understand why it was under strain with that much golfing memorabilia on display. Anyway," Abby waved a hand, "I can call him now. I bet he can get a safety inspector out to you by the end of the week, if not today."

I wasn't expecting a molten ball of chocolate to suddenly become lodged in my chest; sweet, warm, and melting. Its sudden presence was because of Abby. Abby being so indignant on my behalf and wanting to do me such an enormous favour. That must mean she liked me at least a little, right?

"You don't have to do that," I said quickly, feeling a twinge of guilt. Abby shouldn't use her contacts for me when technically, I had my own. Not that she knew that.

"He told me to hit him up if I ever needed anything!" Abby said, shrugging. "Now I need something."

"You should save that for when you need it," I objected. "Not waste it on me."

But Abby just looked at me. "I don't think it's a waste."

And that intensified the molten chocolate ball feeling in my chest. The sticky sweetness melted right down to my stomach as I looked at her, and yeah, I was having feelings that went way beyond acknowledging that Abby was, objectively speaking, hot. I *liked* her. Maybe even more than I had at fifteen. God damnit, Danni was going to be insufferable when I admitted it.

"Besides, it'll make me feel better to be able to do something," Abby went on, shaking her head as though aware that she had said something a little too emotionally intense. "I hate not being able to move around like usual!" She indicated her foot, still in its walking cast. "I can't get anything done."

"Well, that's a lie," I said, teasing. "I saw you cross out twelve things in your notebook yesterday."

"I can't get *enough* done," Abby corrected herself. "It's bullshit!"

"It really bothers you, doesn't it?" I said with a slight frown. "Not being able to power through your day like usual."

"It does," Abby said, screwing her mouth up. "I know it bothers me more than most people, but I…" She trailed off, looking at me with an expression that bordered on helpless. Which was not an expression Abby typically wore.

"I won't ask why," I said quietly. "But if you ever want to tell me, I'm listening."

"Thanks," Abby said, her eyes meeting mine for a moment before she looked away. "Anyway, I should make that call. Help you get Beach Garage all squared away."

"Thank you, Abby," I said, looking into those clear blue eyes again. "It's really kind of you."

"Us little guys have to stick together," Abby said, biting her lip. "You know, with our small businesses and no one to fall back on. It's only right."

"Yeah," I said quickly, but my insides went from melting to twisting with guilt. I wasn't really a little guy at all, and I had plenty to fall back on. "But still, thank you."

"It's not a problem," Abby said, giving me a small smile. "And besides, it's totally selfish too. I want somewhere to eat in Brekkie Beach other than Nick and Nikki's. Wheatgrass and fig brownies just aren't my jam. If I can ever afford to eat out again." She gave a rueful laugh, but that made me feel even more guilty.

"Is everything okay with your cash flow?" I asked carefully. "I mean, I know it's always tight when you're expanding, but you're not in trouble, are you?"

"Of course not!" Abby shook her head and snorted as though desperate to prove how far from trouble she was. But she did it a little too quickly, and I couldn't help being concerned. "I'm not going to starve any time soon."

"Well, I'd never let that happen. I mean, I'm opening a restaurant. I'd have to be a massive arsehole to let my housemate starve when we've got tons of leftovers every day. And I try not to be a massive arsehole."

"Oh, I don't think you're an arsehole at all." Abby's lips twitched. "But don't worry, I won't tell anyone. I know you've got a rep to maintain."

I laughed. "Thanks, Abby."

But the twisting in my stomach didn't stop, and I couldn't help thinking that maybe I really was a massive arsehole for not telling her the truth.

· ♥ · ♥ · ♥ · ♥ · ♥ ·

"When is the Fire Safety Inspection Officer coming?" Mindy asked, looking down at her watch. "I thought he was supposed to be here by now."

"Ah," I said, swallowing hard. "Apparently, he's on unexpected personal leave and won't be back for a few months."

Mindy swore, and though I didn't know the sign she used, I would have been able to tell it was a swear word even without her verbal confirmation.

"What are we going to do?" David asked, frantic. "We open in a month!"

"I know," I said, signing slowly along with my words. "It's going to be okay. Abby knows the Deputy Mayor at Council. She's calling him to get someone out here this week."

David and Mindy looked at each other and then at me.

"What?" I said, exasperated by their silent stares.

"That's nice of her." David raised his eyebrows.

"Very nice of her indeed," Mindy repeated. "For someone who's just a housemate."

"She is nice!" I shot back, even though I had thought the same thing. "And maybe she feels like she owes me after I drove her to the doctor. Even though she doesn't."

Mindy and David exchanged another look, and I rolled my eyes.

"I know what you're thinking, but it's not like that." Even if my feelings when I was in Abby's proximity were rapidly coming to convince me that perhaps it *was* like that. Very much like that actually. "She's not interested in… She doesn't think of me that way."

"Why not?" David managed to convey his disbelief in the way he signed.

"Because..." I sighed. "Because she's too busy." As I said the words, I realised how lame they sounded.

David gave a loud chuckle, and Mindy joined him. "Being busy doesn't mean you can't like someone," she said. "And it sounds like she's keen on you."

"It does mean you're not interested in anything happening, though," I objected. "And she's definitely not."

"We'll see." David crossed his arms, looking irritatingly smug.

Before I could argue any more, my phone rang, flashing an unfamiliar number. I answered quickly, hoping it was someone from Council telling me there was an inspector coming tomorrow.

"Is that Wyatt Parsons?"

"Uh, yes," I said, leaving the kitchen to take the phone call. "Who's this?"

"Belinda Stevens, from the *Herald* Food and Wine team," the woman said. "Is this an okay time to talk?"

"Sure," I said. Someone from a newspaper wanted to talk about my restaurant. That could only be a good thing, right? "Is this about Beach Garage's opening?"

"Yes, it is," Belinda said. "We're looking at doing a feature article about your new venture, how you've broken off from the family business—"

"Is that all you're interested in?" I interrupted. "That I'm a Parsons doing something other than working for Parsons Property?"

"Well, we'd include some details about your menu too!" Belinda sounded offended. "It would definitely be good publicity. People will be interested that this restaurant isn't under the Parsons Property umbrella."

I gritted my teeth. I should have expected this, but I hadn't, which made me feel like an idiot. I just hadn't anticipated that the media would be interested in why I was opening a restaurant that wasn't owned, funded, and run by Parsons Property.

"Look, that's not something I want to focus on," I said bluntly. "You're welcome to come out here and meet my head chef, and I can tell you about how we've transformed an abandoned garage into a gourmet dining experience, but I'm not going to talk about my family."

"Has there been a rift because of your new project?" Belinda seized upon the idea eagerly. "Is this your rebellion against your father being CEO for so long?"

"No," I said shortly. "I've got a great team here who are highly talented, and I'm sure Beach Garage will be a huge success because of them. I want people to care about our food, not about who my parents are."

Belinda was silent for a long moment. "You should know that we can put out the feature whether or not you choose to speak to us."

"You can," I said evenly. "Or you can wait until we're open and come and interview me then, and we'll give you all the quotes and photos you could possibly want."

Another silence. "I'll be in touch," Belinda said finally, and the call ended.

I let out a groan and sat down on one of the metal chairs I had stacked up to install the smoke alarm days before.

"What's up?" Mindy asked, coming to sit beside me. "Was that a journalist?"

"Yes," I said because there was no point lying to her. "They wanted to do a story about us. Except it wouldn't be about us, it would be about how we're not part of Parsons Property."

"It would still be great to get something in the paper before our opening." Mindy scrunched up her nose. "Why did you turn it down?"

"Because..." I sighed. "Because Abby doesn't know about Parsons Property. She thinks I'm just a regular guy with a big dream."

Mindy whacked me on the arm. "Why the hell didn't you tell her the truth?" she admonished. "I can't believe you'd lie to someone about that! And how long do you think you can keep her from finding out? If she googled your name, she'd know instantly! Like I did."

"I know!" I said, groaning again. "And I didn't lie to her. Well, not exactly. Abby assumed, and then she was going on about rich arseholes who don't understand what it's like to run a small business with your savings on the line and no back up. It was after I just moved in, and I couldn't tell her that actually, I was one of those rich arseholes."

"Oh, Wyatt." Mindy shook her head and squeezed my arm harder than could be considered strictly comforting. "What a mess."

"And now it's gone on too long to just drop it in casually," I said. "And it's not like I'm using the family money or anything for this. I'm finally doing something on my own, and I don't want her to look at me like I'm just some rich kid with a hobby."

"You really care what she thinks of you, don't you?" Mindy clicked her tongue and scratched at the tattoo on her neck usually covered by her neat bob. "Because you do like her."

"I do," I said, rubbing my face with the heels of my palms. "And I will tell her, of course, I will. Just...just not right now. I don't want her to be angry with me when she's got a broken foot. She won't let me look after her if she's angry with me."

"So, you're not telling her for her own good?" Mindy snorted. "Sounds like bullshit, but okay."

"Just not yet," I said. "I will tell her. Just..."

"Not yet," Mindy finished. "You'd better do it soon, boss. The longer you leave it, the worse it will be."

I grunted, but I knew my neck-tattoo sporting restaurant manager was absolutely right.

·♥·♥·♥·♥·♥·

Wyatt: are you on the sofa?

Abby: yes of course i am

Wyatt: send a photo to prove it

Abby: why don't you believe me?!

Wyatt: because i'm starting to know you pretty well. send a photo

Abby: okay, fine. i'm having a meeting with josie. but she's not letting me lift anything!

Abby: <photo of Abby seated in a chair with a laptop open and Josie giving a thumbs up behind her>

Abby: satisfied?

Wyatt: i expected worse, so i suppose so

Wyatt: if you can manage to go all day without doing anything strenuous, i'll bring you a reward

Abby: that's very condescending!

Abby: ...but what kind of reward?

Wyatt: if i told you it involved cheese. would that be enough of an enticement to rest?

Abby: cheese is my one weakness. how did you know?

Wyatt: like i said, i'm getting to know you pretty well <winky face emoji>

A sharp tap on the shoulder and I looked up, startled. David was standing in front of me.

"Who are you texting?"

"No one," I said. A little too quickly.

"I bet it's Abby." David looked smug.

"I could have told you that," Mindy broke in.

"I was just checking to make sure she's getting some rest!" I protested. "She did break her foot, you know."

"We know." Mindy rolled her eyes. "And we both know you're sweet on her too, but the rest of those signs you bought aren't going to install themselves on the wall, are they?" She pointed to where the vintage tin signs were still stacked up. Next to them was a power drill and a ladder.

"I thought I was the boss!" I said, but picked up the drill anyway.

"You are." Mindy gave me another uncomfortably firm arm squeeze. "But I'm the restaurant manager, and there's not going to be a restaurant to manage if you don't get your arse into gear."

"Fine!" I said, dragging the ladder behind me as I went. "I'll get started on these."

"I can take a photo of you with the drill if you want," Mindy suggested. "I bet Abby would like to see you looking masculine and industrious."

"That's not necessary." But then I beckoned David over. "Is there anything with cheese on the menu you need to test?"

"Since when are you so interested in cheese?"

"Just a question," I said, trying to act like it was no big deal. "But is there?"

David rolled his eyes theatrically. "I'm sure I can do something. For Abby, isn't it?"

"I didn't say that."

But the look on Mindy and David's faces told me I didn't have to.

9 Abby

"Where are you off to?"

I turned around, startled. Rosy-fingered dawn had barely broken, and I had been sure that it was far too early for Wyatt to be up after a late night at the restaurant.

"I've got a big job in the Southern Highlands," I said, pausing from where I had been double-checking my boxes contained the right amount of shelf dividers, acrylic tubs, and labels before I loaded them into the van. "It's an early start."

"Why didn't you ask me to help you load up?" Wyatt frowned, having clearly spotted the boxes. "You promised me you'd take it easy."

"I did!" I insisted. "For two days, I sat around the house and rested. But I couldn't turn down a three-day job like this just because of my boot." I stuck out my foot, scowling at the offensive grey foam walking cast. "And my foot feels fine."

"A three-day job?" Wyatt scoffed. "That sounds like the opposite of resting."

"I'm sick of resting. I told you, it bothers me to sit around doing nothing. I've got my reasons."

"And I'm not asking," Wyatt said. "Because I know you'll tell me when – and if – you're ready."

His words made my insides heat up like someone had taken a blow torch to them, intent on turning my organs into a crème brûlée. Right then, I wanted to tell him what I had never told anyone. What I barely even liked to admit to myself. But I had a job to do and so pushed the feeling down.

"I'm just worried about your foot," Wyatt went on. "If you push yourself too hard, it won't heal properly. And then you'll be stuck resting for who knows how long, and you'll hate it."

"I'll be fine." I needed to reassure him, apparently. "Josie will be with me. Come on, you know how it is. I can't just turn down a big job. I'm trying to keep things in the black before the online store goes live, and Josie has to be paid!"

"Is it really that bad?" Wyatt had an odd expression like he was thinking about something but not saying it. "I know you're dedicated, but if you're saying yes to work you can't physically do for financial reasons, then maybe—"

"It's not that bad," I said quickly, even though it really kind of was. If I didn't do this job, there was a good chance my savings account would fall into the single digits before the launch of my online store. "And I can absolutely physically do this. Josie's a freaking workhorse! And she's a grandma. A grandma would never let me push myself too hard."

Wyatt gave me a cautious smile at that. "If you're sure," he said. "Because I could lend—"

"Absolutely not," I said fiercely. "I don't need a loan, and even if I did, I'd never take it from someone trying to start their own business. You probably need it more than I do! At least I've got money coming in. Yours is just going out until you open!"

Wyatt shifted uncomfortably and looked away. "I just don't want you to push yourself too hard," he said quietly.

"I won't," I said, even though that wasn't necessarily a promise I could keep. "I'm not even going to be driving; Josie's going to take over as soon as I get to her place."

"Well, that's a relief." Wyatt's shoulders seemed to relax slightly.

"Organised Home Co has always been profitable," I said, folding my arms. "This is a temporary cashflow issue. I've invested a lot in product stock, and I'm still training Josie to do jobs independently. Once she can work on her own and the online store opens, it'll be fine. Better than fine." I paused. "Well, so long as people actually buy things from the store. But my research indicates they will."

"I'm sure they will." Wyatt gave me an encouraging nod. "If you tell them to, they'll be scared not to."

"I'll take that as a compliment."

"I definitely meant it as one," Wyatt said, and he took a step closer to me, making my breath hitch. "You're a force of nature, Abby Finch."

I swallowed hard because what the hell did you say to that? "Thanks," I whispered, my voice oddly husky.

"I'm going to put the rest of these boxes in for you, though, and you're going to sit down and not argue with me." Wyatt was smirking again like he knew I wouldn't try to refuse.

"Fine," I said, but I jutted out my chin. "Only because you complimented me, though."

"Huh," Wyatt said, still smirking. "So that's how I can get you to do what I want? I'll keep that in mind."

And with that, I quickly made my way to the driver's seat before my face could betray just what his words had done to my body.

· ♥ · ♥ · ♥ · ♥ · ♥ ·

"Don't lift that!" Josie scolded, shooting me a scowl.

"It's not heavy," I objected. "I've been letting you take all the heavy ones."

"You're in a cast; you shouldn't be lifting anything!"

"It's a walking boot!" I pointed to the foam covering my foot. "Not a cast."

"Still," Josie looked concerned. "Are you sure you should be doing this?"

"Absolutely sure," I said. "And look, now I'm sitting down." I carefully lowered myself to the floor of the enormous, ornate bathroom that sported more gold hardware than the average rapper's neck. All around me were rows upon rows of bath and beauty products that we had extracted from the overstuffed bathroom cabinets. "I'm going to sit and arrange these in the containers. That's pretty much resting!"

"You're a worry." Josie shook her head. "But if you're going to work on this, are you happy for me to go and make a start on that storage room? It's going to take a while."

"You don't want me to do it with you?" The storage room was stuffed to the ceiling with boxes of childhood art, toys that had probably been recalled for safety reasons, enough bedlinen to outfit a medium-sized hotel, and optimistically-purchased exercise equipment that had been quickly abandoned.

"Oh, I'll need you for the final stage," Josie reassured me. "But I can definitely get things sorted into categories."

"If you're sure." Competent – very competent – as Josie was, I had a hard time letting go. That was ridiculous; the whole point of hiring Josie was that she could do jobs on her own. I knew I had to, and yet...

Before Josie could reassure me once again, the bathroom door opened.

"Hello, my dears." Cynthia, a middle-aged woman in a silk kaftan featuring metallic embroidery and a bold print of flamingos, looked down at us with a benevolent smile. "I've made you some tea. You two should take a break; you must be exhausted!"

"That's very kind of you," I said, hopping up to take my cup of tea. It was too milky, and I suspected Cynthia had put in enough sugar to please an ant colony, but I wasn't going to complain. Some of my clients gave me filthy looks if I dared refill my water bottle from their precious kitchen sinks.

"What a treat, someone making me a cup of tea!" Josie said, picking up her own. "You're a legend."

Cynthia looked pleased to be called a legend, but when she looked around the bathroom, she gasped at the piles littering the floor. "Goodness me, was all of that really in my cabinets?"

"It was," I said, giving her a smile. "And the good news is, it'll be easy for you to decide what to chuck out because these—" I pointed to a large pile. "Are expired. Like, five years ago expired. I don't think they'd be safe to use."

"Oh, dear." Cynthia's fingers went to her mouth. "I get so excited when those lovely young ladies in the shop show me new things, but I never seem to find the time to try them out."

"Happens to everyone," I said, not wanting Cynthia to feel bad for hoarding crumbling eyeshadow palettes and questionable anti-aging products. "That's what we're here for, to help you. When I'm finished, you'll be able to see exactly what you have every time you open the bathroom cupboards."

"You certainly know what you're doing." Cynthia nodded approvingly. "I am sorry it's such a mess. Since the kids moved out, I just..." She waved a hand. "I suppose I've been ignoring the problem."

"That's what we're here for," Josie said, patting Cynthia's arm. "Thanks for the tea. That's got me ready to start on your storage room."

"Are you sure you two ladies can handle it?" Cynthia looked worried. "Surely we could get a man in to help with the heavy lifting."

"No need for a man." Josie flexed an admittedly impressive wiry bicep. I noticed, then, that she was wearing a black silk blouse shot with pink rather than one of her usual faded t-shirts. I felt a flood of warmth, knowing she must have chosen it from those bags I had given her. It had been the right thing to do; the blouse seemed to have given her the confidence to laugh and joke with Cynthia like they were old friends.

"You do look very strong," Cynthia admitted. "I don't know how you ladies manage it, but I take my hat off to you! I'll be in the sunroom if you need me. I'll make some sandwiches for lunch, and you can take a proper break."

"That's very kind of you," I said. "And the next time you come in here, you'll have a whole new bathroom."

Cynthia clasped her hands. "I can't wait!" She bustled off, Josie following her out.

Then it was just me, hundreds of beauty products, and acrylic tray dividers waiting to be filled. I grinned, sticking in my earphones and cranking up a suitably peppy playlist; I was in my element.

· ♥ · ♥ · ♥ · ♥ · ♥ ·

"Well, I think that's enough for today." Josie stood up and stretched hugely. Her bob was even more tousled than usual, and she was suppressing a yawn.

"We've got through a lot," I admitted, even though I was reluctant to leave just yet. "But maybe we could—"

"Abby, you might be my boss, but I've got a good thirty years on you," Josie interrupted. "So, I'm telling you we're done for today. You're crazy enough working your arse off with a broken foot. But we're stopping. Now."

I paused and managed a smile. "Well, if you're going to use the grandma voice on me, I can't really argue, can I?"

"Oh, that's not the grandma voice," Josie chuckled. "That was the mum voice. Big difference!"

"True," I said. "You're probably right, even if I don't want to admit it."

"I am," Josie agreed. "And I know you promised that housemate of yours you wouldn't push yourself too hard. I'd hate to have to tell him you lied."

I let out a slow breath. "I shouldn't have told you about Wyatt," I said, wrinkling my nose.

"But you did. And I'm glad you did. It's nice to get a bit of vicarious romance, with you having a handsome blast from the past show up and wanting to look after you. It's not like I'm going to ever let another man into my life!"

"He's not a man in my life," I objected. "Well, he's technically a man, and he's in my house, but he's not..." I shook my head firmly. "I'm not interested in anything happening with him. This business is my boyfriend, and I can only handle one at a time."

"You're too young to be married to your job."

"I'm not married to my job!" I baulked. "But we're serious. Definitely living together."

"Your job should be a casual relationship at best. A reliable booty call," Josie told me, snorting at the thought. "You've definitely got to make room for the real deal."

"Maybe when things are more settled," I said, not wanting to think about it. "But right now? The only man I'm interested in is the web designer; I need him to finish the online store!"

Josie sighed and nudged a stack of sports equipment with her foot. "I'm going to leave this stuff for Cynthia to check, so she can confirm she's ready to get rid of it. I mean, what does she want with a skateboard?"

I knelt down to look at the skateboard. A few scratches on the sides, but otherwise, unused. "If Cynthia wants to get rid of it, I could find a home for this," I said, testing one wheel with my finger.

"Oh no, you don't!" Josie was aghast. "Do I have to break out the mum voice again? You've got a bloody broken foot!"

"Not for me!" I said quickly. "Just...I have a friend who likes to skate. Well, they did. But they haven't for a while, and it might be fun to remind them of their skateboarding days."

"A friend, huh?" Josie gave me a look that left me in no doubt that she had guessed exactly who I was talking about. "Well, that's very thoughtful of you. I bet *they* would appreciate it."

But I just made another non-committal noise and tried my best not to think about the man who was *not* in my life and what it might be like to see him skate again.

· ♥ · ♥ · ♥ · ♥ · ♥ ·

When I pulled up outside the house, it was dark. But I could see the lights were on inside, and my stomach did a little flip-flop at the thought that Wyatt was home. He'd shoot me that lazy grin, or maybe even a smirk, and he'd ask if I had taken it easy today like he told me to—

"Stupid," I said out loud, even as I flipped down the mirror and smoothed my hands through my hair, which had come loose from the very tight bun I had started the day with. Mascara was smudged under my eyes, and I fixed it quickly and wondered if I should put on some lipstick.

"That would be too obvious," I muttered. "Why would I have fresh lipstick after working all day? He's going to think I'm trying to impress him." Which I wasn't, obviously. He had seen me with zero makeup and a bag of peas on my foot. Why was I even thinking about how I looked in front of my maddeningly handsome housemate?

I shot my reflection an exasperated look and firmly told myself I was absolutely not looking forward to seeing him.

"Hello?" I called out as I turned my key in the door. I could smell something hearty in the kitchen, but I couldn't see the familiar tall bulk of a man as I looked around the empty living area.

"Gotcha!" Two sets of arms grabbed me, and I jumped in shock, ready to fight whoever had broken into my house and...cooked for me?

Tessa and Michelle had a hold of each of my arms, and both were giving me thoroughly unimpressed looks.

"What," Michelle asked me with a scowl, "is that?" She pointed at my boot-clad foot.

"Uh," I said. "Just a sprain."

"Well, that's a lie." Tessa released my arm and bent down to examine the boot. "It's a walking cast. They give these out for fractures, not sprains."

"How do you know that?" Michelle looked impressed.

"I wrote an autobiography for a long-distance runner," Tessa explained. "He was always injuring himself. I'm pretty much an expert on leg injuries."

"You fractured your foot!" Michelle shot me an accusing glare. "And you didn't tell us!"

"What are you two doing here?" I pushed Michelle away and collapsed onto the sofa, folding my arms and trying to give my sisters the look that had always cowed them into submission as kids. It didn't work.

"Dylan saw you at the petrol station and said you had some sort of cast," Tessa said. "So, I called Michelle and asked if she knew anything about it."

"And we thought it was very fishy we had barely heard from you the last few days," Michelle added. "So, we came over."

"You broke in!" I corrected. "That's, like, illegal."

Tessa snorted. "Hardly!" She waved a set of keys at me. "You gave me your spare keys."

"For emergencies!"

"This is clearly an emergency!" Michelle looked ready to throttle me. "Abby! Why on earth didn't you tell us about this? You must have had to go to the hospital and—"

"Did Wyatt take you?" Tessa cut in, her eyes going wide. "I bet he did, didn't he?"

"I wasn't in the hospital!" I objected. "All that happened was that a client dropped something on my foot on a job a few days ago. And I was going to just rest it, but Wyatt insisted I see a doctor and..." I shook my head. "I didn't tell you two because I knew you'd make a big deal out of it. Just like you are. Right now."

"Only because you didn't tell us!" Michelle threw up her hands. "And I bet that doctor told you to rest, which you clearly haven't been doing."

"You need to look after yourself, Abby." Tessa sighed. "Especially since you won't let anyone else look after you."

I thought of Wyatt, forcing me to rest on the sofa and watch reality TV. How he had made me promise not to leave the house for two days. I decided it was best my sisters didn't know about that. "I hate resting," I said instead. "Resting is bullshit. But I've been careful! Josie did all the heavy lifting today! Mostly, I was sitting on my arse and sorting stuff into boxes. And you know I love that."

"That's true." Tessa sat beside me, frowning with sisterly concern. "But it's not the point."

"Then what is the point?"

"The point is that you're always all up in our business, telling us what to do, but when something serious happens to you, you don't even tell us!" Michelle looked torn between fury and deep sadness. "And that's such bullshit, Abby. Don't you think we love you every bit as much as you love us?"

I opened my mouth but abruptly closed it again. Instead, I looked down at my hands. "I just didn't want you to worry about me," I said. "Or stop me from getting on with things. I've got so much to do, and—"

"And you won't let anyone help you, and you won't take a break," Tessa sighed again. "Because you think you can't stop for a moment, or you'll break down like some kind of maniacal wind-up toy."

"I've legitimately got a lot to do! It's not like I'm busy just for the sake of being busy, I'm going through a huge business expansion, and I quite literally can't afford to sit around doing nothing just because of a tiny injury—"

"Hardly tiny," Michelle said, but her face was softening. "Look, I get it. I really do. I damn near sold my soul to my old job, and I thought it was worth it. But it wasn't. A job is never worth your physical and mental health."

"You didn't listen to me when I told you that," I pointed out.

"Well, no," Michelle admitted, smiling ruefully. "But I should have."

"Now you admit it."

"Look, I hate to interrupt this, but Abby? I'm going to force-feed you macaroni cheese right now," Tessa cut in. "Also, we brought wine."

I groaned. "This is exactly what I didn't want you to do!"

"What, show we care about you?" Tessa was in the kitchen, spooning baked macaroni cheese into a bowl. And damn it, my treacherous stomach rumbled. Maybe Tessa wasn't quite at the level of Wyatt's insanely talented head chef, but her macaroni cheese was the single most comforting comfort food on the planet. "Yeah, having sisters who care must be awful for you."

"The worst," Michelle said, producing a bottle of wine and three glasses. I saw that it was my favourite rosé which I seldom bought because it was more than thirty dollars a bottle. And that made my heart melt, even if I felt guilty for the unnecessary expense. "Poor, suffering Abby. She's got to put up with her sisters caring about her."

"Well, now you're making me feel like an arsehole," I said, accepting the bowl Tessa put in my hands. "It's not that I don't appreciate it. Of course I do! But you two have your own busy lives, and I don't want you to waste your time worrying about me."

"It's not a waste." Tessa sat beside me and passed a bowl of macaroni to Michelle, who attacked it with a sound of wanton lust. "You're the self-esteem goddess! You can't say it's a waste, us wanting to look after you sometimes."

"You'll always be our big sister," Michelle said, filling my glass almost to the top. "But we're all grown-ups now. And that means sometimes we're going to be the ones looking after you. And you're going to accept it."

"I am, am I?"

"You are." Michelle nodded firmly around a mouthful of macaroni. "God, this is good. I love carbohydrates."

"Anyway," Tessa went on. "Why don't you tell us about how Wyatt took you to the doctor? That was very caring of him."

I looked down at the bowl of macaroni and gritted my teeth.

Wyatt had been *very* caring. And I had no idea what to do with the feelings that fact gave me.

10 Wyatt

Technically, the restaurant was closed on Mondays. And that was why I had given Mindy and David the day off. I, of course, still had a list of things to do there that would have filled several pages of Abby's little notebook if I ever bothered to write them down. But it had been an exhausting few days and I had decided my to-do list at the restaurant could wait until I caught up on some much-needed sleep.

At least, that was the excuse I gave myself when I finally woke up and discovered it was after ten. Scrambling into jeans and a t-shirt, I hurtled down the stairs and was surprised to see Abby at the dining room table. Yes, she had her laptop in front of her, but her injured foot was propped on a chair, and she was at least sitting still. Had she actually listened to me?

"Good morning, sunshine," Abby said, looking up and smiling.

And shit, that smile did things to me. First, it made me wish I had chosen a t-shirt that wasn't oversized and proclaiming my love for Corona beer. Then it made my stomach twist, my chest grow tight, and finally, it produced an answering smile that was neither a lazy grin nor a smirk. It was an open-mouthed, foolish, happy smile that probably made me look utterly gormless. I was in serious trouble when it came to Abby Finch.

"Morning," I said, looking away before Abby could judge my facial expression too deeply. "I didn't think you'd be here."

Abby made a sound of amusement. "Some dude told me he'd reward me with cheesy foodstuffs if I rested," she said, sounding like she wanted to laugh. "And, apparently, a certain kind of woman can be controlled with cheese. I'm powerless to resist."

"Powerless to resist, huh?" I said, looking at her from over the coffee machine. Pods. It needed pods. "That doesn't sound like you."

"Don't tell anyone," Abby chided. Then she stood up, gingerly putting weight on her foot as she bent down to pull something from under the table. "So, I got you something."

"You don't have to get me anything," I said automatically. But I was already curious about what Abby could possibly be about to give me. My heart sped up, and I hadn't even had my double-shot espresso yet.

"It's just a freebie from my job the other day," Abby said. "No different to you bringing me risotto." She turned around, and I saw she was holding—

"A skateboard?"

"You told me you hadn't skated since you were a teenager," Abby reminded me. "I thought you should try it again. For nostalgia, or whatever."

As she handed it to me, I was struck by a wave of sense memory. I was fifteen again and had just attempted an unwise jump and had fallen on my arse, my board rolling away at top speed. I had been sitting there, dazed, and then a pretty girl whose name I didn't yet know had approached me, holding out my board and looking at me with those same blue eyes I was seeing right now.

I swallowed hard. "Thanks, Abby," I said. "That's... that's very thoughtful of you."

"It's no big deal." Abby shifted uncomfortably at my thanks. "I mean, it would have gone in the trash pile if I hadn't saved it, so it's not like—" She cut herself off. "So, can you still do a kickflip?"

"I doubt it. I could barely do a kickflip back then!"

"Muscle memory," Abby assured me. "I bet it all comes back to you. It's like riding a bike!"

"I'm flattered by your faith in my muscles," I raised my eyebrows, and Abby returned my gaze. Damn it, Danni would be crowing with triumph because there were more than sparks flying between the two of us now. A fireworks display might erupt at any moment, right there in the kitchen. I swallowed hard.

"Well, it does look like you put a lot of effort into them," Abby said, her eyes moving over my chest underneath the unfortunate t-shirt and cranking up the potential for pyrotechnics to eleven.

But the moment was interrupted by a horrible, mechanical grinding sound that startled me.

"Machine's out of water," Abby said, diagnosing the problem instantly. "Rookie error." She shot me something that looked like my very own smirk.

"Guess I was distracted this morning," I said, moving to refill the machine and willing to let Abby interpret that remark however she wanted to.

Abby made a soft sound, giving me one final look before she returned to her laptop.

"I've got to get to the restaurant later to try and set up the EFTPOS system," I said, slipping another pod into the coffee machine. "But I want to take this bad boy out first." I held up the skateboard, making the wheels spin.

"You should," Abby nodded. "You're always telling me taking breaks is a good thing."

"Problem is, I haven't lived in Brekkie Beach that long," I ventured. "I might need a local to show me a good place to try it out. Would you come with me?"

There was a brief pause, and Abby opened her mouth, but I rushed on.

"I know you've got a shit-ton to do," I said. "But let's face it, it'll be ten minutes tops before I'm on my arse and covered in gravel burns. And I'll get you a decent coffee for your trouble."

Abby laughed, but her eyes were fixed on mine. "You'd be a terrible negotiator," she said, her eyes crinkled with amusement. "Improving on the first offer before the other party responds." She paused again. "Especially since I was going to say yes."

"You'll come with me?"

"Absolutely," Abby said. "What kind of housemate would I be if I missed the opportunity to see you fall flat on your arse? My list can wait." She tapped the notebook with a pink felt tip pen, the hint of a smile playing on her lips.

I laughed, but the thought that Abby would agree to take time out of her precious schedule just for me inflated my chest. My heart and lungs were gone, replaced with helium balloons that threatened to lift me off the ground and totally throw off any attempts to show off on my new skateboard.

· ♥ · ♥ · ♥ · ♥ · ♥ ·

"Okay, skater boy," Abby was sitting on a bench, cradling an extra-large, extra strong flat white from Nick and Nikki's and sporting a big smile that gave my chest that helium-filled feeling again. "Show me what you got."

"Let me finish this!" I said, gulping what was left of my own coffee. "Seriously, I need all the chemical help I can get."

"Don't tell me you're nervous."

"Aren't we all nervous about the potential for bodily harm once we're over thirty?" I quipped. "Well, not you, obviously."

"Guess I'll always be fifteen at heart."

And did she mean something by that? It was hard to tell when it came to Abby.

Setting down my coffee cup, I stepped onto the board, testing the weight. I took a few quick steps and then took my right foot off the ground, arms out. With intense concentration, I could skate in a straight line for almost six seconds before losing my balance. Honestly, that was better than I had expected.

A whistling cheer came from the bench, and I turned to see Abby whooping, clearly enjoying herself. And at that moment, I knew I'd definitely risk bodily harm if it got that kind of reaction from her.

"How does it feel?" Abby called. "Like riding a bike?"

"More like riding a horse," I said. "And I bloody hate horses."

"You're doing pretty well!"

And I knew she was just being encouraging, but I liked to hear it just the same.

"Do an ollie!" Abby gave me a double thumbs up, seemingly convinced I could pull off the jump.

And it was probably a bad idea, but the urge to impress the pretty girl watching me was apparently no less strong at thirty-two than it had been at fifteen. In fact, it was a whole lot worse.

I had never been one to back down from a challenge. Gathering speed, I flipped up the board just like I had back as a teenager in Adelaide and—

I managed to jump about two inches into the air. I wasn't fully convinced the wheels had become airborne. But at least I hadn't fallen flat. Yet.

"Again!" Abby demanded, and the sight of her face, alive and happy, her cheeks pink and her eyes dancing with mischievous excitement, convinced me that maybe I could get some decent air if I just...

"Shit!" I swore, staggering into the side of the bench as my attempt to impress Abby resulted in me losing my balance completely.

"It was a good try." Abby sounded like she was trying to be supportive.

"I don't think I'm going to be the next Tony Hawk any time soon."

"He's even older than us!"

"Skating is definitely a use it or lose it kind of skill," I said, smiling ruefully.

"I think your fifteen-year-old self definitely had more skills on the board."

"Well, adult me is better at a lot of other things," I said, my heart thumping in my chest in a way that had nothing to do with the adrenaline of my failed ollie. "I'm a much better kisser, for a start."

"Is that so?" Abby's body had turned towards mine, and I was suddenly very aware that the only barrier between us was the skateboard across my knees.

In the little skate park just beside the beach, with the soft spring sunshine above, the smell of salt in the air, the sound of waves crashing and seagulls demanding their fair share of snacks from the few beachgoers below, I looked at Abby and moved just a little closer. I reached out to tuck one loose strand of hair behind her ear. "I can prove it." Our mouths were so close I could feel her breath on my chin and—

"Bro, do a kickflip! It'll be sick; I'll make a TikTok!"

What could have been a moment that changed everything was broken by the arrival of a trio of preteens. Each of them clutched a skateboard adorned with a heavy layer of stickers, and the ambient sounds of crashing waves were broken by their excited chatter.

Abby leaned away from me. "We've got company."

"Yeah," I said, picking up my board and looking away. "And I promised I wouldn't take up too much of your time. We should head back."

"Not going to try that ollie one more time?"

"In front of them?" I let out a breath. "No way. That's another thing about the dark side of thirty. Kids scare the hell out of you."

Abby just laughed. "I guess they do."

As we began the walk back to the house that fate had determined we share, I knew I should feel grateful that the preteen interruption had stopped me from doing something I couldn't take back. But all I felt was deeply disappointed.

· ♥ · ♥ · ♥ · ♥ · ♥ ·

After a day spent fighting with my internet service provider and swearing at technology in general, Beach Garage's shiny new EFTPOS machine and all-singing, all-dancing point-of-sale system was fully functional. Exhausted in a way I never was from manual labour, I had refused David and Mindy's offer of a drink at the Brekkie Beach Hotel and returned to the house instead.

I knew Abby was inside when I saw the van parked out the front. And that made me swallow hard.

Carefully, I turned the key in the door and made my way inside to the sound of pop music blasting from the kitchen. I could see Abby, her face turned towards a tripod propped on the kitchen counter. And she was...

...dancing? Yes, she was definitely dancing, despite her foot still being encased in the walking cast. Footwork, it seemed, was not required for this particular dance; it was all about the sway of her hips, not to mention the movements of her leggings-clad bottom. She held a sheet of shiny gold labels in one hand and a glass jar in the other, the immaculately organised pantry open behind her.

When she spotted me, Abby stopped mid-dance, her arms falling to her sides and her face contorting between embarrassment and acute physical agony.

"Hi," I said, eyebrows raised.

Abby groaned. "You weren't supposed to see me doing that. No one is!"

"But you're filming it for the internet," I said. "Or, at least, I assume so."

"It's for TikTok." Abby groaned again. "And I know it's ridiculous, but I get a ton of views when I make stuff like this. Facebook and Instagram are so much easier; I can get heaps of likes on flat lay photos and quick tips. But for TikTok, the algorithm demands I participate in those stupid dance trends."

"You do all that work on social media?" I shouldn't have been surprised.

"Of course I do." Abby looked at me like she didn't understand the question. "Social content marketing is a huge part of my business. Most of my clients come from social media. Especially now, with the online store about to open. All these people who love what I do but could never afford to hire me can buy a little piece of the Organised Home Co vibe. At least, that's the plan."

"You never stop, do you?" I was half-impressed, half-concerned. "Don't get me wrong, I'm super impressed by your work ethic, but..." I shook my head. "But seriously, you never stop."

"I like being busy," Abby said, setting down the glass jar and sheet of labels. "And this business is my baby. I've got to put in a ton of hours, or it won't succeed."

"But I don't think I've ever seen you take a real break, just to relax," I said, taking a seat at the dining table. "The only time I've ever seen you watch TV was when you had a broken foot, and I still had to force you."

"I watch TV!" Abby protested. "Well, I like having it on in the background when I'm working on—"

"That doesn't count," I cut her off.

"I hang out with my sisters," Abby said, listing on her fingers. "And I do Pilates. I go for walks by the beach."

"Okay, those things aren't technically working," I admitted. "But they're not taking a break, either. I've never met someone who does as much as you."

"I'll take that as a compliment," Abby said, fiddling with her tripod.

"I guess it is," I said. "But I'm still worried about you. I know I said I wouldn't pry, but I have to wonder. Are you afraid of what might happen if you stop for even a little while?"

Abby stopped fiddling, standing stock-still, motionless, her mouth open.

"That's it, isn't it?" I pressed. "You're afraid to stop. But I don't get that," I went on, "because it seems like you're not afraid of anything."

"I'm afraid of some things," Abby said, her voice so quiet I almost couldn't hear her. And maybe I shouldn't push her, but I had to know. My growing feelings for the woman standing in our shared kitchen made me desperate to know everything about her. Including this.

I rose from my chair, making my way slowly towards her like I'd approach a nervous, skittish feral cat so it didn't run away before I could tend to its battle wounds. If I was the kind of guy who nursed feral cats, which I really wasn't.

"What are you afraid of, Abby?" I asked softly, leaning against the counter beside her. "You know I won't judge you."

Abby swallowed hard, looking down at the imitation granite counter. "Myself, I guess."

"Yourself?" That surprised me. "I can't imagine why."

Abby squeezed her eyes shut and opened them slowly like she was making sure I really was there with her and wasn't a highly realistic hologram. "There was a time when..." She shook her head. "When I did just stop. And I didn't do anything. I could barely get out of bed. Didn't go to my classes, didn't see any friends, almost failed out of uni for not handing in assignments, my room was a mess, and I...just didn't do anything. I couldn't. It was like I was locked in my own body. I'd try to make myself just get up and go, but I *couldn't*." She closed her eyes once more. "I never want to feel like that again."

I took a quick breath. "Was it..." I swallowed. "Were you depressed?"

Abby looked away. "I guess so. It came out of nowhere," she said. "I lost everything in my life so fast because it took everything out of me. Made me a different person – a person I hated – and I just couldn't do anything about it."

I swore softly. "But you got through it. I mean, you clearly got through it."

"Kind of," Abby said, looking down at her hands. "I tried to get out of it on my own, but I..." She shut her eyes. "I had to take medication in the end." She sounded like she had just admitted to having once killed a man in Reno just to watch him die.

"Well, that sounds like the smartest thing to do in that situation," I said cautiously. "Why wouldn't you take medication if it could help you? It's no big deal. Tons of people take medication."

"Because I wanted to do it on my own!" Abby shot back, one hand moving to her face as though she wanted to cover it. "But I couldn't. I needed those bloody pills for years! And even now, ten years later, I'm still scared that it might come back and ruin everything in my life. And maybe the next time, the medication won't work, and I'll just break down. And never get back up."

"Abby..." I didn't know what to say. Instead, I reached out and took her hand in mine, squeezing that warm, industrious little hand between my palms. "I think you're incredible."

Abby let out a soft breath, looking up at me with wide blue eyes. "I want to agree with you." She gave a sad smile. "Because, usually, my self-esteem is kind of legendary. But I hate that I have to live with this fear."

"Being afraid doesn't mean you're not brave as hell," I said. "And you are. Brave as hell, that is."

"I try." Abby's voice was a hoarse whisper, and I was still holding her hand in mine. I didn't want to let it go. Was I brave enough to do what I wanted to, now that she had shared something so personal with me? Could I reach out and pull her close, to kiss her and show her just how much my kissing prowess had improved in the last seventeen years?

I took a step closer to her, about to do something that could change both of our lives forever, and—

My bloody phone began to ring, buzzing excitedly in my pocket like it wanted to worm its way out and make a death leap for the floor.

Abby pulled her hand back, shaking her head as though waking from a daze.

"Shit," I said, fumbling it out of my pocket. And it was double shit when I saw who was calling.

My mother.

Abby saw the name flash across the screen and looked at me questioningly. I quickly rejected the call, setting my phone down and giving it a death stare that I hoped would prevent it from getting any more ideas about ringing at inappropriate moments.

"Your mum?"

"My mum," I confirmed. And I was going to have to give her some explanation, wasn't I? "Uh, my parents don't really—" I took a breath. "They don't really approve of what I'm doing with the restaurant. We had an argument, things were said, and..." I sighed, hoping that was explanation enough.

Abby nodded vehemently. "I get it," she said. "They don't want you to do something risky, right? They probably wanted you to stick with a stable job."

"Pretty much." Even now – especially now – I couldn't tell her the whole truth. Not when she had just shared something so private with me. She'd be furious I hadn't told her before, and rightly so. I'd tell her, I really would. Soon. But not right now. "And I know I'll have to speak to them again eventually, but I can't get it into it right now, not with Beach Garage opening in a month. I don't have the emotional bandwidth."

Abby let out a soft sound. "That's very self-aware of you," she said approvingly.

"I don't know about that," I said. "I just don't want to get into another argument and say things I can't take back. Mum thinks I should apologise for what I said to my dad, especially about Uncle Byron, but I don't do apologies."

"You don't do apologies?" Abby raised her eyebrows. "Like, ever?"

"Well, if I bumped into someone on the street, sure," I said, realising that I probably sounded like a gigantic arsehole by announcing I never apologised. "But I don't apologise when I'm not sorry, just to keep the peace. If I made a decision, or said something, I'll stand by it, even if other people don't like it."

"Hm." Abby appeared to be chewing this over. "I guess that makes sense, so long as you're very careful about what you do and say."

"I try to be," I said, not wanting to think about the mess I was digging myself into by not telling her the truth about my family. That was a problem for another time. "And I'm definitely not going to apologise to my dad for leaving the family business. Or what I said to him, even if he didn't want to hear it."

"It must have been hard, working with your family," Abby offered after a moment's pause. "My parents don't even know what I do. Pretty sure Dad thinks I'm a cleaner."

"Ouch," I said, grimacing.

"Not that there's anything wrong with that," Abby said quickly. "But they've never really been the most involved parents. We used to stay with my Nana a lot, growing up."

"That must have been hard."

"Nah." Abby shook her head, that defiant look on her face again. "Nana was kick-arse. It was for the best."

"Well, then, I guess I'm glad she was there for you."

"Anyway, I'd better get back to work," Abby said. She shot me a rueful smile. "Gotta keep going, right?"

"I'm going to get you to relax one of these days."

"Is that a challenge?"

"Absolutely," I said. "And I know you're competitive, but so am I."

Abby just laughed. "May the best woman win."

And as I watched her disappear up the stairs, all I could do was stuff my phone into my pocket and curse my parents for ruining what might have been.

· ♥ · ♥ · ♥ · ♥ · ♥ ·

Later that night, my phone buzzed again. This time, it was a message; I couldn't just reject that. Technically, I could have deleted it without reading it, but curiosity got the best of me.

Mum: we just want to talk, darling. i know you must still be angry, but we love you and only want the best for you. if you'd just apologise to your dad, this could all be over

I felt a pang of guilt in my chest at her words because I knew it was true that my parents did still love me. Of course, they did. They weren't bad parents – not at all. They simply had a very specific vision of the way they expected me to live my life and couldn't understand why I'd want to do anything else.

"But I have nothing to apologise for," I scowled, staring at my phone. "I'm not sorry for wanting something of my own."

This time, my phone stayed resolutely silent.

And that was a relief. The last thing I needed was for my parents to come down here and try to make peace in person. If Charles and Diana Parsons (yes, those really were their names, and yes, it was the butt of many jokes) descended on Brekkie Beach, there was no way I could hide the truth about my family.

I needed to tell Abby; I knew that. But when I did, I wanted it to be on my terms and certainly not on theirs.

11 Abby

"Just pay your freaking invoice!" I groaned, massaging my temples. "How hard is it? You've got shit tons of money, Donna! You promised you'd put the payment through yesterday!"

But when I refreshed the screen, no payment appeared. I hadn't expected it to, but I was still annoyed. And worried. My invoices clearly stated that clients had seven days to pay, and I knew that Donna had more money than I could ever dream of, even if the Organised Home Co became a global empire.

"Pay me, bitch!" I jabbed a finger at the computer screen, but that did nothing but leave a mark. There was nothing else for it. I was going to have to call her again. In defiance of a thousand opinion articles about what was wrong with millennials, I wasn't afraid of making phone calls. Still,

I hated that I had to put so much time and energy into getting this woman to do something that would make no difference to her and provide a life-saving transfusion to my bank balance.

I swiped my thumb over the screen, and the phone began to ring.

"Hello?" A plummy voice drew out the word so that it had three syllables rather than the usual two.

"Hi, Donna," I said, forcing my voice to sound measured and calm. "This is Abby Finch from the Organised Home Co. I'm calling to chase up your payment for our work with you last month. It still hasn't come through and—"

"Oh, hello, darling!" Donna said, sounding genuinely pleased to hear from me. "I've just been frantic here, frantic! I was at the most marvellous gallery opening last night, didn't get in until two, can you imagine?" She let out a little laugh. "I've just been flat chat."

"I understand that," I said, even though I really didn't. I'd sell a kidney before I left an invoice unpaid, and I knew that Donna spent at least a kidney's worth of money on clothes every single month. "But our invoice terms are seven days, and it's been a month. Your payment is now quite overdue and—"

"Oh, darling!" Donna interrupted me again. "Of course, I'm going to get that through to you; you don't have to worry. Once I get a chance to sit down, of course. I'm just on my way out to lunch with the girls, so I'll have to let you go. Don't stress, darling! It causes wrinkles, you know."

"I just need—" I began again, but Donna ended the call.

I let out a colourful string of swearing and seriously considered throwing my phone at the wall. I didn't, of course. I couldn't afford to replace it, and rage-induced damage wasn't covered under the warranty.

"Problem?" Wyatt had entered the room while I had been distracted by the phone. If I was the kind of woman who got embarrassed about swearing in front of a man, I would have been.

"You could say that," I said, setting down my phone with a sigh. "I've been chasing up this invoice for more than a month. My terms are seven days, and I don't usually have problems. I tell them to pay, and they pay."

"I bet they do." Wyatt looked amused. "I can just imagine those Eastern Suburbs ladies quaking in their Jimmy Choos when you tell them what's required."

"Well, this one definitely isn't." I sighed again. "I don't think she's got any trouble with actually paying it, but she just can't be bothered. The money is nothing to her, but it would make a huge difference to me right now."

Wyatt frowned. "Did she say why she can't pay?"

"Oh, she says she will. But she's always 'busy' whenever I call her," I said, clenching my teeth in a way that was likely bad for my fillings. "She clearly doesn't think it's important because it's pocket change to a woman like her."

"Right." Wyatt nodded in a way that indicated he had made a decision. "What's this Donna's phone number?"

"Why do you need to know?" I looked at him suspiciously. "I can handle this; you don't need to get involved."

"I know I don't." Wyatt raised his eyebrows. "But you should let me try. After all, you did me that huge favour with Council. It's the least I could do." He made a grab for my phone.

"But you did me a favour before that, taking me to the doctor," I said, still not wanting to hand over the phone.

"Are we really being that transactional?" Wyatt looked amused. "I thought we were friends, Abby." His dark eyes were fixed on me, and there was something beneath his smirk. Something...deeper.

"We are friends," I said, my tongue feeling oddly thick in my mouth. "I just don't like being in debt to anyone."

"Well, in that case, you can do me a favour. I didn't sleep well and I've got a long day ahead of me, onboarding kitchen hands. Giving me the chance to intimidate this Donna would make me feel much better." Wyatt managed to look pleading, once again reaching for the phone. "It's almost as good as a kick-boxing session."

I rolled my eyes. "I know exactly what you're doing."

"Of course you do." Wyatt said. "But you're going to let me anyway."

"Am I?" I crossed my arms and raised my eyebrows. Were we flirting again? Was this just a game to him, or was it something more? And hell, what was it to me?

"Yep." Wyatt's hand shot out quickly and grabbed my phone, tapping Donna's number into his own and pressing the glowing green icon.

"I didn't say yes!"

"Shh, I'm on a business call, Abby," Wyatt said, grinning delightedly. "You know better than to interrupt me."

I rolled my eyes so hard it almost hurt, but I couldn't help returning his grin as I watched him.

"Is that Donna Bentley?" Wyatt asked, his voice suddenly going from teasing to terse. "This is Wyatt Parsons. I'm representing Ms Abby Finch regarding your breach of contract and failure to make payment."

My mouth dropped open. He was seriously doing this?

"Oh, but it is a legal matter, Mrs Bentley. Your failure to make payment within the contract's terms is extremely serious. Ms Finch has been very patient, but if the full amount is not paid today, we will begin proceedings, or—" Wyatt's voice became dangerous. "We will be forced to make public your failure to pay Ms Finch. Which I imagine could be rather embarrassing."

I could hear Donna's squeak of protest through the phone, and I couldn't help the stab of triumph that went through me at the sound. Donna wasn't brushing Wyatt off with her 'darlings', that was for sure.

"I'm sure you and Mr Bentley don't want to face that sort of public embarrassment or a drawn-out legal proceeding," Wyatt went on, his voice becoming smooth. "Which is why I'm willing to let this matter drop, assuming that the full amount, plus a twenty-five per cent late payment charge is in Miss Finch's bank account by the close of business today."

Another pause.

"I'm glad you're able to make time in your busy schedule for that, Mrs Bentley," Wyatt said. "I'll be sure to check with my client that the payment has been received. And if not—" His voice went cold once more. "You'll be hearing from me again *very* soon."

With a swipe of his thumb, Wyatt ended the call, looking all kinds of smug. And I *hated* smug men. I couldn't stand them. But on Wyatt? Smug just made him look more appealing than ever. He hadn't shaved this morning, and the stubble dusting his chin made me want to run my hands over him and—

"I'd be astonished if you don't get that payment in the next ten minutes." Wyatt was clearly pleased with himself.

"I can't believe you impersonated a lawyer!" I said, addressing the least of what he had just done for me.

"I didn't, actually." Wyatt raised his eyebrows. "I just said I was representing you. Which I was."

"You know all the lingo," I said. "Sounded pretty legit."

"Well, I did do two years of law before switching to business," Wyatt explained. "Much to my parents' dismay."

"They wanted you to be a lawyer?"

"They wanted me to have a law degree."

"You do look like a lawyer," I said, scrutinising Wyatt momentarily. "Is that a Burberry shirt? A very successful lawyer!"

Wyatt looked down at the embroidered logo as though surprised to see it. "This?" he plucked at the shirt. "Uh, I think it's from a market in Bali."

"Oh, right," I said, still looking at the shirt. "It's a good knock-off! My sister – Michelle – used to send us fake Ferragamos and Gucci bags from her work trips to Shanghai, but they didn't look that real."

"Guess I just got lucky." Wyatt shrugged. "It was a while ago, anyway. Family holiday."

"Nice," I said, with a hint of envy. The idea of my parents taking me and my sisters anywhere as adults was laughable.

"It was." Wyatt still looked uncomfortable. "But I guess family holidays aren't going to happen anymore, not since I... Well, you know."

"I guess there are perks to having parents who aren't very involved," I said, wanting to put my hand out and touch him but not quite trusting myself to do it. "My mum and dad never pressured me to do anything when I finished school. Actually, they were kind of shocked when I told them I had."

"That must have been hard." Wyatt looked concerned, sitting beside me with that oddly soft and tender expression that I wasn't used to receiving from anyone, let alone someone like him.

"Not really." I didn't want him to feel sorry for me. "Like I told you, we mostly lived with my Nana. She was our parent, really. Mum and Dad were more like aunties and uncles who came to visit sometimes. And besides, I had my sisters."

"I always wished I had a brother or sister," Wyatt said, his mouth quirking. "Being an only child when your parents expect a lot from you is...." He searched for a word.

"Shitty?" I suggested.

"I was going to say challenging, but shitty is a much better word," Wyatt said. "Anyway." He cleared his throat, like talking about his family was something he wanted to cough up and get rid of like a ball of phlegm. "Check and see if Donna's paid you."

I swiped open my phone, logged into my poor, suffering bank account app with my fingerprint, and refreshed.

"Holy shit, she actually paid!" My eyes went wide. "Your whole lawyer thing worked!"

"I don't think it was that," Wyatt said. "It was the threat of public shaming that really got to her. She's happy to avoid paying her bills, but she couldn't stand the thought of her friends thinking she couldn't."

"Public shaming," I repeated. "I'll have to remember that one for the future."

"Oh, I'm more than happy to be your legal representative again," Wyatt said. "Any time you need me." And with those words, his eyes were fixed on mine like he wanted me to take a deeper meaning from them.

I looked away, unwilling or unable to return that look. I couldn't let this get out of hand, no matter what I might be feeling. I didn't have time for feelings, even ones for the man sharing my house. I couldn't let anything happen, not now.

"Well, now that the Organised Home Co is safely in the black for a couple more weeks, let me take you out to thank you," I said instead.

"You don't need to do that," Wyatt said. "And I thought we established that you were the one who did me a favour."

"We both know that isn't true," I said. "Come on, let me do it. Mind you, I'm only offering coffee and maybe a weird protein ball. You can call it market research or competitor analysis if you want."

Wyatt laughed. "Well, I suppose I can allow that."

"Are you free now?" I surprised myself as I stood up.

"I've got to get to the restaurant." Wyatt looked genuinely disappointed. "Later today? Three-ish, maybe?"

"I can do three," I said, giving him a look that I hoped impressed upon him the importance of time management. "I don't do 'ish'."

"Of course not," Wyatt said, and his eyes got that intense look again. "Now I've got something to look forward to. See you at three."

And as he left, I could only sit there with a chest full of squirming, nebulous feelings and wonder if having coffee with me was really something Wyatt would look forward to.

· ♥ · ♥ · ♥ · ♥ · ♥ ·

As I made my way down to the coffee shop that kept Brekkie Beach's inhabitants caffeinated and perky, I had to admit there was a certain spring in my boot-clad step. I would have liked to say it was simply because my business was no longer facing imminent financial ruin, but I knew it was more than that.

Wyatt had *helped* me. And what's more, I had let him. The phone call itself had been only a few minutes long, but I had spent a lot longer than that trying to figure out how it made me feel, not to mention what I should do about those feelings.

Okay, so Wyatt was handsome and charming. And he got bonus points for teenage nostalgia, but I had met plenty of handsome and charming men before. I knew all about those twin qualities, and they had landed me in trouble. If handsome and charming was all Wyatt was bringing to the table, I wouldn't be spending so much of my time thinking about him.

I paused to scowl at the front porch of an enormous beachfront mansion. The house must have cost a fortune to build, but the overall impression of grandeur was marred by the clutter of shoes, surfboards, scooters, and bikes around the door. It would be so easy to install a few good shelves and even a bike rack, I thought. Maybe I should leave them a card.

What kind of lives were lived in those mansions, I wondered? Certainly nothing like mine. Wyatt understood that. He, too, had put everything he had into the small business that was his dream, with nothing and no one to fall back on. He was brave enough, driven enough, to try and be successful on his own terms rather than playing it safe, and working for someone else. And that was certainly a rarer quality than handsome or charming.

But there was something more, too. I hadn't been able to identify it at first, but when I found Wyatt sitting at the kitchen table, fiddling with the light-up smoke alarm that turned the room into a low-budget rave, something inside me had just...

...melted. Wyatt clearly had a big heart and a strong sense of justice. He *cared* about people. He saw the world as it was and was dissatisfied. My housemate had taken a chance on the people that society said didn't make good employees. And he did it because it was the right thing to do. Because it mattered to him.

And that? That quality was what was making me like him so much, despite my best efforts not to, more than the fact that he was handsome, charming, or even driven. And when he turned that big, caring heart on me? Looking out for me, even *looking after* me, which I usually hated? Shit, I was in serious trouble.

A big heart was harder to find than any other male organ.

Of course, I had to push all of those thoughts – and the fluttering sensations in my stomach they produced – away when I turned the corner and saw Wyatt was already in the coffee shop, leaning on the counter and chatting with Nick and Nikki.

"Hey," I said, pushing open the door.

"Hi," Wyatt greeted me with a broad smile that made the corners of his eyes crinkle. And while handsome wasn't the most impressive thing about the guy, it wasn't like I didn't appreciate it. That smile made my lower regions tingle in a way that probably had nothing to do with his big heart. "I was chatting to these two about Beach Garage, and how I want us to be complementary, not in competition."

"Oh, we'd hardly consider ourselves in competition with a full-service restaurant with a proper chef," Nikki said with a cheerful smile.

"And we'll never be able to make coffee as good as yours," Wyatt said warmly.

"Compliment accepted," Nick said, giving Wyatt an ironic salute. "Now, what were you saying about that program you used to find some of your staff? We're looking at bringing in a junior barista."

"I'll give you the details," Wyatt said, pulling out his phone. "It's called See Past, and the idea is to match capable people with employers who don't see disability or a difficult history as a barrier. Employers who won't act like they're doing some special big favour by giving a job to someone who might struggle to find one otherwise."

"I like that," Nikki said, nodding enthusiastically. "I've got a cousin who's only ever been able to get a job in fast food, and he could give so much more. It's not right."

"No," Wyatt agreed. "It isn't."

"We'll look into it." Nick was earnest. "Now, what can I get for you two? A large flat white with an extra shot for you, Abby? And a double espresso for Wyatt?"

"You've got an excellent memory," I said, but I was distracted by the fluttering in my stomach. The look on Wyatt's face as he advocated for people less fortunate than himself? Well, it turned out that was even more of an aphrodisiac than his chiselled jawline or well-muscled chest.

"We'll bring them over," Nick said, and Wyatt and I took our seats at the milk crates that masqueraded as appropriate seating.

"I hate to say it because Nick and Nikki are lovely, but I really hope your restaurant will have proper chairs," I said in a low voice, awkwardly arranging my still-booted foot to the side of the weather-beaten industrial spool that served as a table. "And tables."

Wyatt suppressed a snort. "You'll be pleased to know that our tables and the chairs don't have any past lives. Well, except at the restaurant that used to own them. But I think that's allowable."

"Good," I said, and then thought of something. "You would have made a good lawyer, you know."

"Why's that?" Wyatt quirked his mouth. "Because I got Donna to pay your invoice?"

"No, because you're good at convincing people to do things," I said. "Like getting Nick and Nikki interested in that employment program."

"Well, they asked me how I had gone about finding my staff, and we just got talking, and..." Wyatt shrugged. "I didn't have to do much convincing, to be honest. They were interested."

"A lot of people opening a restaurant would never have done what you have," I said, looking at him and resisting the urge to bite my lip. "You've put all your savings into this; you could be forgiven for hiring staff the traditional way. It's...it's kind of awesome, actually."

At my words, Wyatt shifted uncomfortably in his seat. He wasn't looking at me; instead, he stared at the opposite wall, which sported a pegboard dotted with tiny shelves, each bearing a succulent in a pot that appeared to have been someone's first attempt at pottery.

"It's not like I'm some great humanitarian, Abby," Wyatt said finally, looking at me. "I mean, yeah, I wanted to make sure people like my uncle get the opportunities that were denied to him. But I told you, there's a lot of very selfish, capitalist-pig reasons why it's a good idea."

"So you say. But I'm still impressed."

And at that, Wyatt smiled. "Well, if I've impressed you, I must be doing something right."

"I'm not that hard to please!" I protested. After all, I didn't like to think of myself as high maintenance.

"Oh, but you are," Wyatt said. "You've got very high standards of how people should behave because you hold yourself to those standards. And I'm glad to meet with your approval. At least in my business practices. I won't presume to think that I might meet with your personal approval." He was grinning as he said it, but there was an undercurrent in his voice like he really did care what I thought of him.

"You do, actually," I said, and when had my voice got all husky? I swallowed hard, suddenly very aware of how close he was to me, and how those hazel eyes were fixed on me, his mouth tensed like he was about to say something important. Very important.

"Large flat white, extra shot, and a double espresso!" Nikki interrupted, setting them down.

"Thanks," I said quickly in something like my normal voice. The moment had broken, but I could no longer deny how the first person I had ever kissed was making me feel.

And I still didn't know what to do about it.

· ♥ · ♥ · ♥ · ♥ · ♥ ·

Michelle: how's the foot, limpy?

Abby: i'm not limping!

Tessa: that's a good sign. how much longer are you in the boot?

Michelle: how much longer did the doctor say to wear it? because i know that's very different from how much longer you're actually planning to wear it

Abby: two weeks <frowning emoji>

Abby: but i feel fine, i don't see why i have to keep it on. it's a pain in the arse

Tessa: how did your arse get onto your foot?! <laughing emoji>

Abby: <eye roll emoji>

Tessa: sorry, that was bad

Michelle: you better not take that boot off before you're supposed to

Michelle: i bet wyatt would be sad if you did <winky face emoji>

Abby: he did say that, actually

Tessa: that's very sweet!

Michelle: are you still pretending you don't like him?

Michelle: abby?

Michelle: answer me!

Abby: fine

Abby: maybe i do like him. a bit

Tessa: coming from you, that's a declaration of undying love

Abby: it bloody well isn't!

Michelle: this is so perfect! your first kiss might be your last kiss

Michelle: as in you two will end up together forever, not like you're going to kiss him again and then die

Abby: i had worked that out, thanks

Tessa: so, are you going to tell him?

Michelle: you always said the best way to show a man you're interested is to just take your top off. when is that happening?

Abby: it's not. okay, so i like him. but it's a bad time for me to get involved with anyone. i've got the website launch and a ton of jobs coming up. i seriously do not have the capacity for anyone, whether i like them or not

```
Michelle: or you're afraid of
putting yourself out there, and
you're coming up with excuses
```

Tessa: ^^ sounds like something i would do. abby is too kick-arse for that

Abby: thanks

Abby: i really am busy. and i've got a lot on. maybe when things have settled down. it's not like it's a good time for him either, his restaurant is about to open and he's working crazy hours, so...

Abby: it's a bad time

```
Michelle: but you two live together!
he's conveniently located! how can
you not have time for someone living
in your house?!
```

Tessa: that's a very good point, actually. abby, listen to michelle!

```
Michelle: <halo emoji>
```

Abby: it isn't. it's not about spending time with him, it's about distractions. and i can't afford any right now. literally can't afford. time is money!

```
Michelle: do you need a loan?
```

Abby: no! i've told you before, i can handle this on my own

Michelle: <eye roll emoji> and i've told you before that taking a loan to expand your business isn't a handout, it's a sound business decision. i do work in finance!

Abby: i don't need a loan. once the online store opens, it should be fine. but until things are settled, i can't go and let myself get distracted by anyone

Tessa: i think it's okay to wait until things are a bit quieter

Tessa: that is, if you can. if you two really do like each other and you're in close proximity, things will happen. they always do

Michelle: too right!

Abby: things will not just happen. i won't let them

Michelle: sure <eye roll emoji>

Tessa: i think we should make sure you look extra glam at the restaurant opening though

Tessa: just in case

Michelle: <heart eyes emoji>

Abby: sometimes i wish i had brothers who'd beat up any guy who looked at me the wrong way

Michelle: but instead, you got us!

Tessa: and i know you wouldn't have it any other way <heart emoji>

12 Wyatt

I was kneeling on the polished concrete floor, scrubbing frantically at the place where a bottle of red wine had broken just minutes before.

"Fucking hell," I swore. "Just what I don't need for tonight."

The stain was resisting the soda water, which the internet had told me was a quick and easy way to remove red wine stains. So far, I had succeeded only in soaking the knees of my favourite jeans in red wine.

"Hello?" A familiar voice called out, echoing in the space that would hopefully be a functional restaurant by the time people started arriving. "I've got coffee!"

I looked up to see Abby, clad in her usual leggings and tank top, holding a tray of coffees. In the doorway, with the light behind her, she looked like an angel despite the walking boot still on her injured foot. And I sat there, gawping at her and thinking about things that one definitely wouldn't do to an angel. Then I collected myself, picked my jaw up off the floor, and managed to greet my housemate.

"Hi," I said, standing up in my stained jeans.

"How's it all going?" Abby asked, looking around the room with approval. "This space looks fantastic."

"It's going," I said, gritting my teeth. "I thought we had everything ready, but there's still a mountain of shit to do before we officially kick off tonight. David is ready to have a breakdown because the supplier delivered the wrong kind of pork loin, and Mindy can't get a hold of two of the waiters who are scheduled to come in...right now, actually."

Abby made a noise of sympathy. "Well, I can't really help with that," she said. "But I've got coffee!"

"You're an angel," I said, taking the proffered cup and gulping it down.

"How dare you?" Abby pretended to be offended. "I told you I'm an abomination, not an angel!"

I snorted, thinking of how unangelic my thoughts about her were. "I was keeping it together pretty well until I smashed that bloody bottle of wine, and it stained the floor. I'm starting to think polished concrete was a bad idea."

Abby frowned, stooping down to examine the mottled red stain. She sniffed and frowned again. "Did you use soda water on this?"

"Yeah, that's what the internet said to do."

"The internet is a dirty, rotten liar," Abby proclaimed. "Pork loins and waiters, I can't help you with. But stain removal? I'm pretty much a pro. I have to be. Do you know how often soy sauce takes a kamikaze dive from an overstuffed pantry? What we need is warm, soapy water and a stiff brush. Soda water is for carpet stains."

"I think I can find a stiff brush," I said, trying not to think about what else might be stiff in her presence. "Thank you, Abby."

"No worries," she said, shooting me a warm smile. "I'm just showing off."

"But you brought me coffee," I said. "So you're pretty much saving my arse right here. If I can get through tonight without it being a total disaster, I can breathe a little before we open for dinner next week."

"It's going to be fine," Abby rose to her feet, and I couldn't help but notice how close her leggings-clad body was to mine. "You've put the work in. You hired great people. You need to trust that."

"Thanks," I said, letting out a slow breath. "I just hope people like the food. And the vibe. And you know, everything."

"Well, at least five people will," Abby said. "My sisters and their boyfriends are coming, and I've told them they need to talk very loudly about how great everything is, even if you give people food poisoning."

I laughed, feeling a surge of something more than gratitude. "And here I am, thanking you again."

"I shared it on all my socials, too," Abby went on. "Which is good because loads of my clients aren't broke like we are, so they can actually come here and spend money."

And there it was, the wince. And the sick twist of guilt. She still thought I was broke and I still hadn't said anything to dissuade her of that notion.

"I'm not broke, exactly," I ventured.

"Oh, I know." Abby waved a hand. "It's all about cash flow. But you've put your savings into this, and I know how that can feel. Trust me, I know. And I wouldn't be a good housemate if I wasn't encouraging every rich person I know to come and drop a load of coin here."

"You're more than a good housemate, Abby," I said, knowing that now was not the right time to tell her how much more she was to me. I didn't know when the right time would be, but with mere hours until our launch party, I needed to focus on Beach Garage and not on my growing feelings. "Thanks again."

"You're welcome," Abby said simply, looking at me with those wide blue eyes. "I'll see you later, okay? Don't stress too much. After all, there's not much you can do now."

"I know you mean that to be comforting, but..." I sighed. "I just want it to go well. And not just for me."

"I know." Abby reached out to wrap her fingers around my bare arm for a moment, her touch making sparks ignite under my skin. "But it's going to be great. I'm sure of it."

As I watched her leave, my arm still tingling from her touch, I just hoped that Abby was right.

· ♥ · ♥ · ♥ · ♥ · ♥ ·

"It's packed!" Danni called over the noise of the crowd. "You can't be disappointed with this turnout." She took a gulp of her wine.

And she was right. The old garage, now transformed into a fresh, modern space, was full of people. Friend groups in their twenties with greedy fingers grasping for the free booze, middle-aged couples out for their weekly date night, and older people dressed up smartly for the occasion were pointing at the vintage alcohol signs on the wall approvingly. The air was thick with the smell of David's creations, and I could already see smiles and gasps of delight in response to the little sample pots of risotto that our waiters – tracked down by Mindy – were serving up.

"It's great," I said, nodding. "I just hope we've got enough food for all these people."

"Hey, you made it very clear you were offering taste tests, not a full meal," Danni said. "Stop worrying. You should be stoked. Loads of people here, and it's a great vibe. Although..."

"What?" I looked at her with concern. "What is it?"

"My mum might be coming," she admitted. "Possibly with an inappropriately younger man. I think she's been on those sugar baby websites, which is all kinds of traumatising."

"Shit," I whispered. "Not about the younger man, although that's disturbing too, but—"

"I know." Danni wrinkled her nose. "You don't want her reporting back to your dad about what you're doing."

"It's not that!" I said. "I don't care if my parents hear all about this. I just don't want Abby to meet your mum. If she does, then she'll work out that the family business is a whole lot bigger than I let on."

"You still haven't told her?" Danni let out a disgusted sound. "Wyatt, what is wrong with you?"

"We definitely don't have time to go into that," I said. "Look, I will tell her, but can you promise me you'll run interference tonight if it looks like your mum might be getting too near Abby?"

"This would be so much simpler if you had just told her the truth." Danni poked me. "But fine. So long as you tell Abby soon, okay?"

"I will," I promised. "Now I've got to get out there and mingle."

"Look for Abby, you mean." She gave me a knowing smile. "I know you, dude."

"Just don't drink all the booze and keep your mum away from Abby," I said, almost pleading.

"I will," she said. "But you owe me."

Smiling my thanks, I made my way back into the thronging crowd. And I did need to greet my potential future customers and turn up the charm, but Danni hadn't been wrong when she said that I was also looking for Abby, not very subtly. It wasn't like Abby to be late, and I felt sure that I would have seen her if she had been here, even in this crowd.

As I was interrogated about vegan options by a woman with blonde dreadlocks and an unblinking stare, I spotted Abby.

And damn, I had thought she looked good in leggings and a ponytail.

Tonight, Abby didn't look like she organised people's homes for a living. In a fitted red dress that showed off those long legs of hers, she looked like every single one of my dirtiest fantasies come to life. Her hair hung in soft waves around her face, and her lips were pink, glossy, and impossibly inviting.

"You really should look at going fully plant-based," the woman in front of me said, still not blinking. "Instead of supporting an industry based on suffering and—"

"I'll take it into consideration," I said quickly. "If you'll just excuse me."

I didn't allow her to reply and wove my way through the crowd.

"Hi," I said, leaning down to brush my lips over Abby's cheek, even though I never had before. The dress seemed to bring out the gentleman in me. "Thank you so much for coming."

"Of course I came," Abby said, looking up at me through her lashes. "And don't start with me about not wearing the boot tonight. You can't expect me to wear a dress like this with that bloody thing. I compromised by wearing flat shoes, and I swear I'll put the boot back on when I get home."

"I didn't even notice," I admitted. "You look..." I took a breath. "I think you know exactly how good you look."

"I've got some idea." Abby gave me a tiny wink that went straight to my groin. "But I like hearing it just the same."

"You're stunning, Abby," I said. "I'll say it as often as you want."

"Well, there's an offer I can't refuse," Abby said, letting out a soft breath. "And you look pretty great yourself. Every bit the sleek and polished business owner." She reached out to run her fingers over my clean-shaven cheek for just a moment. Her touch was electric, sending sparks of desire flooding through my chest – and much lower.

"I thought I'd better play the part," I said, delighted she was flirting with me.

"I think I prefer the designer stubble, though," Abby said, screwing up her mouth with a thoughtful expression.

"I'll keep that in mind," I said, my hand going to my chin. If I could have grown my stubble back instantly by sheer force of will, just to please her, I would have.

"Anyway, I'll leave you to your adoring public," Abby said, smiling. "I know you're busy, and I have to stop my sisters from scoffing everything in sight."

"You don't have to—"

But before I could protest any further, Abby had disappeared between circles of people, and I was captured by an older gentleman intent on telling me, in some detail, about the garage that had once operated here and what second-rate work they had done on his Holden Monaro.

Despite my best efforts, I couldn't get near Abby again for a long time. However, I did see Danni skilfully engaging her mother – and a man who didn't look much older than me – in a conversation that took them from the opposite end of the room from where Abby was chatting with two women who must be her sisters. When I looked over, both sisters looked at me with open interest. What had she told them about me, I wondered? Were they simply curious to see who the gangly teenager their sister had once snogged had grown up to be, or was it something more?

A sharp poke from Mindy pulled me out of my reverie. "Time for your speech," she said. For the benefit of the Holden Monaro-owning man, she gave a charming smile. "I'll just borrow Wyatt here."

"It's not a speech," I said under my breath as she led me through the crowd and towards a raised platform that had been part of the original garage. I had decided to leave it intact for the sake of authenticity and the possibility of live music. "Just thanking people for being here."

"Whatever it is." Mindy rolled her eyes. "It's time to do it, so these people know they can leave and only come back when they're paying for their food."

As I stood up on the platform, I could see Abby's face in the crowd as she bit into a black truffle and porchetta arancini ball, her eyes closed in absolute bliss. I felt a low tug and wondered if I'd ever have the opportunity to make her look like that without the help of David's cooking.

Abruptly, the soft jazz stopped playing, and I cleared my throat. "If I could grab your attention for just a moment!"

I had eschewed a microphone in favour of simply speaking very loudly. The conversation died away, and suddenly, all eyes were on me. But I wasn't looking at the crowd.

Only one set of eyes interested me, and they were bright blue and now very much open.

"I just wanted to say a huge thank you to all of you for coming along tonight to support the opening of Beach Garage," I began, and there was a brief murmur of approval in response.

"Opening a place like this has been a dream of mine since I was a kid," I said, even though that wasn't strictly true. "And I couldn't imagine a better place to do it than here in beautiful Brekkie Beach." That seemed to please the crowd.

"I do hope you're enjoying a taste of what Beach Garage has on the menu, and I hope we'll see you back here when we open for dinner next Tuesday." Lots of nods, which were hardly a commitment, but certainly pleasing to see.

"And I'd like to thank the team here for making my dream possible. While I've always wanted to open a restaurant, I'd be the first to admit that making the food or running the place is way beyond my talents."

A polite titter of laughter.

"And so, I'd like to say a special thank you to David Evans, our Head Chef, and Mindy June, our restaurant manager, for making Beach Garage a reality."

Abby was nodding in encouragement and seemed to know that I was looking right at her, despite the distance. A smattering of applause, and then I knew it was time to finish before I lost the crowd's attention entirely.

"And I'd like to thank all of you, the Brekkie Beach community, for welcoming us into your beautiful town, and I hope we'll be seeing a whole lot more of each other. Thank you!"

Polite applause, a few cheers, and then conversation once again erupted around us. As I stepped down from the platform, my aunt - and her young companion – made a beeline for me. To my horror, I could see Abby winding her way over to me in the corner of my peripheral vision.

"Doesn't this all look delightful?" Sondra gave me a loud kiss on the cheek, three Hermes bangles clattering on her wrist. Coco Chanel had once said that to be truly stylish, you ought to take off one accessory before leaving the house, but Auntie Sondra clearly thought she knew better than Coco Chanel. "And the food's bloody nice, too! You're a clever boy, Wyatt!"

"Bloody nice food," Sondra's young man echoed, raising his glass to me. In his uncomfortably tight red jeans, and loud shirt, he was taking his role as Sondra's companion exceptionally seriously.

"Thanks," I said, wondering how quickly I could end this conversation without being rude.

"It's a shame your mum and dad aren't here," Sondra went on, and I cringed. "I know you had some words about all this, but I think they'd be proud of you. Look at what you've managed to put together, all on your own!"

"Well, it's hardly on my own," I said, relieved to see that Danni had caught Abby's arm and was asking her something in a low whisper. "I've got a great team here and—"

"You know what I mean," Sondra said, patting my cheek. "Anyway, I'll leave you to it, but I just wanted to say I'm proud of you."

"So proud of you," her companion parroted, as though he, personally, felt a familial pride in my achievement. I managed a weak smile in response, relief flooding through me as they moved away.

Then a soft hand was on my arm. "Great speech," Abby leaned up to whisper the words, which I supposed made sense, given the crowd, but it still sent a shiver through me.

"Hardly a speech," I said, turning to her. "But I'd be an arsehole not to thank the team."

"But you did well," Abby insisted. "Particularly given most people fear public speaking more than death. So, it's an achievement."

"In that case, thank you."

"I'll leave you to it," Abby said, about to escape through the crowd again, and I let out an audible groan. She paused, looking at me in confusion. "What is it?"

"Nothing," I said. "Just, I have to go and talk to strangers. And I'd rather talk to you."

"You can always talk to me!" Abby made a face. "I mean, I do live in your house."

"Still..." I said, wanting to reach out and pull her to me. I didn't know if I was buoyant from the success of the launch, or if it was just that my feelings were becoming so intense I couldn't deny them any longer. "I'd rather be with you."

Abby looked at me for a long moment. "I'll see you later," she said, and I couldn't help thinking that sounded like a promise. A promise of something more.

· ♥ · ♥ · ♥ · ♥ · ♥ ·

It was well after the finishing time listed on the Facebook event when the last of our guests trailed out of Beach Garage, and Mindy looked at their retreating backs with distinct distaste.

"I thought they'd never go!" Mindy exclaimed. "Maybe they thought they'd get a free dinner if they stuck around."

"Maybe," I said, distracted. I was looking at where Abby, in the red dress that clung and whispered to the curves of her body, had joined our waiters in clearing tables and collecting wine glasses. She seemed to be part of the team already, laughing and joking with them.

David came out of the kitchen then, picking up a half-empty bottle of wine and settling into a chair. With a happy, though exhausted, grin, he took a long swig straight from the bottle. "That went well."

"Very well," I said. "Let's just hope some of the punters turn up next week. With money."

David laughed. "They will. My food will bring them in," he signed.

"I have to agree with that."

"Your food is addictive," Mindy said. "You try it once, and then you're craving your next fix. Good thing risotto is allowed under my recovery plan."

David and I chuckled at that, and I felt a swell of gratitude to them for making this dream a reality. At that moment, it all felt real. I really had something of my own. Something my parents had no part in. Something that was just mine.

"Abby is still here." David indicated where Abby was now showing the waiters how to stack plates more efficiently.

"Yes," I said. "She's very thoughtful, helping clean up."

Mindy rolled her eyes. "She's waiting for you, more like."

"What are you waiting for? Take her home!" David made a face.

I looked over at Abby once again, and a powerful surge of want swelled inside me. I looked again at David and Mindy. "We've got to get this place cleaned up. I need to—"

"Don't be stupid." Mindy gave me a dismissive look. "We've got this."

"You go and get the girl," David said, nodding emphatically. "Get lost, boss!"

I looked again at Abby.

"If you're sure..."

"We are," Mindy said. "So long as you are."

"I think I am," I said, still staring at Abby. "I think I'm sure."

13 Abby

"You must be so happy with how tonight went," I said, looking up at Wyatt as we approached the little house that fate had determined we share.

"I am," Wyatt said, his voice oddly tight. He had seemed so determined when he had taken my arm and led me out of the restaurant. I had been certain he was about to flatten me against the nearest wall and kiss the hell out of me. But once the night's cool breeze had hit us, he had pulled away, muttering something about needing to get me home so I wasn't putting any more pressure on my foot. And I was feeling disappointed, to say the least.

"Beach Garage is going to be a huge success," I ventured. "Seriously, the crowd was buzzing. I heard this one woman making full-on orgasm noises when she tried the arancini.

It was like that scene in *When Harry Met Sally*. Everyone will want to have what she's having."

Wyatt laughed, but his body was still tense like he was waiting for something. I sighed and pulled my keys from my pocket, opening the door and stepping inside. Wyatt followed me and immediately tripped over the skateboard he had left by the door. I, of course, would have put it on the shoe rack to avoid such tragedies, but I decided not to mention that.

"Shit!" he swore, regaining his balance. "I'm definitely off my game with the skating. I guess seventeen years is a long time."

"It is," I said, looking at him and trying to control my breathing. "But some things don't change."

"Oh?" He looked at me, a question on his lips. "Like what?"

I let out an exasperated sound. "Like I'm still standing here, waiting for you to kiss me!"

Wyatt stared at me for a moment, and then his big hands were on my waist, hot and urgent through the soft fabric. When his lips captured mine, they weren't tentative and hesitant like they had been seventeen years before. Now they were insistent, sure, and utterly confident as he kissed me. And yes, I was now flattened against the nearest wall, his firm body covering mine, pressing into me.

My lips parted under his, and *god*, he sure hadn't been lying about his kissing prowess improving since our teenage years. His mouth moved over mine in a sensuous rhythm, teasing and making me open for him. I let him plunder my mouth like he was an old-timey pirate seeking treasure and adventure on the high seas. Which wasn't a sexy metaphor at all, and I really needed to get it out of my head.

"I was waiting for you to say that," Wyatt whispered, hot breath on my skin. "I had to be sure this was what you wanted."

"This shouldn't be what I want," I admitted, even as my body celebrated the joining of our lips with a fireworks display that would be illegal in most states. "I told myself I couldn't let anything happen. Not when I've got so much on, but..."

"But?"

"But I have zero self-control when it comes to you, apparently." I angled my hips into him and gasped at the contact. "And I just don't care anymore."

"Good answer." Wyatt's voice was a harsh whisper. "Very good answer."

His mouth was on mine once more and I melted into him, my arms around his neck, my body pressed into his.

"I'm going to take you upstairs," Wyatt murmured. "Got to get you off your feet. Your foot must be sore."

"I'm not thinking about my foot right now, I have to admit." And that was true. As we had walked back to the house, my foot had been twinging, but now? Now all I could feel was desire, hot and heavy, bubbling inside me, ready to erupt. I wasn't even aware of having feet at all.

"Still..." Wyatt pressed a kiss to my neck and then scooped me into his arms like I was a bride he was about to carry over the threshold.

"Show off," I chided, but I was smiling.

"Oh, I totally am," Wyatt replied, his smile meeting my own. "Remember how I tried to do all those kickflips to impress you? The bruises lasted months. But it was worth it," he leaned down to kiss me once more, pausing on the stairs, "because it did get your attention."

"You already had my attention," I told him. "And you still do, right now."

"And I intend to keep it." I gasped as Wyatt kicked open the door to his bedroom (and not just because that would leave a mark on the painted wood) and carefully set me down on his bed, joining me in an instant.

I could feel my body almost shaking with want; I had denied myself this for too long, I thought. The reasons why I couldn't let anything happen with Wyatt hadn't disappeared, but they didn't seem anywhere near as important as they had before. Not compared to the intensity of my feelings for the man before me.

Impatiently, I tugged at his shirt, trying to slide my hands underneath to touch that bare skin, that flat stomach, to feel his body heat against me, but Wyatt caught my hands. I let out an indignant sound as he held them above my head, capturing both my wrists in his big hand like it was easy.

"Nope," he said with a smirk. "I know how much you like to be in control of everything, Abby. But you're not going to be in control of this. Not with me."

I squirmed against him, indignance and fresh desire rushing through me. Was he seriously telling me what to do?

"Because I know—" Wyatt leaned down to kiss my neck, the brush of lips and graze of teeth over the sensitive skin making me squirm. "That giving up your precious control is what you really want right now. Isn't it?"

I made a noise that definitely wasn't a real word. Not even close. Because he was right. I'd never admit it to anyone – not even my sisters – but giving up control to Wyatt was *exactly* what I wanted.

"I..." I could barely breathe; I was utterly overcome with demanding desire. "Yes."

Wyatt's mouth captured mine once more, urgent and demanding. Even as we kissed, even as I pressed my body into him, seeking out more contact, he never let my wrists free. When he finally did release me, it was to roll me over and unzip my dress.

"Do you know how it made me feel seeing you in this dress?" His breath was hot against my neck, making me shiver. "When I had to play the charming business owner and talk to all those irritating people? When all I wanted to do was drag you into the nearest supply closet."

Heat went through me at his words, and I pressed my body back up into him, moaning out loud at the touch. "I think I'm getting some idea of how it made you feel." I turned my head to look at him, and Wyatt chuckled softly.

"You'd be right." With deft fingers, he sent my bra and underwear (yes, red to match my dress) sailing across the room.

"You're so beautiful," Wyatt whispered as he stared down at my naked body, desire darkening his hazel eyes. "I haven't been able to take my eyes off you; it's been driving me crazy."

I squirmed under his gaze, even though I had never been the kind of person to pretend I didn't know I was attractive. But somehow, knowing I was conventionally attractive and having Wyatt call me beautiful were two very different things. "I want to see you." I was almost pleading, reaching up for his shirt again.

But Wyatt just grabbed my hands, pinning them above my head. This time he bent his head to mouth over my neck and then lower still. His breath was hot as his tongue teased my breasts, licking, sucking, grazing his teeth. "I told you, Abby. You don't get to be in charge in this bedroom."

I let out a whine of need, every part of my body loving that I had let myself submit to him but impatient for more just the same.

"Now lie back, and let me enjoy you." Wyatt's voice was an order. "Or I might just have to spank you."

"You wouldn't!" I shot back, even as the thought sent a thrill through me, making me tremble underneath him.

"Oh, but I would." Wyatt's smile was wicked. "And what's more, you'd love it."

I groaned again, unable to form anything like coherent words, and all I could do was let him take his time with me, licking and sucking, biting and nibbling, setting every part of my body on fire until I was writhing in needy frustration.

"I want to touch you!" I hissed, bucking against him. "And I know you want me to."

"Oh, I do," he said. "I really do. But not as much as I want to hear those noises I know you can make for me."

And with that, he pressed his mouth right to the nape of my belly, slinging my legs over his broad shoulders. And god, how was I already naked while he was still fully clothed? Somehow, that made me feel even more vulnerable. In my regular daily life, I *hated* feeling vulnerable. But now, with Wyatt's mouth inches away from where I wanted him so badly, vulnerable didn't feel like such a bad thing to be.

When he finally pressed his mouth to where I was so wet, so ready for him, I let out a cry, my hips bucking into him, but he stayed me with strong hands. "Stay still," he murmured, hot breath against my inner thighs. "

And all I could do was *let* him. Let my body melt into that perfect, hot mouth as his tongue drew dizzying circles, swirls, and licks over my core, teasing and taunting me. Whenever I tried to move, to buck, to draw him closer, those big hands just gripped me tighter, telling me without words that I wasn't the one in control here. He was. Because just for now, I was letting Wyatt Parsons be the boss of me.

"Wyatt, please!" I cried out, my body squirming because, god, I was so *close*, and I didn't want to come, not yet. "If you keep doing that, you're going to make me come!"

But Wyatt just looked up at me, his lips wet with me, and smirked.

And that was *it*. When Wyatt's mouth captured me once more, and he pressed one long finger inside my body to brush that secret bundle of nerves, I was done. My body convulsed underneath him, and I was flying, sailing, soaring through ecstasy. Wyatt didn't stop until he had wrung every last bit of pleasure from my body, and I was left sweaty and gasping beneath him.

I looked up at him then, my body melting into the mattress, to see he looked just like the proverbial cat who had got the cream. In this metaphor, I was definitely the cream. Hell, I was the whole damn dairy.

"So fucking hot, Abby," Wyatt breathed. He was looking at me like I was an entirely new kind of being, something he had never seen before. He wasn't smirking now. His mouth was open, his smile joyful and natural. "Seeing you let go for me like that."

"I couldn't help it, with you doing that to me." And it was true. Plenty of men had gone down on me before. A few had even tried to take the lead in some kind of BDSM-inspired powerplay. But it had never been like this. It had always felt perfunctory, like something they thought they had to do to get me to return the favour. But no man had ever made me come before I touched him, had wanted to make me feel good, simply for my own sake.

"I've been thinking about it since..." Wyatt shook his head. "Since I met you again that very first morning. When you were very unimpressed with me."

"Really?"

"Really."

I reached out to his shirt once more. "Is this ever going to come off?" I didn't even try to unbutton it this time; I knew that was a losing battle. "Because I really want to see you naked."

Wyatt didn't say a word; he just moved back and stripped off his shirt in a fluid movement. And wow, his body was every bit as impressive in the soft light of his bedroom as the glimpses I had caught previously had promised. Broad shoulders, firm biceps, and a chest that I wanted to lick.

I let out an appreciative moan, reaching up to trace my fingers over his skin and found it hot to my touch. Wyatt took my hand and pressed a kiss to my palm, and I let out a sound of frustration. "Are you ever going to let me touch you?" My voice was almost a whine. I was never this needy, but I had never been faced with something I wanted so much before. "Please, Wyatt."

"I think I could allow a little touching." I could feel his smirk against my skin. "Seeing as you did say please."

I pressed my hands into the muscles of his back as he kissed me, glorying in the feeling of my skin against his skin, pressed so tight that it felt like this could last forever, that nothing could break us apart.

When I reached down to grab his arse, squeezing the firm muscle, Wyatt groaned. "I didn't say you could do that."

"No way I could resist," I said, getting in one more solid squeeze. At that, Wyatt rolled me over to my belly, and I was prone and vulnerable beneath him once more.

"I know all about can't resist." Wyatt was pressing light kisses over my shoulder blades and down my spine as his big hands cupped my bottom, fingers kneading. I was pushing back into him, fresh arousal spiking through me. "Do you know how crazy your leggings drive me, Abby? How much you make me want to touch you? I've been starting to think you do it on purpose."

I gasped, aching for more. "They're very practical for work!"

"Is that so?" There was a brief pause as Wyatt stripped off his jeans and... *God*, I could feel his hard length pressed against my inner thighs, so close to where I wanted him. Was he going to take me like this?

"Condoms!" I gasped out before my brain could completely short-circuit and forget the need for things more practical than my leggings. "I think I have some in my room."

"I've got some." Wyatt reached across to his bedside table and scrabbled in the drawer. I craned my neck, looking back at him. "Don't you trust me to put it on properly?" He gave me an incredulous look.

"I want to *see* you," I whispered, my eyes going wide at the sight of him, thick and hard and so ready for me as he slipped the sheath over himself.

"Yeah?" Wyatt's eyes were dark with desire. "And you like what you see?"

"I do," I whispered. "Can we please just—"

"You're so impatient," Wyatt told me, with a light slap to my bottom that made me cry out in shock and pleasure. Mostly pleasure because that one spank set my nerves on fire, and made my core ache with need for him. Was it really possible for me to be ready again so soon after my first orgasm? Apparently, all my usual rules were off where Wyatt was concerned.

"Wyatt!" My voice was a needy whine, and I didn't care. How could I, when I was entirely under the control of both Wyatt himself and my own desperate lust? I squirmed under him, pressing back into him and moaning at the contact. "Please."

"Well, you did say the magic word." Wyatt's body pressed over mine, and he slipped an arm beneath me, rolling me onto my side. "Spread your legs for me, Abby."

I was barely aware of what my body was doing, but I managed to comply, eagerly spreading my thighs wide for him. When he pressed the tip of himself right against my entrance, he paused, and I groaned in needy frustration. But when he bent down to kiss me, murmuring something about how beautiful I was, with proprietorial hands on my body, I stopped caring.

Then he pushed inside me in one smooth stroke, filling me up completely. I cried out, arching into him, and he groaned out his pleasure. "God, you feel perfect, Abby."

I would have liked to say something back to that, but apparently, my speech facilities had been short-circuited due to pent-up want and extreme pleasure, and all that came out was a needy garble of sounds. My ability to form words didn't return as he moved inside me, every stroke making me gasp. I couldn't take my eyes off his face; Wyatt looked at me like this was the fulfilment of every fantasy, every wish, every daydream he had ever had. That it was all me; all that he wanted was me. Could that possibly be true?

But my capacity for rational thought was the next thing to go, as he reached down with commanding fingertips to tease that nub of pleasure he had worshipped before with his tongue. "Wyatt!" I gasped, just able to form his name.

"You're going to come for me again." He made it sound like a statement of fact. It wasn't even an order; it was simply what *would* happen. "And I'm going to feel it. I want to feel you squeezing tight around me."

And, as it turned out, he was absolutely and completely right.

My body began to tremble, convulse, quake underneath him, and I was letting out sounds I didn't know I was capable of. Every bit of my body was on edge, ready to tumble over. I was so close and—

"Do it." Wyatt's voice was an order now, a command. "Come for me, Abby."

My body's frantic symphony reached its crescendo. I let out a cry as I clenched tight around him, my vision swirling. Every bit of my precious control evaporated as I bucked up into him in dizzying waves, peaks, summits of pleasure.

Wyatt let out a low, rough groan as he released inside me, his body going rigid with his final thrusts.

And then, miraculously, our bodies stilled. Wyatt pressed a soft kiss to my forehead, pulling me close so we were nose to nose.

"Hey." He wasn't smirking now, just smiling with a genuine delight that made my heart swell.

"Hey," I replied, my voice a little shaky. "That was…"

"I know," Wyatt agreed.

"How did you know that I..." I swallowed. "That I wanted it like that?"

"Because I know you." He tucked a loose strand of my dark hair behind one ear. "And I know you'd tell me in no uncertain terms if I had been wrong."

"You weren't wrong. Really weren't wrong."

"You're always in control of everything." Wyatt's voice was soft. "Always the boss. I figured this might be one time you could use a break from that. And I hoped," he paused for a moment, "that you'd trust me enough to let me give that to you."

"I..." I swallowed. "I wouldn't have wanted to let anyone else do that to me." The confession made me squirm, even though it was true.

"Then I'm very lucky," Wyatt said, brushing his lips across mine. "And relieved because there's no way in hell I could stand letting some other guy be the boss of Abby Finch."

"There are no other guys," I said, looking right into those hazel eyes and wanting him to know I meant it. "I wasn't even supposed to let anything happen with you because..."

"Because you're at a critical stage in building your business, and you don't need any distractions?" Wyatt quirked his mouth.

I groaned. "Something like that."

"I promise not to be too distracting." Wyatt still looked amused.

"Well, that's a giant lie." I snuggled closer to him, enjoying the faint smell of his cologne in the crook of his neck. "But you know what?"

"What?"

"I think I could make room for one distraction. Especially given he's so conveniently located," I said, reaching out to brush my fingers over his face.

Wyatt smiled against my fingers. "You think I'm worth your precious time?"

I looked at him for a long moment. "Yes."

·♥·♥·♥·♥·♥·

When I stirred to consciousness the next morning, I was briefly completely disorientated. No silk eye mask, no white noise, no crisp grey duvet. Instead, I was surrounded by navy stripes, sunlight pouring in through thin curtains, and a strong arm holding me against a broad chest. I could feel the soft rise and fall of Wyatt's breathing as the memories of last night came rushing back.

I felt a rush of something in my stomach. Not regret. I definitely didn't regret what had happened last night – my body wouldn't let me, even if my brain had tried to insist. But I was very aware that last night had been significant.

It had changed things irrevocably. It hadn't been a casual hook-up or a drunken mistake. It was...something. Something I didn't know how to define just yet.

I lifted my arm, grateful to see my smart watch still in place. It was just after six, but I knew I'd have to get up soon if I expected to leave the house by seven.

A soft groan made the hair on the back of my neck shift.

"Stop looking at the time," Wyatt told me. "Let's get some more sleep."

"I can't," I said, turning in his embrace so we were face to face. "I've got a job to get to."

Another groan. "What would it take for me to get you to take a sick day?" Wyatt drew me closer so my body was flush against his, and wow, that really did make the idea of a sick day very appealing.

"Not even you could make me cancel a job last minute," I said, though I was regretful. "This is the first day of a three-day job, and we've been planning for Josie to do the next two days solo. But I have to get her set up, make sure she's comfortable with everything, and—"

"But you told me how capable she is," Wyatt complained. "I bet she's ready to work alone."

And that was possibly true. Josie had already proven herself more than capable of following my carefully laid out plans of how to make a wardrobe appear inviting or a fridge look ready for Pinterest. But I had promised her we'd be starting the job together, and I wasn't about to let her down. Not even for my very handsome housemate, who was currently pressing kisses along my neck.

"I really can't," I said, sitting up. "You said you know me. So you know why I can't."

"I do," Wyatt said with a sigh. "And your conscientiousness is one of the things I like so much about you, even if I wish you'd give yourself a break sometimes. But," he smirked, "it was worth a try."

"Full points for effort." I gave him a grin. "And I bet you've got a ton to do at the restaurant."

"You're not wrong." Wyatt sighed. "But I don't have to be in until twelve. I told everyone to take the morning off after last night."

"You're a good boss," I said, touching his face again and wishing the client would cancel last minute, even though that would be terrible for my bank balance. "A good man."

"I'm just glad you think so," Wyatt said, and then his face changed. A slight frown. "Abby..."

"I can't cancel!" I said, cutting him off. "But I'll be back later. Tonight."

"You better be." Wyatt pressed a kiss to my belly, making my skin tingle and desire shoot through me in hot, insistent sparks. "Or I'll hunt you down."

"Stalking isn't an attractive quality."

"Not even on me?" Wyatt gave me a pleading look, and I laughed.

"Jury's still out on that one," I said. "I just..."

"What?"

"I want you to know that I wish I could stay," I said, my words coming out in a tumble. "If I didn't have a job to get to, I'd absolutely stay in bed with you. I wouldn't, you know, tell you I have to watch a content marketing webinar or—"

"Vacuum the interior of your van?" Wyatt suggested. "Thanks, Abby."

"You know what I mean!"

"I do," Wyatt said, oddly serious. "And I wasn't joking. It means a lot that you'd give me some of your precious time. I just have to make sure you won't regret it."

"I think you're worth it," I said quietly, leaning in for one last kiss before leaving the bed full of tempting housemate-turned-something-else and getting ready for my day.

· ♥ · ♥ · ♥ · ♥ · ♥ ·

Michelle: last night was great. cannot wait until beach garage opens, i need like four bowls of that risotto

Tessa: #teamarancini over here

Michelle: and wyatt is totally into you, abby. he couldn't take his eyes off you all night, even when he did that little speech

Tessa: ^^ agreed. when are you going to accept that you two are fated?

`Michelle: do you need me to sing sk8er boi? because i will`

`Michelle: <voice recording sent>`

Abby: anything but that!

Abby: ...something did happen last night, actually

Tessa: !!! why are we having to drag it out of you?! you always tell us when you hooked up with a dude. usually with more detail than i ever wanted to know

`Michelle: FINALLY. was it good? everything your teenage self dreamed of?`

Abby: my teenage self definitely couldn't have dreamed about what happened last night

`Michelle: that good!? damn girl! <confetti emoji> <exploding champagne emoji>`

Tessa: <volcano emoji>?

Abby: all of the above. it was...different. like he knew what i wanted and wanted to make it perfect for me. he really seemed to care about my pleasure

`Michelle: of course he does, he's totally in love with you!`

Abby: let's not get carried away

Tessa: i'm so glad you're getting good sex with a hot guy! please don't tell me you're still claiming you don't have time for anything with him

Abby: well, he did point out he's conveniently located in the house, so it's not like it's a whole lot of extra time required

Michelle: how romantic <eye roll emoji>

Tessa: so, are you two a thing?

Abby: i think so. i mean, he was pretty clear about not wanting me to see other dudes, and i said he was worth making time for. seems like that's a thing

Michelle: i'm surprised you didn't ask him outright. you always say you don't believe in game-playing and miscommunication

Abby: i was in a rush! i will definitely confirm

Tessa: and are you feeling good about all this? about having a proper boyfriend?

Abby: i agreed it was a thing, not that he's a proper boyfriend

Abby: i still don't know if i have space in my life for a full-on boyfriend. but if i was going to have one he'd be the only one i'd want

Michelle: pretty sure that's as romantic as we're going to get from you

Tessa: i think that's very sweet. so when do we get to meet him properly?

Abby: you met him last night!

Tessa: we met him as your housemate last night. not as your "thing"

```
Michelle: tessa's right. omg, we can
do a triple date!
```

Abby: that might be fun, or it might be hell on earth. definitely no time right now for any dates, triple or otherwise. i gtg, lunch break is over and i think there's a nest of wasps in the linen cupboard behind the spare towels

Tessa: that's terrifying!

```
Michelle: i hope you charge extra
for vermin removal!
```

Abby: all part of the job

```
Michelle: and keep us updated on the
wyatt front! i'm so happy for you!
```

Abby: i'm happy too

14 Wyatt

"Look at this!" Mindy thrust her phone into my face, waving it back and forth so I couldn't possibly focus.

"What am I looking at?" I leaned back, trying to see.

"Our Instagram!" Mindy was still waving the phone. "Some of those people who were here last night took a lot of photos, and now we've got all these new followers!"

"Oh, cool," I said, fishing my phone out of my pocket to check. "See, that's what I told you would happen! The free advertising is worth way more than what we spent on the food and booze."

"I know that's what you said," Mindy said. "But I didn't believe it."

"Oh, ye of little faith." I shook my head sadly.

A sharp tap on the shoulder interrupted me, and another phone was thrust into my face. "Look at this!" David demanded, and I could see a video looping across his screen.

I was horrified to discover that the video was, in fact, six seconds of me offering a plate of arancini balls to a group of young women. The caption read, "when the hot chef offers you his delicious balls <heart eyes emoji>".

"But I'm not the chef!" I protested as though that was the only problem with the video.

David made a face. "I know," he said. "But it's had fifty thousand views."

"What?" I must have misunderstood the number, given my signing was still in the intermediate stages. "You mean five thousand?"

"No." David gave me a withering look and put the phone in front of me again. And he was right. Fifty thousand people had viewed a six-second video of me offering up porchetta and truffle-filled arancini balls.

"Fifty thousand?" Mindy looked aghast. "The bloody booking system's going to blow up. We can't deal with those numbers!"

"It's not that bad," I said quickly. "It's TikTok; most of them will be overseas. But hopefully we'll get a couple of bookings out of it."

"Opening night only has a couple of spots left," Mindy said, sounding pleased. "A six o'clock and one at nine-thirty. There's a waitlist for the seven o'clock time slot."

"We have a waiting list?" I was delighted to hear it. "That's a very good thing. I'll put something up online. It'll make people want to come even more if they think they might not be able to get in."

As I sank into a chair to update Beach Garage's social media channels, I could see a silent conversation between David and Mindy in my peripheral vision.

"What?" I asked, looking up.

"What happened when you left with Abby?" David asked.

"Would you stop asking if I said it was none of your business?"

"Nope," Mindy snorted. "You might have a good head for business, but this is what you don't know about having a restaurant. There's no privacy. Everyone knows everyone's business. Now, tell us what happened."

I rolled my eyes. "I think you can guess. And yeah, I should have made a move earlier, but the way it turned out..." I paused. "I wouldn't change a thing."

"Oh, now that's very romantic," Mindy was approving, and David nodded his agreement.

"You were careful, weren't you?" David asked, and I learned just what the sign for "safe sex" was.

"David! Boundaries!"

"I have six brothers and sisters." David shuddered. "So, I always remind people to be safe."

"He's right, you know!" Mindy pointed a finger. "It shouldn't be taboo to talk about safer sex and harm reduction, Wyatt."

"For your information, it was perfectly safe. And that's all I'm going to say about it."

"So, are you two a couple now?" Mindy pressed. "That's the important part, anyway."

I paused, taking a moment to think about her question. Abby *had* told me there weren't any other guys and that I was worth making time for. That seemed to indicate she'd be at least open to having the 'are we a couple' discussion with me.

"We didn't get a chance to talk about it," I said perfectly honestly, although David made a face and Mindy scoffed. "But I hope so."

And as I said the words, a warm feeling rose in my chest. I really did hope that Abby and I could be a couple. Because already, I couldn't stand the thought of letting her go.

· ♥ · ♥ · ♥ · ♥ · ♥ ·

I didn't know when Abby would return that evening, especially since she had sent me an alarming photo of her removing a wasp's nest from a linen closet with only a pair of thin gloves for protection. But even so, I practically jogged back to the little house, hoping she might be there.

When I saw the white van parked out the front, I felt a thrill of glee shoot through me. And not just because I was hoping for an encore of last night's performance. I was just as excited to hear about Abby's day, to give her a hug, to laugh at her impressions of her clients, and discover just what had happened to the wasp's nest.

I wasn't falling anymore; I had well and truly fallen. But I was the opposite of worried. Abby was, I was becoming certain, the one person I wanted to give my heart to. After all these years and meeting hundreds, even thousands of women, the girl I had met in the park at fifteen was the right one for me.

Swallowing hard, I reminded myself that while I could accept that I felt this way, I was reasonably sure it was too early to say any of this to Abby. I ran a hand over my chin and was glad to feel that some of the stubble had re-established itself for Abby's benefit and opened the door.

Nothing could have prepared me for what I found inside.

The lounge room was bathed in the soft glow of candles placed artistically on the coffee table. Soft electronica played from the speakers, and a bottle of wine was decanted with two glasses ready and waiting.

"What's going on in here?" I asked, looking around for Abby.

"Hey!" Her voice came from the kitchen. "Just give me a sec; I've got this charcuterie plate almost ready."

But I didn't wait, walking straight into the kitchen. And there she was, frowning slightly as she rolled a piece of prosciutto into a tight spiral that it was intent on escaping. A platter was set with soft cheese, grapes, what smelled like truffle salami, olives, and freshly chopped sourdough.

"What's all this?" I asked, leaning in to kiss her.

"Well, I'm not much of a cook," Abby said, gesturing at the plate. "But I'm pretty great at arranging, so that's what I'm doing. It's a charcuterie plate. You like charcuterie, right?"

"Of course," I said. "But you didn't have to do all this."

"I know," Abby said simply. "But I wanted to. How many times have you fed me?"

"I run a restaurant."

"I know, but..." Abby had a soft smile playing on her lips. "I wanted to. And besides, you're the one always telling me I should relax. So that's what I thought we could do tonight. Eat cheese and meat. Drink wine. Sit. Talk." She paused. "I won't even jump up and start clearing your plate away the second you stop eating."

"Now that would be an achievement," I teased. "This seriously looks amazing, though. Better than a restaurant. Even mine."

Abby laughed. "I doubt that," she said. "But it's much cheaper. And your budget must be as tight as mine, so I didn't want you to feel like you had to take me out or anything."

And *shit*. There it was. I had almost let myself forget that I still hadn't told Abby the truth about my financial situation. She still thought I was a struggling entrepreneur who had put my life savings into the restaurant, with nothing and no one to fall back on. And while I had put a lot of my personal liquid capital into Beach Garage, the truth was, I had plenty to fall back on. Investment properties paid their rent, shares paid dividends, and term deposits their interest. Not to mention the trust. I couldn't forget the trust.

"What is it?" Abby looked at me. I had been silent too long.

"I should tell you something," I began and then paused. I should tell Abby now. The longer it went on, the worse it would be. I knew that. But, I thought, it would be a difficult conversation. One that had to be handled with the utmost care. Abby had clearly put a lot of effort into setting up a relaxing evening for us. And she *never* relaxed. I'd be some kind of arsehole to ruin all her hard work.

"What do you need to tell me?" Abby touched my arm, looking up at me with concern. "Are you okay?"

"I'm fine," I said. "I just thought I should tell you..." I swallowed. "About my stutter."

"About your stutter?" Abby looked confused.

"Yes," I said, relief and guilt flooding through me in equal measure. "When you told me about what you went through with your depression, I wanted to tell you then, but I..." I swallowed once more. "I guess I'm telling you now. I used to stutter as a kid. Pretty badly, too. You remember that I didn't talk much when we first met?"

"I do," Abby said, still giving me an odd look. "I'm glad you feel like you can tell me, but it's no big deal. Did you think I'd judge you for it or something? You know me better than that!"

"I do," I said quickly. "I didn't think you'd judge me for it; of course not. But I've always been self-conscious about it, even now, when it hasn't bothered me for a long time. It's not very suave, is it?"

"You don't have to be suave twenty-four-seven, Wyatt," she said, pressing a kiss to my cheek. "You do know that, right?"

"I know," I said. "I just...wanted you to know."

"And now I do," Abby said, giving my hand a squeeze. "Does it still affect you?"

"Not for years," I said, shrugging my shoulders and cursing myself for being a coward. "Only when I'm angry or something really awful happens. Like when my uncle died."

At that, Abby abandoned her charcuterie platter to wrap her arms around me, her head under my chin. "I hope I don't ever hear it, then," she said quietly. "But if I did, I hope you know it wouldn't change how I think of you."

"I'm very glad of that," I said, kissing the top of her head.

She pulled back, gentle fingers caressing my chin. "Anything else you need to tell me?" she asked. "While we're at it, we could get all the big revelations over and done with. You already know my biggest secret. And not even my sisters know about that, so you're very special."

I could have told her then. I should have done it. But instead...

"There's nothing else," I said quietly. "Just that I'm happy to be here with you. Right now."

"Mm, good answer." Abby leaned up on the tips of her toes to kiss me, a soft brush of her full lips over mine, giving me a taste of what was to come once the charcuterie had been devoured. Actually, I thought, the charcuterie could wait.

I kissed her again, deeper now, showing her how much I wanted her until she was pressed into me, her heart beating hard against my own.

"Right now?" she whispered, looking up at me with bright blue eyes.

"Right now," I said, my arms tight around her waist. "After all—" I continued, my lips grazing her earlobe, the sweet smell of her hair in my nostrils. "I still haven't had the opportunity to spank you."

And Abby's gasp of want told me that I had said exactly the right thing. I'd tell her the truth; I really would. But not tonight.

"Dude, what's with the radio silence?" Danni made a harumphing that sounded exactly like the ones made by the occupants of her stable. "Did I do something to piss you off?"

"No, of course not!" I said as I made my way down a side street towards Nick and Nikki's, caffeine firmly on my mind. "I've just been busy since the launch and..." I trailed off, hoping she wouldn't ask.

"And shagging Abby," Danni finished, sounding smug. I could almost see her self-satisfied expression through the phone; it was that visceral.

"How did you know that?"

"I didn't until just now. I can't believe you didn't tell me! I'm supposed to be your best friend, dickhead!" Danni was affronted, and I did feel guilty for not telling her right away.

"Well, you did choose to be best friends with a dickhead," I retorted. "I was going to tell you, but like I said, it's been so busy and—"

"And you couldn't text me?" Danni was definitely pissed off. "It happened after the launch party, right? I knew it! When I saw how she was looking at you, I knew you'd end up in bed together. Chemistry, right? It never dies!"

"Well, you were right," I admitted, lingering on the corner, as this wasn't the sort of conversation that I wanted Nick and Nikki to overhear. "It did happen. And it's... I mean, we're kind of a thing now."

"Kind of a thing," Danni repeated, and I could hear her eye roll right through the phone. "So, she didn't have an issue with you being a trust fund brat? See! I told you she'd understand if you were honest about it."

"Uh, well," I began. "I didn't exactly—"

"Please tell me you did not sleep with her without telling her." Danni sounded not angry but disappointed, which was far worse. "Wyatt!"

"I'm going to tell her!" I insisted. "It's not that easy. I mean, we're both so busy, and it's a delicate conversation. I'm trying to find the right time."

"So, you can find time to put your dick in her, but not time to talk to her? That's a terrible excuse."

"I know." I hung my head because, despite my rebuttals, I knew she was right.

"You remember what happened when I didn't tell Sally about my horses, right?" Danni began.

"Sally was the redhead with the piercing on her—"

"That's the one," Danni confirmed. "And she was like, this militant vegan who didn't believe that animals should be enslaved by humans. Had a fight with her housemate about his cat."

"I can't believe you were ever attracted to someone like that."

"She had E-cups and a smile that made me gush like Niagara Falls." Danni sighed. "But I digress. Anyway, I kept it all hidden from her, and told her that I had a lavender farm, not a stable. I even bought a lavender plant so I could present her with a bouquet from my imaginary farm."

"And what happened?"

"Her friend – who I think was secretly in love with her – found me on Instagram and showed her all these pictures of me. Me on horses. Me eating a bacon sandwich. Me wearing a leather jacket."

"And then she keyed your car," I remembered. "I don't think Abby would do that."

"She scratched 'murderer' into the passenger door," Danni corrected. "It was not good."

"This is completely different," I said, looking out at the bright blue waters of Brekkie Beach as I stood on the corner as though they might provide some magical insight into my unfortunate predicament. "That Sally chick was always going to react badly whenever you told her. With Abby, I just need to find the right time."

"Well, you'd better find it soon," Danni said. "Because your mum texted me the other day. She saw all the pictures from your launch and asked me how it went."

"What did you say?"

"I told her it went well, and she sounded so sad. She asked me if I thought you'd ever speak to her again."

"I will. It's just with Dad, I..."

"I know," Danni sounded sad too. "But you'd better call her soon, or she's going to show up in Brekkie Beach and demand an audience. And I bet that's not how you want Abby to find out you're less Jeeves and more Wooster."

"That is a thoroughly outdated reference," I said, addressing what was definitely not the point.

"Find me a better comedic writer than PG Wodehouse, and then we'll talk," Danni objected. "Look, dude, you're my cousin, and I love you like a brother, but you are on a seriously dangerous path here. If it all falls apart, I won't be there to pick up the pieces."

"Yes, you would."

"Okay, yes, I would," Danni admitted. "But wouldn't you rather I didn't have to?"

"True," I said. "Look, I've got to go. I'm going to grab a coffee and...think about things. Come up with a plan to talk to Abby."

"Today?"

"Maybe not today," I hedged. "End of the week."

"Dude!" Danni sounded pained. "Just try not to fuck this up, okay? Abby's awesome!"

"I know," I said. "And I won't fuck it up. Just give me a bit more time."

· ♥ · ♥ · ♥ · ♥ · ♥ ·

I had every intention of talking to Abby about my lack of complete forthrightness regarding my financial situation when I returned from the restaurant late that night. And not just because Danni had texted me every thirty minutes like clockwork to remind me.

I'd tell Abby. I'd explain why I hadn't said anything before. I'd tell her about my fight with my dad, why I had felt like I needed to do something on my own, separate from Parsons Property. She'd understand; I was sure of it. And yes, she'd be pissed off with me for not saying anything before. But I was sure she'd understand if I explained it right.

I was rehearsing the beginning of my little speech in my head as I turned the key in the lock, but when I entered the house, the only light came from the kitchen. Frowning, I looked around for signs of Abby.

There was a note on the counter, and it made me smile. It was written on a sheet of thick paper torn from her ubiquitous notebook in purple pen.

Last minute early job tomorrow. $$$ too good to say no. Had to go to bed early but won't say no to sleepy snuggles if you're in the mood. So long as you don't expect me to have a coherent conversation with you. Abby xx

I let out a sigh as I set down the note. Well, it seemed coherent conversation was most definitely off the agenda. Instead, I'd simply enjoy the sleepy snuggles and try again tomorrow.

One more day couldn't hurt, could it?

15 Abby

I had planned to spend the day checking and re-checking the Organised Home Co online store, ready for the launch. Josie and I would be hosting a live-stream launch party, and if I was going to get enough viewers to ensure the store opened with a bang (ideally a financial bang), I needed the website to be flawless.

But when I had received a call late in the afternoon from a woman who claimed to need me desperately the very next day, it had proved impossible to say no. It was just a simple wardrobe job, even if the wardrobe did sound rather palatial. Eight hours' work at the most, the chance to get more photos of my new product range for social media, and my new client had even promised to pay cash, with a bonus for the late notice.

Like I said, it wasn't the kind of offer I could refuse.

When I rose at an ungodly time of the morning, Wyatt had stirred, mumbling something about me being very pretty, him wishing I was staying in bed, and that he was looking forward to ravishing me later. It had made me smile, more than smile, actually. I had a certain bounce in my step as I made my way down the stairs.

Maybe, when the online store was live and Josie had taken on a full load of projects of her own, I could schedule a day to stay in bed with Wyatt. We'd order greasy, cheap pizza to keep us fuelled and spend every moment exploring each other's bodies or taking indulgent, snuggly naps.

Okay, maybe a half-day.

But the thought gave me an extra dose of motivation as I bounced down the stairs to grab a home-brand energy drink and a protein bar. Maybe, I thought, when things settled down a little, I'd learn to cook or at least meal prep. Perhaps I could become the type of woman who made my own overnight oats in little glass jars rather than the kind of woman who arranged her bulk-pack protein bars in colour order.

When I reached the address that Sondra (definitely not Sandra, she had been unequivocal on that particular point) had given me, I actually gasped. It wasn't like I wasn't used to wealthy clients. After all, only people with a ton of money could afford to hire someone to organise their crap. But this place? I didn't even want to imagine what it would cost to buy a house like this.

On this street, every house was a mansion, and my van looked about as welcome as a sunken soufflé in a three-hatted French restaurant. But this house? It was something else entirely. It appeared to have been built out from a sheer cliff face, clinging to the solid rock by the power of the almighty dollar. It had to be seven stories, each with huge glass windows. As I nervously made my way to the enormous gates, designed to keep riffraff like me out, I spotted a swimming pool that looked ready for the Olympics and a tennis court nicer than anything Wimbledon had to offer.

Pressing the intercom button, I waited and wished I had worn my best leggings. These ones had a spot of silver nail polish right on my left butt cheek.

"Yes?" The voice was different from the one I remembered from the phone, and I wondered if I had the wrong house. That would be most unfortunate in this neighbourhood.

"It's Abby Finch. From the Organised Home Co. I'm here to organise Sondra's wardrobe."

There was a pause, and I felt like I was being scrutinised by the little electronic eyeball. I wasn't sure I'd pass the test.

But the gates opened before me, and I approached the front door. Which appeared to be made of solid marble. Bloody hell, this place made Buckingham Palace look like a dump. Although given what I had heard about the problems with dust and damp in Buckingham Palace, that might not be a fair comparison.

The piece of solid marble revolved, and a woman in a smart black suit became visible.

"Sondra?" I ventured. "I'm Abby." I stuck out my hand, refusing to be overwhelmed by the display of wealth around me.

"I'm Mrs Higgins," the woman corrected me, ignoring my outstretched hand. "Sondra Parsons' housekeeper." Parsons? The same surname as Wyatt, I thought. But it wasn't an uncommon name, and the idea that Wyatt might be related to Sondra was ridiculous.

"Nice to meet you," I said. I had some experience with housekeepers, and most of them regarded me with suspicion, seeming to think I was there to steal their job or that my mere presence insulted their abilities. "It's great you're here, actually. I've found that my clients with regular housekeepers are far more able to maintain the spaces I organise. And maintenance is the key."

At that, Mrs Higgins softened her stiff shoulders very slightly. "That," she said, "will not be a problem. I believe Ms Parsons is expecting you now. If you'll come this way."

I followed her into the hallway, clenching my jaw to avoid gawping like a country bumpkin at the splendour surrounding me. Rich, I knew. But this? This was something else. A fountain took pride of place in the middle of the entrance hall, a frolicking nymph with a gentle stream trickling over her pert breasts. I didn't doubt that it was solid bronze.

There was a gentle beep, and the elevator (yes, a goddamn elevator) suddenly opened. This must be Sondra, I thought, straightening up slightly. If Mrs Higgins had intimidated me, I could only imagine what Sondra would be like.

I was more than a little surprised when a middle-aged woman with bright red hair in a messy topknot, a stud through her nose, and jeans with the knees ripped out came out and greeted me with a bone-crushing hug. "Abby!" She greeted me like I was an old friend. "Thank goodness you're here; my wardrobe is seriously making me mental."

I laughed, mostly in relief. The imposing cliff-clinging house and distinctly uptight Mrs Higgins had made me think I'd spend my day with the kind of rich person who saw me as a temporarily useful cockroach. But Sondra seemed delightful.

"Mental wardrobes are my favourite," I told her, smiling broadly and no longer worried about the spot of nail polish on my butt. "I can't wait to get started."

"Well, in that case, come up in my glass elevator," Sondra chuckled as she pointed at the elevator, raising her eyebrows. "And I'll show you the devastation site. It's like the Chernobyl of clothes, I swear. You need to fix me; I'm a hot mess express."

I was liking Sondra more and more. "My kind of Chernobyl."

"Will you require any refreshments, Ms Finch?" Mrs Higgins stood stiffly as though Sondra was embarrassing her.

"You want a drink, Abby?" Sondra asked. "Sheila makes a mean Irish coffee, but it's probably too early for you. You seem like the kind of woman who has her life together."

"I'm just fine for now," I said. "But maybe later?" After all, who was I to refuse such graciously offered hospitality?

"Could you do me a green smoothie, Sheila?" Sondra asked. "And maybe chuck in a little kick of vodka to make it palatable."

"At once, Ms Parsons."

I stepped into the elevator after Sondra, excitement fluttering inside my chest. Already, I couldn't wait to tell Wyatt about her; how funny that they shared a surname.

"I was looking through your Instagram," Sondra went on. "And you're freaking amazing at this shit; I had no idea a wardrobe could look like that." The elevator rose, and I saw from the illuminated button that Sondra's bedroom – or master suite, as I'm sure a real estate agent would describe it – was on the top floor. The view must be incredible.

"Thanks so much," I said appreciatively. "How did you hear about me, out of interest?"

"Oh, I was chatting to your sister's boyfriend at my nephew's restaurant launch the other night," Sondra said carelessly, hands in her pockets and bangles with a very distinctive 'H' logo rattling on her wrists.

Everything stopped. I couldn't have heard her correctly. That was the only plausible explanation. Or maybe Tessa or Michelle had been to another restaurant launch somewhere else, weeks or even months before, and charming Sondra simply had the timeline wrong.

"Oh, right," I said, swallowing. "That sounds fun. What's the restaurant called?"

"Beach Garage," Sondra said, giving me a big grin. "It's in some place called Brekkie Beach – I had never been there before, but it's quite pretty. I wanted to go along and support dear Wyatt. He's a good boy!"

I stood perfectly still, my bones feeling like they had been replaced with shards of ice. There still had to be some explanation, I thought desperately. Maybe, I thought, Sondra had simply married and divorced someone obscenely wealthy, and Wyatt really was just a regular guy. A small business owner like me.

"I see," I said automatically, ensuring my face betrayed nothing. "I live in Brekkie Beach, too," I said, fishing for information. "I'll have to check out this restaurant. Is your nephew the chef?"

"Wyatt? No!" Sondra shook her head cheerfully. "I don't know if he can even boil an egg! But he's always liked his food; little bugger was into the foie gras even as a toddler. But it's nice to see him do something on his own, after working away at the family firm all these years. Of course, that's what I think. You see, my brother – Wyatt's dad – was pretty pissed off. You know how families are!" She waved a well-jewelled hand. "He even threatened to cut off Wyatt's trust fund, but of course, he didn't go through with that."

And that was it. There was a sharp stabbing pain in my guts, and my skin felt so hot that it might burn anyone who touched it. Wyatt was a trust fund kid from a wealthy family. Not just a wealthy family, but a stupidly, ridiculously wealthy family.

He had *lied* to me.

"Are you okay, Abby?" Sondra looked at me, frowning. "You've gone all red."

"Cramps," I said quickly, my hands going to my stomach. "I'll take some ibuprofen, no big deal."

"Oh, you poor thing," Sondra said sympathetically. "Do you need to sit down? Cramps are such a bugger! Before I had kids, they used to have me curled up in bed like I was dying!"

"No big deal," I said again, forcing my face to remain neutral.

"You know, an Irish coffee would sort you out." Sondra looked conspiratorial. "Loosen up your muscles and all that. I can tell Sheila to make two. I'm not sure I fancy my green smoothie after all."

I looked at Sondra, as my guts really did start cramping like I was being tortured by my uterus and not the lying bastard who was probably still asleep in my bed. "You know what? Irish coffee sounds like an awesome idea."

· ♥ · ♥ · ♥ · ♥ · ♥ ·

I wasn't sure how I made it through the day with Sondra. Muscle memory might explain how I could keep folding lacy negligees into acrylic trays, hanging silk gowns, and grouping Gucci loafers by colours; I could have done that in a coma. The real problem was that as I worked, the lovely, whacky, and charming Sondra serenaded me with stories of her life. Most of which included Wyatt. I discovered he had thrown up on Mickey Mouse on his first family trip to Disney World – or was it the second? He and his cousin Danni, Sondra's daughter, had been caught sneaking into the stables at a polo match – such a funny story! And then there was the 'family business', which I was rapidly coming to discover owned more land and real estate than the average monarch of a mid-sized European nation.

When the job was finally done, and Sondra's wardrobe resembled the kind of boutique that was entered by invitation only, I had been kissed, hugged, had my hair ruffled, and begged to stay for a glass or two of champagne. I had declined, managing to keep it together all the way down in the glass elevator, out through the marble hallway, past the tennis courts and into my shitty white panel van.

When I finally slammed shut the door of my van, I let out a howl that was probably audible to the people who lived nearby. Maybe they'd look out of their floor-to-ceiling windows, wrinkling their aristocratic noses at the lowly person who dared disturb their quiet street's sanctity. But I didn't care.

I started the van, revving it for good measure, and called my sisters. A message might go unanswered, but a call? That was a summons. And I needed to summon my sisters now more than ever.

"What's up?" Tessa sounded like she was out for a walk.

"Hey, Abby!" Michelle joined the call. "I'm just on the ferry, and damn, I don't think I'll ever get used to this view! Freaking stunning! Sydney Harbour is the best!"

"Wyatt," I said through gritted teeth, "is a lying bastard!"

"Woah!" Tessa's voice was concerned. "What happened? Are you okay?"

"What did he do?" Michelle had abandoned all her delight in the harbour. "Where are you?"

"I just met his aunt," I said, swallowing back bile. I felt like I might throw up, though the Irish coffee had been consumed eight hours earlier, and I had declined all subsequent offers of alcohol. "And he's been lying to me this whole time. His family," I spat out the word, "are absolutely loaded. He's a trust fund kid."

There was silence as my two sisters digested this information, and I smacked one hand against the steering wheel impatiently.

"He's never said much about his family, has he?" Tessa began cautiously. "I guess it's kind of a big thing to leave out, but—"

"A big thing to leave out?!" I repeated, furious. "Yeah, it's a big thing to leave out! He told me he was just like me, trying to build a business on his own. That he had put his life savings into it, with no one to fall back on. And all this time, he's a trust fund kid who goes to the bloody polo!"

"Shit." Michelle sounded like she was biting her lip. "I'm sorry, Abby, that's really crappy that he didn't tell you. I wonder why he's living in a share house in Brekkie Beach if he's got all that money."

"Well, that's obvious," I said, rolling my eyes so hard it hurt. "He's playing at being a normal guy. Rich people do that sometimes. It's all a big joke to them, living like us ordinary people for fun. I bet he's been laughing at me all this time with my shitty chickpea dinners and my shitty little business. Bastard!"

"I don't know if that part is true, Abby." Tessa's voice was conciliating. "That he's been laughing at you, I mean. It sounds like he really cares about you from everything you've told us. Maybe he felt like you'd look at him differently if you knew about his family's money."

"Are you making excuses for this dickhead?" My voice rose sharply as I turned a corner and immediately found myself in the traffic jam that was the only path in and out of the leafy waterside enclave where Sondra lived. A traffic jam designed to keep people like me out, I was sure of it. "I can't believe you!"

"No!" Tessa said, aghast. "I'm not defending him! I just don't think he's been laughing at you. But he definitely did the wrong thing by not telling you. You have every right to be angry."

"Damn right, I do," I muttered, scowling at the Tesla in front of me. "That arsehole has watched me worrying over my bank balance, doing everything I can to stay in the black and all the while, he's been making me think he's like me! Bringing me food from his little hobby of a restaurant, like I'm a stray dog!"

"Woah, Abby," Michelle broke in. "Pretty sure he doesn't think you're a stray dog. I agree with Tessa, he shouldn't have lied about this, but that doesn't mean he's been looking down on you."

"You don't know that!" I shot back. "And he had me feeling sorry for him that his parents didn't support his dream. He told me he had a fight with them about the restaurant because they didn't want him to do something on his own. Well, it all makes sense now! Why would Richie Rich want to start a restaurant in some random beach town when he could be on a yacht, snorting cocaine off an heiress?"

"I guess he didn't want that kind of life," Tessa said slowly. "Growing up like that, maybe he wanted to do something that was just his. And he shouldn't have lied!" The last part was said very fast. "But I kind of get it. I mean, Dylan had that whole complex about not wanting to be a photographer because of his famous dad. Maybe Wyatt wanted to do something on his own terms."

I let out a frustrated breath. "Are you seriously defending him, Tessa? What the hell!?"

"But I think she's right," Michelle chimed in. "I bet that's it. He wanted to do something separate from the big family business. I'm not saying it's okay he lied to you. Of course not. But it's understandable why he'd want something of his own."

"He's got a fucking trust fund! Why would he need more things to own?" I was enraged. "I can't believe you're being so understanding!"

"It's not like that," Tessa said quickly. "I still think he's a bastard for lying to you."

"A complete bastard," Michelle added. "Do you want us to come over? We can drink wine, drown ourselves in Sara Lee, and discuss how all men are shit."

"Or you can come to my place," Tessa offered. "So you don't have to see him. I bet Dylan wouldn't mind going to his dad's place, so we can hate men without one in the house."

I softened slightly at that. Despite my sisters being horribly empathetic to the bastard who had lied to me, they were still ready to drop everything to support me.

"No," I said firmly. "I want to see Wyatt. I want to look him in the eye and ask him why he lied to me and hear his pathetic excuses. Then I'm going to tell him just what I think of him."

Another silence.

Michelle sighed. "I guess you'll have to talk to him sometime. Better to get it out of the way."

"And you should definitely tell him what you think of him," Tessa agreed. "He deserves the full Angry Abby experience."

"Definitely," Michelle said. "I'm so sorry, Abby. I know you really liked him."

I let out a sound between a scoff and a scream. "I didn't really like him. It was just...chemicals. And lust. And proximity. He's dead to me now."

But that wasn't true. It had been far more than chemicals, lust, and even proximity. Wyatt, that lying bastard, had wormed his way under my skin. I had shared things with him that I had never told anyone else. I had opened myself up to him. Goddamn it, I had even tried to *relax* for him. I had been falling hard, and now...

"You can come and stay with me after you've confronted him if you like," Tessa said quietly. "I mean, sharing the house with him would be a bit awkward."

"Oh, hell no!" I hissed. "He's going to leave. Not me. It's not like he doesn't have the money for a hotel, is it?"

"I guess so," Tessa said. "I just don't want you to be alone."

"We could come over after," Michelle suggested. "To look after you."

But I just sighed out a long, weary breath. "I can look after myself." I would never make the mistake of letting anyone look after me again.

· ♥ · ♥ · ♥ · ♥ · ♥ ·

I was onto my third glass of wine when I heard keys in the door. Quickly, I shut off the angry girl anthem I had been blasting and abandoned the scrubbing brush I had been using to rage-clean the grout of the kitchen tiles. I was sure the dirt had been put there by Wyatt, and only Wyatt, and I could imagine every deep scour with the brush was right onto his stupid, smug, lying, obnoxiously handsome face.

I was full of self-righteous fury, ready to explode. And maybe slightly drunk. But I deserved to be, after everything he had put me through. When that long body and smiling face appeared, I was ready to scream.

"Hello, gorgeous," Wyatt called out in a tone that made me want to throw things at him. "How was your day?"

I just stood there, staring at him, fury seething under my skin.

"Abby?" Wyatt frowned. "What's wrong?"

I was ready to tell him.

16 Wyatt

I knew something was wrong right away. Abby was looking at me like she wanted to run me over with her van, and there was an almost empty bottle of wine on the kitchen counter. And somehow, before she said a word, I knew.

Abby had found out the truth about my family. And, it seemed, she was displeased.

"How was my day?" Abby shot my own words back at me. "I had a very interesting day, thank you for asking. I had a new client. Sondra Parsons. You might know her."

I winced at that. "I..." I began. "Abby, I can explain—"

"Explain?" Abby was pacing now, turning tight circles in the kitchen. "Explain that your family is richer than god? Explain that you've got a trust fund? Explain that this whole restaurant – this whole thing with me! – is some little game you've been playing? The rich kid pretending to be a regular guy, just for a laugh!"

"Abby, that's not true," I said quickly. "I'm not playing any games."

"Well, that's a lie." I could see that every muscle in her body was tense. "And this is just the first one, I'm sure. I have no idea what else you've been lying about! I can't believe you told me you were just a regular guy with a big dream. Pouring your life savings into your small business. Just a struggling entrepreneur like me!"

"I..." I licked my lips and swallowed hard. "I never said that."

"You never said what?"

"That I put my life savings into the restaurant. I told you I was opening a restaurant and that my family didn't approve. That's all true. My parents don't approve. They don't understand why I'd want to leave the family business or why I'd want something that was just my own. You assumed—"

"I *assumed*?" Abby spat out the word like it was a slur so vile it wasn't even used on anonymous internet message boards. "You lied to me!"

"I didn't lie, exactly," I said, wanting to defend myself. "You made some assumptions! And I was going to tell you everything—"

"I don't believe you for a second!"

"Well, you should!" I shot back, my blood growing hot. I had known she'd be angry, but this felt like an overreaction. "I was going to explain about my family. How I grew up. How I had always wanted something different, especially because of my uncle. But I felt trapped in the family business, and they wouldn't let me leave—"

"Trapped in a gilded cage?" Abby sneered. "Poor little rich boy, who's had everything he could ever want! The only thing you didn't have was the experience of being broke, so you decided to make believe you were and involve me in your sick game!"

"It's not like that!" I shot back. "It was never like that, Abby. It was a lot, leaving the business. My dad was furious. He told me I was ruining my life, doing something pointless and stupid. He even threatened to cut me off—"

"But he didn't," Abby cut in. "Sondra told me all about that. You've still got your precious trust fund!"

"I never asked for one!" My voice was growing louder. "And I didn't use it, for the record. I've only put my own money into the restaurant. Money I earned by working for the family business all these years."

"That doesn't make any difference!" Abby slapped her hand on the kitchen counter, narrowly missing her wine bottle. "Whether you did it with your pocket money from Daddy or your bloody trust! You made me believe you were struggling like me when all the while, you've got all this money. It doesn't matter if your restaurant never makes a dollar, you can just go back to your luxurious life!"

"And you pretend that you don't have any support, that you have to do this all on your own when I know your sisters have been begging you to accept a loan!" I was angry now. The 'daddy's pocket money' comment had hit a nerve, and I was responding in kind. "But you won't accept it because you're too bloody proud and insist on doing everything on your own! No matter how ridiculous that is!"

"Oh, so I'm ridiculous, am I?" Abby was walking towards me now. "I guess normal people do seem ridiculous to you."

"I didn't say you were ridiculous, but it's crazy that you'd rather skip meals and work yourself to death than let your sisters give you a bloody loan!"

"Is that what you think?" Abby looked up at me, her eyes narrowed. "I guess all that bullshit about being impressed by my work ethic was just a ploy to get me into bed. A tumble with a normal person must be easy for a guy like you to arrange. Just flash your Rolex – which I'm sure isn't fake, by the way – and they fall into your arms. I'm sorry you had to go to so much extra effort with me."

"You're acting like I manipulated you into sleeping with me when we both know you wanted it as much as I did!" I said, but her words had cut deep. I had promised myself I wouldn't let anything happen with Abby until I had told her the truth, and I didn't like to break promises to myself. And now that she mentioned it, I had lied about my Rolex. That hadn't been an assumption. "And it had nothing to do with money. You wanted me!"

"Well, I can admit when I make a fucking huge mistake!" Abby said fiercely, and I could see the hints of tears in her eyes. And that made me pause because I had never seen Abby cry. Not even when she was limping around on a broken foot. "I wish I had never met you! Not when I was fifteen, and not now!"

"Then I'll leave," I said, picking up my keys and putting them back in my pocket. "I'll go, if that's what you want."

"Good!" Abby thundered. "I bet the presidential suite is waiting for you, so it's not like I'm putting you to any trouble."

"A-A-Abby!" I didn't even know what I wanted to say. And shit, I was stuttering. That couldn't be good.

"What?" She looked at me then, and I could see the hurt underneath the anger, raw and vulnerable. "What could you possibly have to say to me?"

"I was going to tell you," I said quietly. "I really was."

"It's a bit late for that." She turned back to the kitchen, picking up a scrubbing brush. She didn't look at me again as I let out a long sigh, turned around, and left.

Standing on the footpath outside the little house that had started to feel like home, I swore out loud.

"What the hell am I going to do now?"

♥ . ♥ . ♥ . ♥ . ♥

I was being nudged awake, but consciousness was highly unwelcome. I pushed the hand away, groaning. "I'm sleeping!"

Another nudge, this one more insistent. I opened my eyes and was assaulted by bright light and the face of David, crouching over me with a look of deep concern mixed with profound bemusement. "What are you doing?"

And that was a fair question. Because I had been sleeping under a tablecloth, another bunched up as a lumpy pillow, in the corner of Beach Garage's dining room.

"Uh..." I began, knowing I didn't have the signs to explain. "I was working late, so I slept here."

David gave me a disbelieving and thoroughly unimpressed look. "Why?"

"It seemed like a good idea at the time," I sat up, rolling my neck. My body was aching like I had run a marathon followed by a bare-knuckle boxing match. And I had lost both; that much was clear.

David made a face and toed the empty bottle of wine next to me with the tip of his clog. "You were thirsty."

And that probably explained some of why I was feeling dreadful, even though I knew most of it was to do with my conversation – if you could call it that – with Abby last night.

"I was," I said, sighing and pushing myself up and off the floor. "I'm going to get coffee. You want one?"

"Always." David nodded. But then he frowned. "Are you okay, boss?"

"I'm fine," I insisted, even as my body protested at my movement. When did my bones get replaced by those of a calcium-deprived octogenarian? "I just want some coffee."

After fetching coffee for David and myself, which meant I had to force a cheery smile for Nick and Nikki's benefit, I crossed the road to the petrol station for something I hadn't allowed myself in a very long time.

Leaning against a wall, I took a deep draw on my cigarette and coughed. Well, that served me right, I supposed. I had officially given up smoking when I was twenty-three, but sometimes, when life practised its kickboxing on my most delicate regions, I bought a pack.

I took another drag, managed not to cough, and swiped my thumb over my phone.

"Hey dude," Danni sounded cheerful. "I am so glad you called me right now. My new stable hand wanted to argue about mucking out the stalls. I might punch him if I don't step away for a few minutes. Who the hell thinks that horse manure isn't part of the job description of stable hand?"

"Hey," I said, coughing again. "I th-th-think—"

"Oh, Wyatt," Danni's voice changed in an instant. "What happened?"

"I th-think," I said slowly and cautiously, but it didn't help. "I fu-fu-fucked up."

17 Abby

After confronting Wyatt, I had refused to let my sisters come over, though I was sure Michelle had driven by the house. I had told them I needed space, but space wasn't something my sisters were especially keen on.

That was why, when the doorbell rang the next evening, I knew exactly who was at the door.

"Abby!" Tessa wrapped me up in a tight hug, pressing a kiss to my cheek. "I brought food!"

"And I brought booze!" Michelle joined the hug, leaning her head on my shoulder. "And my best man-hating attitude."

"Me too." Tessa was still hugging me. "Men are pigs!"

"You two are in disgustingly happy long-term relationships," I pointed out, extricating myself from the hug.

"Eh, Patrick left beard clippings in the sink this morning." Michelle shrugged. "I can whip myself up into a rage about that."

"And Dylan used a metal spatula on my favourite non-stick pan," Tessa chimed in. "I bet I can turn that into fury."

"You two are sweet," I said, letting out a sigh and collapsing down onto the sofa. "But you don't have to pretend to hate the male species just to make me feel better. You two found decent dudes. I found a dud."

"I can't believe he didn't tell you," Tessa said from the kitchen. She returned with a stack of cork placemats, setting them down on the coffee table before returning to fetch a baking dish wrapped in foil.

"What's this?" I asked, peeling back the foil. It smelled amazing, whatever the hell it was.

"Cob loaf," Tessa told me. "It's an Australian delicacy. It's bread with hot cheesy dip inside. You tear off pieces and dunk them in. If you think about it, it's like ripping off someone's fingers and using them to sample their internal organs."

"Gross, Tessa." Michelle looked disgusted. "You listen to too much true crime. You know that, right?"

"Don't yuck my yum." Tessa grinned, shooting back the line Michelle herself used so often.

I tore off a piece of bread, dipped it in the thick, creamy concoction, and tasted it. "That's really good," I said, managing to smile at my sister.

"I'm glad you like it." Tessa's expression was earnest. "I wanted to make you something non-restaurant-y."

"That's very thoughtful," I said with a sigh. "Well, there's another thing that sucks about Wyatt being a lying bastard. We finally get a decent restaurant in Brekkie Beach, and I'll never be able to go there." I let out a harrumphing sound, and Michelle pushed a glass of wine into my hand.

"How are you feeling?" she said, taking a seat beside me and helping herself to a piece of cob loaf dipped in the gooey cheese concoction. "Really, I mean. None of this 'I'm fine' bullshit."

"Oh, I'm not fine," I said, shaking my head and gulping the wine. "I'm furious. At him, mostly. But also, at myself, for letting myself open up to a guy who was such a—" I searched for the right words.

"Lying, manipulative bag of dicks?" Tessa supplied with a rueful smile.

"Bag of dicks is the perfect way to describe him," I said. "See, this is why you're such a successful writer."

"That particular phrase hasn't come up in my children's books."

"You shouldn't be angry with yourself for liking him," Michelle said, setting down her wine. "I mean, it seemed so perfect. Your teenage dream appeared after all these years, growing up into such a hottie, and he seemed like a truly decent dude. A dude who really liked you."

"That's the worst part," I said, taking another large gulp of wine. "Wyatt did act like he really liked me! He was annoyingly caring. Like with my foot, bringing me food, asking about my business, and...other stuff."

"What other stuff?" A slight frown appeared between Tessa's eyebrows.

"Nothing." That earned a thoroughly unimpressed look from my sisters. "Just... I told him a bit about some stuff in my past. Stuff I've never told anyone else."

"Stuff you haven't told us?" Michelle looked affronted at the idea. "But you tell us everything! You even told us when your boyfriend in your first year at university had haemorrhoids! In great detail."

"Look, I don't want to get into it right now," I said, feeling guilty for not telling my sisters and furious for having told Wyatt about the worst time in my life. "Please, not now."

"Not now," Tessa repeated, a gentle hand on my arm. "But if you told him things you haven't even told us, I can see why you feel especially betrayed by all this."

"I wish I hadn't told him. I hate that he knows so much about me. He's probably laughing about that too."

"I don't think that's true," Michelle said quietly. "Look, I'm not saying it's okay he lied. I'm definitely not saying that. But my guess is he lied because he liked you and wanted you to feel comfortable with him. Not see him as just some rich guy."

I let out a breath through my teeth. "I can't believe he just sat there, watching me drain my savings and panic about how I was going to pay Josie if my invoices weren't paid, and acted like we were in the same boat! I mean, what's wrong with him!? It's freaking pathological; that's what it is. He's a sociopath!"

"You were panicking about paying Josie?" Michelle repeated. "Abby, you told me you didn't need a loan because you had more than enough saved up!"

"I did!" I bristled. "But stuff happened. The van needed new tires. A couple of big jobs were cancelled last minute. And I decided to double my product order from the factory and increase the ad spend for the launch, so…" I sighed. "It's just kind of tight right now. It'll be fine, so long as nothing else unexpected happens."

"Right." Michelle set down her wine glass. "I'm not giving you a loan. I'm making an investment in your business. I'll get a contract drawn up because I know you'll insist on paying me back with interest. But I'm making the transfer right now."

"No!" I protested. "I don't want any help!"

"Too bad," Tessa squeezed me tighter. "Because if you even try to refuse, I'm going to start hiding cash in your house. In your fridge organisers. Under the cutlery tray.

In your spice jars. And it'll drive you crazy because you'll never know when more is coming."

"Excellent idea." Michelle nodded approvingly. "This isn't up for discussion, Abby. I'm investing in you because I believe in you."

I let out a breath, and decided not to argue, even if I wouldn't let them do it. "When did you get so bossy?"

"I can't imagine who I learned it from," Michelle nudged me. "I want to shake you, but..."

"But what?"

"You're my sister, and you're an idiot sometimes, but I love you, and it kills me to see you like this. Do you want me to go find Wyatt and throw things at him?"

"Ooh, I could get in on that!" Tessa enthused. "I've got lots of ideas! You might not like my true crime obsession, but it's very inspiring for situations like this."

I let out a breath. "Don't bother," I said. "I just... I can't believe he made me feel like—" I cut myself off. "I haven't felt like that about someone before, and it was all a lie."

There was a silence. "Shit, Abby," Tessa breathed. "You're in love with him, aren't you?"

"No!" I said it so loudly I startled even myself. "No, of course not. But..." I swallowed. "Maybe I was going down that road. But obviously not now. Not after finding out that he's a lying shitbag."

Michelle topped up my wine glass. "I'm so sorry," she said. "We're here for you. Whatever you want."

"I just want to forget about all of this," I said, taking a gulp of my wine. "And focus on my business, like I should have been doing all along."

"I don't think you have to worry that you haven't been working hard enough, Abby," Tessa smiled. "We know you."

"I've been distracted," I said. "But not anymore. Business, not boys."

"We're here for you, whatever you want," Michelle said. "Do you want to watch a movie, maybe?"

"There's this great documentary about women who poisoned their cheating husbands," Tessa suggested. "That might cheer you up."

But I just shook my head. "You know what you two could do to help me right now?"

"Anything, Abby," Michelle promised. "Even karaoke, and you know I sing like the unholy lovechild of a dying cat and a foghorn."

"I want to do a run-through for the live stream of the product launch," I said, getting to my feet. "I know I'll do a better job if I rehearse, and I've only got a couple more days. Tessa, you can stand in for Josie, and Michelle, you can hit me up with questions and comments my viewers might send through."

"Seriously?" Tessa looked at me, her mouth puckered.

"You want to work right now?" Michelle looked incredulous. "But we brought booze! And ice cream."

"I definitely want to work," I said, going to the cupboard where I stored my tripod and ring light. "But I'm not saying it has to be a dry rehearsal."

Tessa and Michelle looked at each other and shrugged. "If that's what you want."

"It is," I said, jutting my chin out. "It's the only thing I want."

Even if that wasn't entirely true.

· ♥ · ♥ · ♥ · ♥ · ♥ ·

Everything was, I thought, perfect. I had taken Tessa's advice and borrowed some studio lights from Dylan. They certainly put my ring light to shame, even if they did make me break out in a thin sweat if I got too close. All of my props were in place; t-shirts and towels ready to demonstrate the joy of my shelf dividers, condiments prepared to grace the Lazy Susan that I had rebranded the Efficient Sue, a mess of cables I had tangled ready to be hidden in a concealer, my most social-media worthy beauty products to be placed in acrylic boxes, and every single one of my pans was out of the cupboard, ready to demonstrate the pan stacker.

And just to be festive, a bottle of champagne (okay, not champagne, but cheap sparkling wine) was chilling in an ice bucket, ready to kick off the proceedings.

"It looks good," Josie declared, taking a final lap around the living room. "Actually, it looks bloody fabulous. I feel like I'm on a film set!" Even she was ready for the occasion; her usually shaggy bob had been straightened, and she was wearing a soft blue blouse that I was sure I recognised from our former client's discarded garments, a pair of wide-legged black trousers, and a slick of red lipstick.

"I think it's going to be okay," I said, taking a deep breath. "Engagement has been high on the posts promoting the live stream, and we should gain more viewers as we go. If we're lucky, we might get a few thousand views live, and hopefully more on the recording—"

"Bloody fabulous," Josie said again, smoothing down her blouse. "I never thought I'd be doing something like this! Me, doing an online launch party. My kids couldn't believe it!" She dropped her voice. "I wouldn't have blamed you if you had wanted to have your sisters do this with you instead of me. I'm not exactly glamorous."

I shook my head. "No way! My sisters are gorgeous, but they don't know shit about organising. You're the one I need."

Josie laughed but looked pleased to hear it.

"And besides," I said. "Look at your earrings!" I pointed to the glittery sunbursts hanging from Josie's ears. "I reckon you've got plenty of glamour when you let yourself."

Another throaty laugh. "It seems silly to be vain at my age," Josie said. "But it does make a person feel good, dressing up a bit." She looked around the room, smiling in satisfaction. "But you're the star, Abby. I'm just supporting cast."

"Not feeling much like a star," I admitted. "I'll just be relieved when this is over."

Josie nodded, and then she looked at the stairs. "The fella who lives here with you," she said after a moment, and my body stiffened. "Wyatt knows this is on, right? He won't be wandering in halfway through?"

I swallowed hard. "No," I said quickly. "He's, um, out for the evening. We won't be interrupted."

"That's good," Josie said. "Although he might have been good for engagement, he's a good-looking bloke! Maybe you should have asked him to accidentally drop in wearing nothing but his pants."

I forced a laugh as my insides constricted painfully at the thought of Wyatt, wearing nothing but his pants or otherwise. "Nah," I said, shaking my head. "He'd just be a distraction."

And that was precisely what he had been: a distraction. A distraction I should never have let myself get caught up in. Well, I had learned my lesson the hard way.

"You might be right," Josie agreed. "Nearly time, then, eh? Should I take my place?" She paused. "What is it that they say on film sets? Find my mark?"

"Something like that," I said. But as I fiddled unnecessarily with one of the studio lights, it was all I could do to stop from breaking into angry tears at the thought of Wyatt.

If I was honest with myself, Wyatt had been far more than a distraction.

· ♥ · ♥ · ♥ · ♥ · ♥ ·

I should have been elated. Euphoric, even. Ecstatic, perhaps. Any of those synonyms for overjoyed was how I should have been feeling.

By any possible measure, the live launch of the Organised Home Co online store had been a roaring success. The views had surpassed even my most secret hopes, and my inbox was chock-full of orders. I should have been glad I had doubled the size of my order from the factory – if I hadn't, my millennial pink shelf dividers would have sold out, and the terrazzo patterned cord concealers weren't far behind.

"So why don't I *feel* good?" I asked my shampoo bottle. It didn't respond; it just sat on the shelf, glowering at me. Perhaps it knew I didn't especially like it but had downgraded to it from my preferred sulphate-free organic shampoo in the name of economy. The bastard would probably take a swan dive for my injured foot any time now.

To my horror, I felt a sob wrack my body, catching me by surprise as I stood under the warm spray of water. Before I could stop myself, tears were falling freely, hidden by the stream of water but very much present. I couldn't believe I was crying in the shower like some sort of television drama cliché.

I let my tears flow, my body wracked with sobs, and my arms around my middle, trying desperately to comfort myself. I knew why I was crying, even if I didn't want to admit it. Anger, hurt, disappointment. Wyatt wasn't who I had thought he was, and that *hurt*. I had been falling harder than I wanted to admit to anyone. Maybe even myself. And I wasn't the kind of person who'd let a man break her heart, but if it walks like a duck, quacks like a duck, and cries in the shower like a duck...

Letting out an angry groan, I turned off the water, wiping away the last of my tears. Wrapping myself in a towel, I did something I hadn't done in a long time. I plonked down on my bed, damp and dripping.

"You've got things to do," I told myself, flipping open my notebook. My tasks were listed right there in front of me in purple, green, and aqua. "You need to go through those online orders. Pack up those studio lights, ready to give them back to Dylan. Reply to comments from viewers. Get a grip, Abby Finch! You've got work to do!"

My pep talks seldom failed, yet I found my body, against my will, becoming horizontal on the bed. I didn't want to do anything as much as I knew I *had* to. I flung the notebook across the room and didn't even care when it landed in a way that was sure to bend the pages.

"I shouldn't be doing this," I whispered to my dark, empty bedroom. "I shouldn't be letting myself just..." I couldn't even come up with the words. "I've got things to do."

But my body was utterly impervious to my mind's insistence on activity as I snuggled under the covers with wet, uncombed hair and my skincare routine not even begun. Logically, I knew that one lazy night off didn't mean that I'd fall back into the crippling, stifling paralysis that had robbed me of my precious self-control.

But as I lay there, I couldn't help wondering if this was how it started.

And that just made me hate myself for falling for Wyatt all over again.

18 Wyatt

"Why," I asked, entering the kitchen, "does even your house smell like horses?"

Danni just laughed. "Occupational hazard, I guess. Plus, I nursed a sick foal in your bed."

"That's disgusting," I said, wrinkling up my nose. "You let a horse in the bed?"

"Nah." Danni snorted. "Not really. But if it bothers you so much, you don't have to stay here, you know. You've got a lot of choices. I get that you can't stay in your place at Brekkie Beach, but there's the penthouse in the city, that house in Bondi, the mountain retreat... I'm sure even my mum would let you stay if you agreed to drink with her."

"I don't want to stay anywhere my parents own," I said, my mouth a thin line. "And you know Sondra would invite them over, try to get us to reconcile."

"Would that be such a bad thing?" Danni looked pained. "You did say you'd talk to them again sometime."

"Sometime," I said. "Not now."

"Fine," Danni sighed. "Get a hotel or an Air BnB or something. It's not like you don't have the money."

And that, I thought, was absolutely true. "I don't want an Air BnB," I said rather peevishly.

"You don't want to be alone," Danni corrected, looking right at me. "Because you feel like shit for what you did to Abby."

"I didn't do anything to A-A-A—," I cut myself off, cursing my stutter for choosing to reappear on her name. "She made assumptions, and then she totally overreacted!"

Danni made a noise like a horse about to fart. "Seriously, dude? We're still going with that? I think there's a reason you can't even say her name."

"It was an emotionally distressing situation," I muttered. "That's what brings out the stutter."

"And her name is especially emotionally distressing because you feel guilty about lying to her."

"I didn't lie! Well, not on purpose. She's the one who made such a big deal about doing everything on her own, with no support."

Danni opened her mouth to speak, but I wasn't done.

"But her sisters have offered her loans tons of times. She turned them down. She's too bloody proud, and now she's pissed off with me because she thinks I've had it too easy when she could have accepted help from her family any time she wanted to! And she wouldn't listen when I tried to explain that it was difficult, leaving the family business to do something on my own."

"I still think you owe her an apology," Danni said, taking milk from the fridge and stirring it into the coffee that she still, perversely, made in a French Press. "A big one."

"I don't do apologies," I said. "Especially when I've got nothing to apologise for."

"You're killing me, Wyatt," Danni sighed again. "You think she's proud? You're worse than Mr Darcy!"

"I thought you didn't like period dramas."

"I read, okay?" Danni looked offended. "And no, not just books with horses."

"I'm glad you moved on from *Pony Pals*."

And that earned me a whack. "Dude, if you keep up this attitude, you're not going to be welcome here, either," she said. "I know that somewhere in there, you know you fucked up with Abby. And maybe with your parents, too. But I can see you won't admit it any time soon."

"I need to get to the restaurant," I said, fiddling with my car keys. "Long drive."

"Well, that's your choice." Danni shrugged.

"I am grateful, you know," I said after a moment. "That you're letting me stay here."

"You're like a brother to me, dude," Danni said. "A really annoying brother."

"Can't you at least accept my gratitude?"

"Oh, I can," Danni said. "But you can't stay forever. There's no way I can bring women back here with you lumbering around the place."

・♥・♥・♥・♥・♥・

It took more than an hour to get from Danni's stables to Beach Garage, which was entirely too long alone with my thoughts. The podcast I had put on about building a resilient team culture in the food industry had utterly failed to distract me, and by the time I passed the 'Welcome to Brekkie Beach' sign, I doubt I could have even named the guru who had been interviewed.

I needed to get to work. With Beach Garage now open for dinner and starting lunch service next week, it was an all-hands-on-deck situation. I certainly wasn't above playing kitchen hand, chopping up some garlic or arranging garnishes if that was what was required. I longed for the busy, thriving kitchen, for the sounds of bells indicating an order was up, for Mindy's firm voice directing our new waiters from table to table. Anything, I thought, was better than being alone in my head.

Flicking off the podcast, I chanced a look out of the window at the rolling waves and glistening sand of Brekkie Beach itself. A woman stood on the shore's edge, looking out into the ocean. Even in a bulky windbreaker and hat, I knew who it was. When she turned, I could see Abby wearing dark glasses and clutching a coffee cup in both hands, her mouth a thin line.

For a moment, I wanted to pull over or even park in the middle of the street like the rich, entitled arsehole she thought I was, run to her and—

And what, exactly? Apologise? It wasn't my fault she had overreacted like that. And she had made assumptions! And okay, maybe I had given her reason to believe those assumptions. The Rolex on my wrist that I had pretended was a fake. The car I drove wasn't borrowed from a friend. My Armani loafers weren't cheap knockoffs from a tropical holiday destination. All of those things had been lies, even if I had never technically told her that I was a struggling, on-the-verge-of-broke entrepreneur like she was.

I shook my head and focused on the road once more. Just another few minutes, and I'd be in the heat and bustle of the restaurant.

At least everyone there still liked me.

· ♥ · ♥ · ♥ · ♥ · ♥ ·

A tap on the shoulder, and I looked up to see David, a huge grin on his face. "What's up?" I asked, looking up from where I had been playing bartender. I was beginning to think that we would need an actual bartender; people in Brekkie Beach certainly liked to drink.

"Look at this!" A phone was shoved in my face.

"Oh, we got a review," I said, scrolling through the phone. "A good review!"

"A very good review." David jabbed his finger at the screen again, and I saw the words, "Head Chef David Evans has created a classic yet imaginative menu that is sure to delight every palate."

"That's awesome!" I said. "Who is this person?"

"A food blogger," David explained. "With a lot of followers."

"That should keep the bookings coming in." It was an *excellent* review. The food blogger in question had even liked how I had transformed a disused industrial space into a thriving, picturesque dining hub. Well, that was nice.

"Oi!" Mindy interrupted. "Rush might be over, but why are we standing around staring at phones? We've still got punters on the floor."

David rolled his eyes, took back his phone, and saluted Mindy. "Sorry, Mindy."

"He was just showing me a good review," I explained. "Some food blogger with tons of followers had a great time here the other night. Should be good for bookings."

"Food blogger, eh?" Mindy scratched her chin. "What happened to that journalist who wanted to do a story on this place?"

I swallowed. "She's sent a few more emails, and I...I guess I haven't had time to follow up."

"Wyatt!" Mindy looked ready to whack me. "That's bloody critical marketing! You call that journo and get her in here!"

"I guess I could," I said, but I had an uneasy feeling in my stomach. I had put off the persistent journalist because I hadn't wanted Abby to find out the truth about my family's money. But now, I supposed it didn't matter. It wasn't like she could think any worse of me, could she?

"You go and do that right now; I'll get someone else on those drinks orders." Mindy steered me away from the prep area and towards the storage room that contained a desk and was thus dubbed 'the office'.

I sighed, sitting down on the stool by the desk. No reason not to email the journalist. Even if she did publish an article that made me sound like a rebel-without-a-cause trust fund kid opening a restaurant just to pass the time.

It didn't matter anymore; Abby already hated me.

19 Abby

"I'm thrilled you've come, of course." Janice, my client, was twisting her hands together and shooting me furtive glances like she wasn't entirely sure she wanted me here. "But I do feel a bit embarrassed that everything's in such a state."

"It's no problem!" I said, my voice hearty. "If everyone had their house in perfect order, I wouldn't have a job."

Janice nodded, swallowing hard. "It didn't use to be like this," she said, looking at me like it was important I believed her. "I always had things nice and tidy, but when my husband left, I..." She shook her head. "I let it all go. It's really shameful how bad it's become. I don't know what he'd say about this if he was here."

I felt a stab of sympathy for the woman in front of me. In her flowing white linen trousers, delicate silk tank top, and bejewelled sandals, she looked every bit the well-heeled lady of leisure. But I could see that Janice had been through something that had shaken her to the core; her face was drawn and her trousers low on her hips like she had lost a lot of weight in a short time, and I could see where she kept reaching to twist a ring on her finger. A ring that was no longer there.

"I don't think anyone can be expected to make housekeeping their top priority when they're going through a difficult time," I said, swallowing hard against the lump in my throat. "And you've told me it's just the cupboards that are bad. I can't see much clutter around the place; you've done well."

"I've just shoved everything away," Janice said, and she reached out to open what I assumed was a cutlery drawer, but currently contained:

– An unopened tube of mascara
– Six pens
– The offer of a Platinum credit card
– Three yellow socks, none of which matched each other
– A spice rub for grilled prawns
– Two birthday cards
– A mass of knives, forks, and spoons hidden underneath

"Miscellaneous drawers are my favourite," I said to Janice, trying to get her to smile. "I hope all your drawers look like this; I'll be in heaven."

Janice did manage a small smile at that. "I don't know how you do it," she said, leaning against the kitchen counter. "Cleaning up other people's mess all day. When I can't even take care of my own."

"You'd be surprised by how many people struggle with keeping things in order," I said, beginning to remove the varied items from the drawer. No time like the present to start, I thought. "I've worked with barristers who can't find a pair of matching shoes, CEOs with fridges full of out-of-date ingredients, tech gurus who can't sit on their own sofas. It's nothing to be ashamed of."

"You're very kind." Janice took a breath. "But I can't help feeling ashamed of myself. I never thought I'd be in my sixties and alone. And my daughters are sweet, coming to check in on me, but they have their own lives. I don't want to be a burden."

"Think of this as the chance to make a fresh start," I said, extracting a wooden ruler from where it was wedged beneath the disused cutlery tray. "I'm here to make your home work for you again, so you can do whatever you want with your life and not worry about it."

"It would be nice to be able to host my book club here," Janice ventured. "I used to entertain a lot, but I couldn't do it now, not with the house the way it is. And I so enjoyed cooking, but now it seems like too much effort because I can't even find a chopping board when I want one."

"By the end of today," I told Janice, "this kitchen will be ready for you to cook up a storm. Why don't you message your book club, and tell them that you'll host the next meeting right here?"

"Do you really think I could?" Janice looked at me, her eyes glassy like she might cry.

"I'm absolutely certain," I assured her. "This is a fresh start. You can do whatever you want."

Janice gave me a watery smile and retreated with her phone. I was glad I could reassure her, but I wished it was as easy to make myself believe the same thing. My cupboards were immaculate, my clothes a delight of colour order, and my life organised to the last detail. But when I woke up in the morning, I felt like I was trying to escape a vat of thick syrup. All my motivation was gone, and all I could do was force myself to put one foot in front of the other and go on with my life, pretending to be okay.

Four hours later, Janice's kitchen had been reborn. Three enormous garbage bags were full already, and I had a nasty cut from a stray paring knife (how had it ended up in the freezer?), but Janice was elated.

"I just can't believe you did this so fast!" she said, opening her pantry to sigh at the results. "I thought the kitchen alone would take days!"

"I love my work," I said, taking a sip from my water bottle. "Now, I'm going to get started on your bathrooms."

"Oh, do take a break," Janice wheedled. "Can I make you tea or coffee? I know where all my mugs are now!"

I didn't need a break, and I found that staying busy was the only thing that stopped my feelings from overwhelming me, but I could see that it was important to Janice that she could use her kitchen again for the first time in too long. If she was going to feel ready to host her book club, making tea for me was the first step. "A tea would be lovely."

"You sit down at the breakfast bar, and I'll rustle it up." I could see the change in Janice already. Somehow, as she reached into the cupboard for mugs and saw her teabags arranged in neat acrylic containers, she seemed to grow taller. Or maybe her posture was simply no longer hunched.

"So, how many daughters do you have?" I asked because one thing I had learned in my years of organising was that people loved to talk about their kids.

"Just two," Janice said as she flicked on the kettle. "Marisa's in finance, and she's doing very well. And Samantha—" She paused. "Samantha's a special education teacher. My husband never liked that she didn't want to do something more prestigious, but I..." Janice raised her chin defiantly. "I'm very proud of her for doing something that makes a difference. She loves working with those kids, and they just adore her."

"That's awesome," I said, nodding encouragingly. But that made me think of Wyatt and his determination to give people like his uncle better opportunities. Some light stalking had revealed he had been the Director of Operations of the Eastern Australia Portfolio at Parsons Property Inc. Until he had decided to leave that behind to open a restaurant in a sleepy beachside town and employ people most companies wouldn't bother with. He had swapped long lunches and an office with harbour views for hauling second-hand tables in a horse float and playing kitchen hand.

"The world needs people who care enough to do jobs like that," I said quickly when I realised my thoughts had kept me silent too long.

"Yes," Janice agreed. "Samantha's got a huge heart, and that's special."

Wyatt's big heart, hidden underneath that smirk and charm, had been what had made me fall so hard for the guy. And it wasn't like that heart had disappeared, even after I had discovered the truth. His being a rich kid with an easy life didn't change the fact that he genuinely cared about giving opportunities to the people society swept aside. It infuriated me that someone who obviously *cared* so much about others had lied to me. Because I knew, despite my anger and hurt, that Wyatt wasn't an arsehole. No one who did what he had could be a complete arsehole. So why had he chosen to act like an arsehole by lying to me? He had lied over and over again, and he didn't even seem to be all that sorry. Was I not worth the truth? Not worth an apology?

But Wyatt didn't do apologies. And he wasn't going to start now.

I made a conscious effort to unclench my fists and smile at Janice as she placed a cup of tea in front of me. "There you are," she said. "And I've got some biscuits, too."

"Thank you." The way Janice set down the little plate of biscuits made me feel like my chest might just cave in on itself and collapse. I couldn't help but think of how Wyatt had brought tasty treats from the restaurant for me. I had never let anyone take care of me, but he had wormed his way into my life and insisted I let him do it. And I had permitted him. Why had I allowed that man into my life and heart like I never had for anyone else?

A niggling thought in the back of my brain had some ideas, but I chose to ignore them as I took a gulp of my tea. "Thanks," I said again. "This is very kind of you."

"Oh no." Janice swept aside my gratitude. "It's you I should be thanking. This kitchen..." She waved a hand. "I can't believe how much better it's made me feel already."

I swallowed down a mouthful of biscuit, though not the pain in my chest. "Just wait until I've finished with your bathrooms."

I was more than a little tempted to turn around and go right back to the quiet, meticulously organised, and very much empty house that I no longer shared with Wyatt. Usually, the chance to catch up with both my sisters for a night of good food, good wine, and bad TV was a treat. But tonight?

"I don't feel like it," I muttered, making my way up the hill to the house where Tessa lived with Dylan. Technically it was Dylan's house (he was rich too, not that it seemed to bother Tessa), but somehow, the house seemed just as much my sister's as it did his.

"I just want to..." But I didn't have words to finish that sentence. Except maybe 'go home and lie in bed with all the lights off', but I had sworn to myself that I'd never do that again. I would never let myself sit around and do nothing when I had commitments, responsibilities, and a colour-coded to-do list that spanned two full pages. I hadn't let depression creep back into my life for ten years, and I wouldn't let it now just because of Wyatt turning out to be a lying bastard. Well, maybe not a bastard. Lying liar sounded lame, but it was the best I could come up with. Wyatt being a lying liar would not break me now.

Would it?

"There you are!" Tessa opened the door and caught me in a tight hug. "Not like you to be late."

"Long day," I said shortly. "But I'm here. And ready to have fun."

Tessa wrinkled her nose. "You don't have to be fun. We'd want to spend time with you just the same."

I brushed aside her words, making my way into the familiar living room. I could see Tessa had made another cob loaf, and Michelle was already seated, bread in hand as she dipped into the magnificently gooey creation.

"Hey!" she said, waving her bread at me. "Come and try this! Tessa put bacon in it this time. It's freaking next level."

"It definitely smells like it," I said, forcing an enthusiastic expression onto my face and joining her.

"And that sounds like my cue to leave you ladies to it," Dylan said, taking a beer from the fridge. "I'll be in the dark room. With music on. You can say whatever you want about me in peace, my darling."

Tessa laughed and leaned up to kiss him. "You know I'd only say nice things."

"Oh, I don't know." Dylan pretended to consider the matter. "I did leave some potato peelings in the sink the other day. And a damp towel in my gym bag."

I wrinkled my nose. "It's going to smell all musty," I chastised him. "Get it out in the sun, it's a natural disinfectant."

"Already onto it." Dylan gave me a salute. "I'm sure Tessa can come up with some more bad habits I've got to complain about. It's very healthy to have a good vent."

He smiled at the three of us warmly and disappeared down the stairs.

"It's good that he gives you space to hang out with us like this," Michelle said, tearing a piece of bread from the side of the loaf and munching on it with evident satisfaction. "I mean, we are sort of kicking him out of his own living room."

"He offered," Tessa said. "Just like I make myself scarce when he and Tad want to have a boy's night. Which mostly involves plugging in an old PlayStation and shouting that they've banged each other's mothers when they get a good headshot."

I let out a snort. "Men."

"Oh, I think they get in some meaningful stuff too." Tessa sat opposite me. "But even for modern feminist men like Dylan, they've still got to have an activity that they pretend they're focused on while they talk to each other."

"Speaking of meaningful," Michelle cut in, opening a bottle of rosé and pouring it into three glasses. "How are you feeling, Abby?"

"Fine," I said quickly. "Great, actually. The online store has been a huge success. The orders that have come in so far are well above my predictions."

"That's awesome!" Tessa said, giving me an encouraging smile. "I knew it would be a big hit. I mean, who can resist a terrazzo cord concealer?"

"Or a velvet scarf organiser," Michelle said. "But you know that's not what I meant. How are you feeling about Wyatt?"

"Nothing's changed," I said with a shrug, even though that wasn't entirely true. "I'm still angry. Hurt, too. Mostly just mad at myself for getting involved with him in the first place. It's fine; I'll get over it."

"But are you really okay?" Tessa asked, looking at me with tender concern. "I know it's really affected you, so—"

"If you're asking if I'm lying in bed all day doing nothing, the answer's absolutely not," I said with a quick toss of my ponytail. "I'm just focusing on work. Like I always should have been. And yeah, I feel like shit when I think about it. But I'm not going to let it destroy my life."

"Well, that's pretty damn impressive," Tessa said. "That you're still doing everything that you do. But my psychologist would tell you that you need to make space to work through your feelings."

I let out a grunt. "There's plenty of space inside me for feelings," I said. "They can work themselves through. I don't have time to sit around writing in a dream journal or some bullshit."

"Wow, way to dismiss all of Tessa's work with her psych," Michelle chided.

"I didn't mean it like that," I said quickly. "I'm very proud of Tessa for doing so much work on her anxiety, but it's different for me. I'm absolutely fine; I just had a bad experience with a man. It's not like I have an underlying mental health issue to address."

"Are you sure about that?" Michelle gave me a piercing look that startled me.

"What do you mean?"

"I've been thinking about what you said," Michelle said. "About how you've told Wyatt things you've never told us." She took a gulp of wine. "And I wondered if that might be it."

Tessa's eyes were wide. "Is that true, Abby? I've wondered myself, sometimes. I mean, you're always in motion, working, or exercising, or cleaning, or something. Almost like you're afraid something bad will happen if you do stop."

"I just like to stay busy," I muttered, looking into my wine glass. But I knew the game was up. I had kept my sisters in the dark for too long, and the truth would burst out soon enough, like a beanbag set upon by bouncing toddlers.

"Why do you never take a break, Abby? And I won't accept 'no rest for the wicked' or 'I'll have plenty of time to rest when I'm dead'." Michelle raised her eyebrows.

I sighed. It was time to come clean. "When I was at uni, I...went through a rough time, I guess. I felt like I couldn't get out of bed and couldn't study. It just all seemed pointless. My boyfriend broke up with me because I was no fun anymore, and I can't even say he was wrong."

"Abby..." Tessa placed a gentle hand on my shoulder. "That sounds like depression."

"It was," I said, quickly shoving a piece of bread into my mouth, barely tasting the bacon. "I know it was. And it was horrible, like I was paralysed in my own body, and I just...didn't care. When I got out of it, I swore I'd never feel like that again. So that's why I don't like taking breaks."

"Why did you never tell us about this?" Michelle looked furious. "That's huge!"

"Because you were still doing your A-Levels," I shot back. "And Tessa was..."

"In uni as well and would have taken the train down to see you if you had ever told me what was going on," Tessa finished, frowning. "Why didn't you tell me?"

"I couldn't!" I insisted. "When it was happening, I didn't tell anyone. And then when I finally started taking medication and—"

"You were taking medication?" Tessa's mouth dropped open. "And you never told me? Not even when I was freaking out about taking anti-depressants. Abby!"

"It was a long time ago!" I protested, even though I knew that was a crappy excuse. "And I didn't want to make what you were going through all about me."

"It would have made me feel a whole lot better about starting Zoloft if you had told me," Tessa said quietly.

"And I think I know why you didn't tell us." Michelle's arms were folded. "It's because you think you've always got to be the strong one. The big sister. Always in control, no doubts, no fears. And maybe that was true when we were kids, but we're all adults, Abby! You don't need to play that part anymore!"

I groaned, covering my face with my hands. "I'm sorry," I said quietly. "It's not that I didn't think about telling you. I wanted to forget that part of my life. It scared me, you know? Really scared me that my own brain could take me hostage and destroy everything I was working so hard for."

"Oh, Abby." Tessa wrapped an arm around me. "I get that. I just wish you had told us."

"Did you ever see anyone about it?" Michelle pressed, unwilling to move on from the topic.

"No." I shook my head firmly. "I went to the university health service. They gave me some generic SSRIs, which I took for a while. Things got better. And that was the end of it."

"I think you should consider seeing someone now." Michelle was looking at me like she couldn't decide whether to glare or hug me.

"Because Wyatt lied to me?" I snorted. "That's ridiculous! You don't go to a psychologist because the guy you were seeing turned out to be a liar."

"Not because of Wyatt. Because you have some pretty messed up beliefs about always having to be in control, and that you're never allowed to relax," Michelle pointed out. "And that's totally psychologist territory, right Tess?"

"Probably." Tessa looked at me apologetically. "It might not be such a bad idea, Abby."

"I don't need a psychologist!" I knew I was a hypocrite because I had hounded Tessa to see one not long ago. "I don't think it would make any difference."

"Neither did I," Tessa said thoughtfully. "But it did."

"Maybe we should make you," Michelle suggested, taking a sip of her wine. "I'll tie you to a chair, and Tessa, you can get – what's her name, Jillian? – in to make Abby stop thinking she's never allowed to be vulnerable or relax."

I rolled my eyes. "Just try making me do anything. See how that goes for you."

"Didn't Wyatt make you see a doctor about your foot?"

"And look how that turned out!"

"Well, it turned out well for your foot," Tessa pointed out. "Why did you let him convince you to do things and not us?"

I rolled my shoulders, fiddling with the stem of my wineglass. "I don't know," I answered honestly. "Maybe he didn't, really. Maybe it was just stuff I would have done anyway."

"Bullshit," Michelle proclaimed. "You'd never have gone to a doctor without him insisting."

"Okay, maybe it was because I liked him and trusted him!" I spat out. "And I shouldn't have! So, stop bugging me about it, okay? I know! I know how bad it is that I trusted someone who was such a goddamn liar. I get it!"

"That wasn't what I meant," Michelle said. "I'm sorry; I didn't mean to make you feel worse about all this."

"You didn't," I said. "Make me feel worse, that is. I don't think there's a worse I could be feeling, even if I put a lot of effort into it. It's just hard, knowing that I trusted someone who..." I paused. "I mean, he's not a total bastard, obviously, because he really does care about people. But not me. He lied to me! And he wasn't sorry."

"Oh, Abby." Tessa let out a sigh. "It's worse when you can't even hate them, isn't it?"

"I still hate him," I said, totally untruthfully. "For lying to me."

"Is it the lying or him not being sorry that really upsets you?" Michelle asked, perceptive as ever. "Because I think they both bother you."

"I don't know," I said quietly.

"Would it make any difference if he did apologise?" Michelle asked. "Like, could you ever forgive him?"

"It's not going to happen. He doesn't do apologies," I said, shaking my head and standing up. "Anyway, enough of this whole depressing discussion. Where's the remote? We've got reality TV to catcall."

But even as my sisters began to gleefully shit-talk the surgically-enhanced wannabe influencers who were pretending to find true love while watched by thousands of TV viewers, I couldn't help turning over Michelle's question again and again in my head.

Like, could you ever forgive him?

But the truth was, I had absolutely no idea.

• ♥ • ♥ • ♥ • ♥ • ♥ •

"I do like this paper you've got," Josie said approvingly, adding a big sticker with the Organised Home Co logo to the package shelf dividers she had just carefully wrapped. "What colour would you call it? Bronze?"

"Soft gold," I said. "A hint of luxury without being too in your face. That's the idea, anyway."

"Well, it's very nice," Josie said, sliding the wrapped package into an express post envelope and sticking down the mailing label, her tongue between her teeth as she carefully aligned it to be exactly even.

"It's a good thing you like it because we've got at least fifty more orders to get out," I said, tapping the pile of receipts and mailing labels I had already printed. Then I paused. "You know, you don't have to do this stuff if you'd rather not. I put occasional packing duties in the job description, but we've been doing this every night this week."

"I don't mind a bit of packing," Josie said stoutly, frowning as she read through the next order. "Bloody hell, six cable concealers? Who needs six cable concealers?" She moved away from the table, which had become our makeshift packing space, to count out just how many we had left. "And you should be pleased, really. Everything's selling like hotcakes! You'll need to order more product from the factory."

"It is going well," I said. "And that's a huge relief because I invested so much in the stock and the website, but..."

"But what?" Josie looked at me, frowning. "You're not pleased?"

"I am!" I said quickly. "Just, I need to order more stock because it's moving so fast, but the sales don't hit the account until the end of the month, and if we order more, we'll need a bigger storage space, and maybe a casual to help with packing and..." I swallowed. "It's just cash flow. Obviously, we can afford it, but the timing is..."

"Ah," Josie nodded serenely. "But you'll work that out. You're good at all this. And didn't you say your sister was in finance? I bet she can give you some advice on that sort of thing. Me, I managed the family budget for years, but I don't know much about how it works in a business."

I made a non-committal noise, and Josie continued. "But I will say," she went on, "that I don't think people will wait if what they want is out of stock. The internet has spoiled the lot of us. They'll just find what they want somewhere else."

And that was precisely what I had been fretting about. "You're not wrong."

"So, you'll order more stock?" Josie asked, smiling brightly. "How exciting! You'll be needing your own warehouse before you know it!"

"Let's not get carried away," I said quickly, chewing my lip. "Actually, if you don't mind, I might just call my sister. The one in finance."

"Oh, I'm quite happy here," Josie sighed contentedly. "Nice glass of wine, my show on in the background? I could do this all night."

"I'll definitely hire a casual before I let that happen," I assured her, before getting up and moving out to the front porch for what I knew would be an awkward phone call.

My hands shook slightly as I slipped my phone from my pocket, but I knew I had to do this. It might hurt my pride to make this call, but maybe, I thought, my pride could take a little hit. Hadn't my sisters told me they were desperate for me to ask for help when I needed it?

"Michelle, it's Abby," I began, and let out a long breath. "Is it still okay for you to give me a small loan?"

20 Wyatt

It was meant to be my day off. After all, with a Head Chef like David, and a Restaurant Manager like Mindy, there was no real need for me, as the mere owner, to be present as often as I was. But since the showdown with Abby, I had practically moved into Beach Garage. Sometimes I even slept in the storeroom when I thought Danni might be getting sick of me. At least I had a roll-out camping mattress and sleeping bag now, so the tablecloths were safe.

But after I had put myself through a gruelling workout at the gym (the obnoxious yellow plexiglass and throbbing music did nothing to improve my mood) and then sat in Nick and Nikki's for an hour while flicking through Beach Garage's social media pages, I had been unable to resist the siren call of the busy restaurant. It was almost lunch rush.

They'd have some need for me, I was sure of it. I'd clear plates if I had to. Anything was better than sitting around alone.

"What's crack-a-lacking?" I said, pushing my way into the busy kitchen. "Thought you could use a hand with the rush."

Mindy came in then, took one look at me, and frowned. "You're not supposed to be here."

"And yet here I am," I said. "What, am I unwelcome in my own establishment? That's very cruel."

"No, but..." Mindy inclined her head, and I followed her into the storeroom that served as an office, concerned.

"What is it?" I asked in a low voice.

"We just seated a table of two," she said, not quite meeting my eyes. "They asked if the owner was in and seemed disappointed when Sandi said no. She mentioned it to me because she thought it was odd. I'm sure it's your parents, Wyatt. Bloke's a dead ringer for you."

My insides froze like I had been hit squarely by a curse from a Disney ice queen, possibly in full song.

"Oh," I said, swallowing hard. "That's...unexpected."

"Look, I don't know what the situation is." Mindy crossed her arms, obviously uncomfortable. "But I'm guessing you had a falling out with them when you started this place."

"Something like that," I mumbled. "They didn't approve of me leaving the family business. Didn't see why I'd want to do something like this."

"I know a thing or two about families not approving," Mindy ventured. "And it's not my place, but..."

"It's always your place," I said, frowning slightly as I looked at Mindy. "You know you can say whatever you want to me. What is it?"

"It's just that you never know how long you've got to make things right when you argue with family," Mindy said. "So, you should consider taking the chance while you can. While they're still around." She swallowed hard, looking away from me, and there was a shadow of the past, a haunting pain, clearly visible in those crinkled eyes.

I didn't know the details, but Mindy had mentioned before that she had lost her sister, and that had sent her tumbling down the dark road she had worked so hard to free herself from. I wondered if perhaps she and her sister hadn't been on speaking terms when it happened, and my heart ached at the thought.

"Thanks," I said, touching her arm for a moment. "I know it must be hard to talk about."

"Not really." Mindy shrugged, wiping her eyes with the back of her hand. "It hurts like hell, but it's not hard to talk about. And if telling you my story means you don't make the same mistakes, well..." She shrugged again. "That makes it a bit less shit for me."

I nodded and squared my shoulders. "I should go and see them," I said, reaching for the door. "At least hear what they have to say."

"Good," Mindy said, patting my arm encouragingly. "But try not to have a shouting match in front of the lunch crowd. It would be terrible for our reputation." She raised her eyebrows.

"I promise," I said, managing a small smile in response.

"Good," Mindy said again. "Now, get the hell out of my kitchen."

Swallowing again, I made my way through the kitchen, avoiding a kitchen hand swearing passionately at an uncooperative piece of asparagus and managing not to bump David as he tested a rack of lamb with a meat thermometer.

I spotted my parents before they saw me. My mother and father were sitting at a second-hand table on un-cushioned chairs, clutching menus and talking in low voices. I pulled an empty chair to join them and sat down.

"Hi," I said quietly. I didn't stutter; I was ready to have this conversation.

"Wyatt!" My mother's eyes went round. "The waitress said you weren't here today."

"Is that what you were hoping?" I asked, still not looking at my father.

"Of course not," she said, shaking her head. "We wanted to see you. And to see your restaurant. It's not at all what I expected, but it's rather charming. Isn't it, Chuck?" She looked anxiously at my father, and I met his eyes for just a moment.

"It's very nice," my father said before taking his water glass with a long gulp.

"I'm proud of it," I said quietly. "We've been booked out most evenings so far. Good reviews on the food. Though I can't take credit for all of that."

Diana inclined her head. "We saw that article in the *Herald*."

I winced. As I had feared, the article had primarily focused on the fact that I had left the family business to open Beach Garage, but at least there had been some nice glossy atmospheric photos and a gushing description of David's hand-rolled gnocchi.

"I didn't want to air dirty laundry," I said carefully. "But it was good publicity, so I..."

"I can see that." My mother sighed. "I don't think I – we – realised how important this was to you. It was hard to understand why you'd want to leave the family business, but..." She paused. "I think I understand now."

"I don't like how it all happened," I said, fiddling with my hands under the table. "Leaving suddenly like that wasn't the best way I could have done things. But every time I had tried to give notice, you just—" I looked at my father then, and he nodded gravely.

"I refused to accept it," he said. "Because I didn't see why you'd want to leave. We'd given you everything a young man could want, and—" He cut himself off, sighing. "I'm sorry I couldn't understand that what you really wanted was something of your own. To do things on your own terms. And to honour your uncle, of course."

"Dad," I let out a breath. "Are you seriously apologising?" I gave him a wry smile. "I thought a Parsons never apologised."

"Well, never in business." My father raised his eyebrows. "But maybe apologies aren't so bad when you want to make things right with the people you love."

And I knew he was talking about me. I knew that. But all the same, my gut clenched as I thought of Abby, at the way she had looked so *hurt* under all that fury. I had told myself I had nothing to apologise for. That, I was starting to see, might be one of the most epic mistakes of my life, including the time I had let Danni shave my head the night before my graduation ceremony at university.

"Then I'm sorry too," I said before I could think better of it. "For how I left. And for what I said to you. Especially about Uncle Byron. I know you cared about him a lot."

"I did." Charles shifted uncomfortably. "And I should have pushed my father harder to change his mind. I know you think I didn't do anything, but I did try—" He paused, looking away. "I could have done more. And by the time it was my choice..."

"It was too late," I finished. "That's why I wanted to do this now. So that other people, like Byron, get a fair go.

And I wanted to build something on my own, not just coast on how lucky I've always been."

"You're a good man, Wyatt. Probably a better man than me. And I'm proud that you're my son." He put a hand on my arm, and I felt a rush of something go through me. As much as I had been too stubborn to admit it, I had *missed* my parents. Missed them terribly. They weren't perfect, not even close. But I knew they really did care about me.

"I'm proud to be your son," I said, my voice hoarse. "And I...I'm really glad you're here."

"We're glad to be here too," Diana said. "It's a pretty little place, this Brekkie Beach. I hadn't even heard of it, but it's sweet. And the people seem very friendly."

I swallowed hard. "They are," I said. "Anyway, what are you going to order?"

"The risotto looks very nice," my mother said. "And your father was interested in that slow-cooked lamb shank."

"Good choices," I said. "How would you feel about me crashing your lunch date? And I could take you to meet the team and see the kitchen after lunch."

"We'd be delighted," Charles said, his hand again on my arm. He huffed out a long breath. "Though, to be honest with you, right now, I really need a drink."

"I think we all do."

· ♥ · ♥ · ♥ · ♥ · ♥ ·

In the end, my parents stayed for almost three hours. As it turned out, there was a lot of family gossip I had missed out on. My second cousin had been arrested for climbing a large-scale public artwork while travelling in Germany. His excuse of 'I thought you were supposed to!' had not gone down well with the local police. My aunt Davina, who lived between Los Angeles and London, had gone through yet another 'non-invasive' cosmetic procedure, and her lips were now so swollen she could only drink through a straw. And then my mother had mentioned Auntie Sondra raving about her delightful experience with a professional organiser.

"Do you think we should get this woman in, Wyatt?" Diana had asked.

"No," I had said quickly. "I mean, I don't think you need a professional organiser. Auntie Sondra's always in chaos; you're not like that."

"I suppose not," my mother had said. "But the photos she sent of her wardrobe were very impressive."

The thought of my mother hiring Abby was too much to bear, and so I had quickly changed the subject, hoping – almost praying – that she'd forget all about it.

But I couldn't forget about Abby.

On the long drive back to Danni's stables, I caught a glimpse of myself in the rear-view mirror and swore.

"What the fuck am I doing?" I asked my reflection. "I did lie to her. Of course I did. Why couldn't I just admit it and apologise?"

I swallowed hard, the idea of apologising still making me smart like I had been whacked with a ruler.

"Maybe apologies aren't so bad when you want to make things right with someone you love," I repeated my father's words, trying very hard to keep my eyes focused on the road ahead.

When I arrived, Danni wasn't in the house, which could only mean one thing. I'd have to brave the stables – and their equine occupants – if I wanted to talk to my best friend. I swapped my shoes for a pair of too-small gumboots and made my way through grass and mud, the smell of horse intensifying with every step.

"Hey," I said, raising a hand and not getting too close when I spotted Danni currycombing a mare (at least, I assumed it was a mare – I wasn't keen on getting close enough to make any definitive judgements regarding horse genitalia) and making crooning noises as she did.

"Wyatt Parsons, are you seriously in my stable right now?" Danni pretended to stagger backwards in shock, but I could see her surprise was genuine. "Are you okay? I know you'd never willingly come in here without the threat of something even more terrifying than my babies."

"I'm not scared of them," I said, even as a whinnying snort from a nearby stall made my skin crawl. "I just don't especially like them."

"And I will allow you to keep up that fiction in front of other people, but not me." Danni rolled her eyes. "Come on, what's up? You'd never be in here if something wasn't up."

"My parents came to the restaurant today," I said, taking a stool and setting it a reasonable distance from Danni and her hairdressing client.

"No shit!" Danni's eyes widened. "What happened? I hope you're insured; I bet the damages were huge."

"We talked," I said. "And it was…kind of anti-climactic, actually. I think Dad finally understood why it was so important to do my own thing. Because of Uncle Byron. I mean, I was angry with Dad for how he acted when I quit, but…" I sighed. "I don't know. It just didn't seem like such a big deal anymore."

"This is good." Danni nodded, frowning. "Definitely good."

"Dad said he was sorry."

"Seriously?" Danni dropped the currycomb. "Your dad actually apologised? What happened to Parsons never apologise?"

"He said something about how it was a good rule for business but a shitty rule when it stopped you from making it right with someone you love," I said slowly. "I was as shocked as you. I don't think I realised how hurt he was, you know? I thought it was all pride, but now I think maybe he was hurt that I didn't want to work with him anymore."

"Men," Danni scoffed as she smoothed over a flank of hard muscle that gave me an unpleasant mental image of how hard the spotted mare could kick. Or trample me, given half the chance. "Of course he was hurt! When you left, it was like you were rejecting him and everything he had worked for."

"And I told him I was sorry, too. For how I handled it."

"You apologised? Two Parsons apologising on the one day? Pretty sure this is a sign of the apocalypse." Danni snorted, but then was serious. "That's a pretty big deal, Wyatt."

"I know," I said. "And my brain's been a mess, trying to work out if..." I sighed. "If I could..."

"Apologise to Abby?" Danni supplied. "Yeah, dude, you should! I've been telling you that from the start! You fucked up and hurt her; she deserves an apology."

"I know she does," I said quickly. "That's not the thing I'm trying to work out. I'm definitely going to apologise, but what I can't work out is if there's anything I could say, anything I could do, that might make her give me another chance. Because I think—" I stood up, took a deep breath, and forced myself to walk up close to the terrifying beast to look my best friend in the eye. "I think I'm in love with her."

"Oh, shit!" Danni's voice was so loud that she startled the horse. The mare whinnied and stamped her feet, making me immediately retreat back a few steps. "Sorry, girl, I wasn't expecting to hear that." She ran a comforting hand over the spotted back. "Damn, Wyatt. That's...that's a lot."

"Just my luck, huh? I finally fall for real, and it's for someone who despises the very sight of me. She'd probably throw a shelf divider at me if I tried to talk to her."

"Better a shelf divider than a terrazzo cable organiser," Danni joked. "I watched some of her live stream. And ordered a bunch of product for the office. She was very compelling."

"She was," I said, not wanting to admit that not only had I watched Abby's live product launch but downloaded it and watched it again, over and over, trying to see if there was something behind that bold, confident smile that might ever forgive me. "So, what the hell am I supposed to do? I mean, I can go to see her, but I don't think she'll even hear me out. She was absolutely furious with me."

"And she had every right to be, despite all your bullshit about not doing anything wrong and her making assumptions and—"

"I know," I winced. "I know. I messed up. I did lie. And yes, she did make an assumption right at the start, but after that I lied to her. Because I didn't want her to see me differently. I just wanted her to like me."

"And she did." Danni sighed, setting down her currycomb again. "You said she opened up to you with stuff she's never told anyone else. That's a big deal. And she let you look after her, and she's so not that kind of person. It sounds like she had some pretty big warm and fuzzy feelings for you."

"I think she did before she found out." I shook my head. "I don't think she feels that way anymore."

"Probably not." Danni shrugged. "But if you can show her you're sorry – properly sorry – and take responsibility, you might be able to get her to give you another chance. And then she might feel that way about you again."

"If she'll even speak to me."

"Yeah, she might slam the door in your face," Danni agreed, her face thoughtful. "You should definitely bring a gift. That might soften her up a bit."

"I think she'd hate that," I said. "I mean, bringing her a gift after I lied about money?" But then I paused. "Maybe I could cook her something special."

"Food is definitely the way to a woman's heart. Do you remember when I spent a week trying to make gluten-free white chocolate and macadamia cookies because that woman I was crushing on – Sasha, the show jumper – mentioned they were the thing she missed the most after she found out she had coeliac disease?"

"I remember you making me taste a lot of really horrible cookies," I said. "Did it work?"

"Nope, she was straight," Danni said matter of factly. "Not even cookies can change someone's sexual orientation. But I think food is a good start. Because it's not about money, it's about taking time to do something for her. You should give it a shot."

"Give it a shot," I repeated. "So, what should I cook to make Abby forgive me and give me another chance?"

Danni let out a snort. "How would I know, dude?" She paused. "But I'm definitely up for taste testing. It's the least you could do after I've let you crash here."

"True," I said. "I think I'm going to go to that farmer's market I saw on the way here, to get inspired."

"You just want to get away from my horses."

"Also true," I said, cringing at the horse and making for the open doors.

"Hey, Wyatt?"

I turned around, and Danni was giving me a strange look. "You stopped stuttering on her name. I reckon that's a good sign."

I huffed out a breath. "I hope so."

It probably was a good sign. But it didn't change the fact that Abby might never speak to me again, regardless of what I cooked for her.

And I couldn't imagine going through my whole life without Abby now that I had found her again.

21 Abby

"So, how's it going there?" I asked, holding the phone to my ear with my shoulder. "Everything okay?"

"Just fine," Josie said in her clipped, no-nonsense tone. "Quite a delightful job setting up a butler's pantry from scratch. No mess to clear out, getting it right from the start. I just hope they keep it that way."

"The pictures looked great," I said. "Thanks for posting those."

"I used that little light you gave me and everything," Josie said, a hint of pride in her voice.

"You're a natural," I said warmly, even though I would have angled the camera a little lower. But I had to accept that growing my business meant that not everything would be done my way. And that was an ongoing struggle. "So now you've just got the rest of the kitchen, right?"

"Just that." Josie chuckled. "It's bloody enormous, and they've got appliances I've never even heard of. But I had a chat with the two of them about what they use the most, so I'm sure I'll be able to do a good job."

"I'm certain of it," I said. "But if you're unsure about anything, you can always call me." Maybe I wasn't so great at letting go. "Not that you have to or anything!"

But Josie just laughed. "You need to trust that you've trained me well, Abby."

"I do!" I said, trying to sound convincing. "I'm sorry, it's kind of hard for me. I'm trying to get the right balance between being supportive and available and not micro-managing. I'm still pretty new to this whole boss thing."

"For what it's worth, I think you're doing an excellent job," Josie said. "Now, I'd better get back to it. I've got three different blenders to position!"

The call ended, and I let out a sigh, but it wasn't an unhappy one. Well not entirely unhappy, anyway. I was…satisfied? That wasn't quite right either. But I was starting to feel less anxious about Organised Home Co becoming insolvent. The online store was spitting out orders almost faster than I could fill them. Accepting a loan from Michelle had been the right call; I needed the additional stock. Still, I couldn't count on ongoing sales remaining at their current level, as nice as that would be. There was a decent chance they'd drop off after the initial rush, and

I wasn't the kind of businessperson to count my terrazzo cord organisers before they sold.

But I couldn't deny it felt good to see my business account safely in the black again. It wasn't like I'd be able to upgrade my van to the Peugeot Expert of my dreams (with custom decals, of course) any time soon, but now I could safely buy a coffee at Nick and Nikki's without worrying about the cost. That was good progress.

I let out another sigh, this one less happy. It had been more than a week, and I still couldn't stop thinking about Wyatt. If anything, it had gotten worse. When my anger had died down, and only hurt and confusion remained, I had no idea what to do with my feelings. I had started walking past the restaurant more times than I'd admit willingly – even to my sisters – but had never actually gone inside. But I had gotten close enough to see Beach Garage was doing a brisk trade. The outdoor tables on the new concrete slab were always full of people consuming hand-rolled pasta or slow-cooked lamb, their faces showing their delighted satisfaction under the soft fairy lights.

I didn't even know what I'd say to Wyatt if I did see him. Did I want to ask him for an explanation of why he had lied to me? Ask him if he really had been planning to tell me? Ask him if he genuinely cared about me or if I had just been a convenient distraction? Would the answers to those questions make any difference?

"It doesn't matter," I told myself firmly, standing up, stretching, and making my way to the Great Wall of Boxes that had turned the living room into something like a child's fort on steroids. I was waiting to take possession of a new, larger storage unit, but until then, the eyesore dominated the room.

Maybe I should lean into the box fort thing. I could make a little cave, chuck in some throw cushions and a blanket, and sit inside with a glass of wine and my laptop showing any reality TV show that wasn't *Selling Sunset* (which now made me think of Wyatt). Would that be self-care, I wondered, or just utterly pathetic?

"It's a fine line," I muttered, getting up to help myself to the wine and think further on the matter of the box fort.

As I poured the wine, a soft knock on the door made me pause. It didn't sound like either of my sisters. Michelle pounded and called out, and Tessa always texted first. I felt a strange, squeezing sensation in my chest at the thought that it might be Wyatt, which I tried to ignore as I went to the door, my wine abandoned.

Even if it was him, it wasn't like I could assume he had come to speak to me. After all, Wyatt had left a lot of his stuff here. And yes, I had broken the sacred rule of housemates by taking a quick look in his room, but I had immediately fled because the smell of him made me want to cry and throw things simultaneously.

Looking at the looming shadow through the glass, I decided it *probably was* Wyatt. The height was right, and I could recognise those broad shoulders even in cameo. Right. I took a breath, smoothed my hair, and decided to be extremely casual and nonchalant about seeing him. Even if my insides were squirming like the nest of baby mice I had once found in a client's prized vintage cowboy boot.

I opened the door to find Wyatt standing before me, both hands clutching a covered baking dish. His face looked tight and drawn, and there were dark circles under his eyes like he hadn't been sleeping well. His stubble, too, was longer than usual (though he still looked annoyingly handsome). I should have been glad he was clearly suffering, but a treacherous part of me – a very large part – wanted to ask him if he was okay.

"Hi," I said, moving back to let him enter.

"Hello, Abby," he said, stepping inside cautiously like he thought I was about to slam the door so fast it broke his nose. And while I had entertained a very similar fantasy, I had no intention of being quite that violent.

There was a silence during which Wyatt looked at everything except me, and I stood with my arms crossed, pretending I wasn't looking at him.

"Lots of boxes," he said finally, nodding at the living area.

"Yeah," I said, suddenly glad I hadn't constructed the box fort of my dreams. That would have been somewhere well beyond embarrassing. "I had to order more stock for the online store, and I'm just waiting to get access to a bigger storage locker. It won't be here long."

"That's not what I..." Wyatt paused. "Sounds like it's going well, then. Your online store."

"Pretty well," I said, wondering why he was asking. "You don't need to make small talk, you know. If you came to get your stuff, you can just get it."

Wyatt looked taken aback. "That's not why I came," he said, and I could see him swallowing hard, his Adam's apple bobbing. "I wanted to talk to you."

That strange squeezing feeling intensified, like a particularly ravenous boa constrictor was underneath my rib cage and intent on crushing each of my internal organs into a messy paste. "Oh."

"Can we..." Wyatt indicated the couch, which was partially hidden by boxes. "Can we sit down?"

"Okay." My voice sounded stiff and forced. Was I going to get an explanation? An apology was too much to hope for, surely.

I sat down carefully at one end of the sofa, crossing my legs underneath me and wishing that I had had both the time and the money for a decent pedicure. Half of my toes were orange, while the other half were their sad natural pink and not especially well maintained. I tried to tell myself that I didn't care what Wyatt thought of my toenail maintenance, but I shifted my position to hide my toes just the same.

Wyatt, for his part, didn't seem to be interested in my toes; he just stared at the covered dish on his lap. He was looking at the foil like it held the secrets to the universe. What was in there, I wondered?

"I wanted to talk to you," Wyatt began and cleared his throat. "About what happened between us. The way you found out about my family, it was..." He paused and shook his head. "I was going to tell you. That night, actually. And I hate that you found out like that instead, with Auntie Sondra. You were right to be angry with me."

I let out a breath. "I was angry," I said flatly. "Because you lied to me. Or withheld the truth, if that's how you want to—"

"No, I did lie," Wyatt said, shifting in his seat. "And that was a seriously shitty thing to do. And I... I'm sorry for that. Truly sorry."

My eyes widened. "I thought you didn't do apologies."

"I didn't," Wyatt said, giving me the faintest hint of a rueful grin. "My dad always said that if you're confident in your decisions, you should never have anything to apologise for. But I made a shitty, awful split-second decision to not tell you the truth. And then that forced me to keep lying again and again. I'm not..." He sighed. "I know you have no reason to believe me, but I'm not the lying type, generally speaking."

"Well, I do appreciate the apology," I said slowly. "Especially since I know it's not something you make a habit of." I looked down at my hands – also in need of a manicure – and then back up at him. "But why did you do it? Did you think I'd hate you just for being lucky enough to be born into money? I know I bitch about my rich clients, but I'm not the judgemental type."

"I guess..." Wyatt sighed again. "Because when you said I was a struggling entrepreneur with a dream, just like you, I wanted it to be true. I liked that you saw me that way. And I justified it to myself that even if I wasn't broke, I had left my family company and gone out on my own. And it has been a struggle, doing my own thing without their help. But it was still a lie. I just... I didn't want to change how you saw me."

"You wanted me to like you?" I twisted my mouth. "I think that's probably the most common reason people have for lying. That, and getting out of trouble."

"I always planned to tell you the truth," Wyatt said quickly, his eyes wide and honest. "Danni can confirm that; you don't have to take my word for it. She was always badgering me about when I'd tell you, but I was waiting for the right time. But it never seemed to come, and then..." He sighed. "Then the launch party happened, and I knew then that I had seriously fucked up, getting involved with you without telling the truth. And I did want to make it right."

The squeezing in my chest lessened slightly as I looked at him. He looked so earnest, so insistent, that I wanted to believe him. I *did* believe him. And what's more, I was coming perilously close to forgiving him.

"I wish you had," I said quietly, unable to look him in the eyes any longer. "I mean, I would have been angry, but a whole lot less angry than the way I did find out."

"I hate that you found out like that," Wyatt said. "Before I could explain. And that you thought I had been laughing at you or trying to manipulate you. I would never do that. I think you're absolutely incredible, Abby Finch. I was just trying to be the kind of man you might consider making room for in your very busy schedule."

I tried to huff out a breath of laughter, but it sounded like a sob. Why did Wyatt have to go and say things like that? All those feelings I had been trying to stamp down like errant grapes in an old-fashioned wine tub were flooding through me now, demanding acknowledgment.

"And I guess I'm asking if there's any chance you might forgive me," Wyatt said, those hazel eyes fixed on me. "I don't mean right away because I know how badly I messed up. And you're probably still angry with me. But I want to know if there's a chance. I'm willing to wait, however long it takes. Because I..."

He reached out then, taking my hand between his. I lifted my chin, and his eyes met mine. "Because I'm in love with you, Abby. I've never felt like this about anyone before. So, I've got to know if there's any chance you could see yourself caring about a rich trust fund arsehole because I'm pretty sure my life is going to suck if you're not in it."

All the breath went out of me in a great whoosh, and I just stared at him. "Are you freaking serious right now?!"

And crap, I hadn't meant to say it quite like that, but I had never been the best at controlling what came out of my mouth. That clearly hadn't been the response Wyatt was hoping for because he drew his hand back as though he had touched a cast iron pan hot from Beach Garage's industrial oven.

"Uh, yeah," he said. "Very serious, in fact. But if you can't imagine forgiving me, I get it. It's my fault; I'm the one who lied and—"

"No, that's not what I..." I shook my head. "I just really wasn't expecting you to say...that."

"That I'm in love with you?" His mouth quirked as he said it again, and the words made my face grow hot, and my stomach tighten almost painfully. "God, Abby, how could I not be? You're so smart, so independent, and so driven. And you make me laugh more than anyone ever has. You're a force of nature and kind of terrifying. In a good way. A really good way. You care so much and live so fiercely. And when you shared with me about what you went through, it just made me love you more. Is that enough of an explanation?"

I let out a quick breath. "That's a lot of reasons." I swallowed hard, shaking my head again. "I...I can definitely see myself forgiving you."

"Well, that's a start," Wyatt raised his eyebrows. "So, what do I have to do to convince you to give me another chance?" He held up the baking dish. "I brought this. Rhubarb and apple crumble because you told me that it's impossible to get in Australia unless Tessa makes it, and she doesn't like rhubarb. I was going to try and tempt you with it if you refused to speak to me, but—"

"I don't need crumble to want to give you another chance," I said, taking the crumble from him and putting it on the coffee table without so much as a coaster. "Although I'm very touched that you remembered me telling you that."

"So, you want to give this another shot?" Wyatt's face lit up. "Really? I was sure I'd have to do a whole lot of penance before you'd even consider it. Not that I'm not grateful, but you were so angry with me. Why are you giving me another chance?"

I groaned, wrinkling up my nose. "Isn't that obvious?" I asked him. "Because I'm in love with you, Wyatt. I think I have been for a while, even if I didn't want to admit it. I didn't stop caring when I found out the truth, even though I was so angry and hurt. I had a whole lot of feelings to work through, but now I—"

But I didn't get to finish what I was saying because firm lips were pressed against mine in a kiss that was about a million times more technically skilled than our first as blushing teenagers but no less full of wonder and possibility.

When Wyatt drew back, big hands cradled my face. "I love you, Abby," he murmured. "And I promise I'll never lie to you again. Or do anything else that might make you hate me because I want to keep you in my life. Always."

"I never hated you," I whispered, resting my forehead against his. "I tried to. I wanted to. But...I couldn't."

"I'm very glad about that," he said with a tiny chuckle. "I don't like to think about what you might have done to me if you had."

"I..." I sighed. "I thought about some of what you said, too. Even though I didn't want to hear it. About how I wasn't really all on my own; I just didn't want to accept help."

"I'm sorry, that was a shitty thing to say. I was trying to justify myself, and—"

"But you were right, too," I told him. "I accepted a loan from Michelle, anyway. Well, an investment. She was insistent on the terminology because she knew I hated the idea of a loan. I did it so I could order more stock for the online store, and—" I swallowed. "I should have done it a few months ago. You were right."

"I won't tell anyone," Wyatt's lips quirked. "I promise."

"Better not."

"So, are you going to try this crumble?" Wyatt pulled back the foil. "I made six batches before Danni and I decided it was good enough. She told me that if I ever bring rhubarb into her house again, she's going to lock me in the stable."

"It smells amazing," I said, eyeing the crisp, golden brown top of the crumble, cracked by rivers of dark red rhubarb beneath. "But the thing is... I'm not hungry right now."

"Oh?" Wyatt caught my meaning immediately, running a hand up my bare leg and making my skin dance and tingle. "Not hungry?"

"Not at all," I whispered, leaning in to kiss him again.

I gasped out loud as he pulled me close, hooking my legs around him and standing up with me clinging to him like a koala. "Carrying me around, huh?"

"Not letting you go, more like," Wyatt murmured, his lips brushing over my neck. "And you're still going to try that crumble later. Even if I have to force-feed you."

I let out a laugh, even as hot desire swept through me. "You're the only person who can make me do anything, you know."

"I'm very glad to hear that," Wyatt told me, carrying me up the stairs effortlessly. "And you're the only person who can make me apologise. So, I'd say we were pretty evenly matched, huh?"

"Yeah," I whispered, kissing him again. "We're definitely a good match."

22 Wyatt

"How's it all going in here?" I asked, watching David as he gently prodded a truly glorious-looking piece of prime rib, testing the surface tension.

David gave me an incredulous look. "Busy!" he signed. "Why are you in my kitchen?"

"Ouch!" I laughed. "But point taken, I'll leave you alone."

David nodded in satisfaction, moving past me to show a kitchen hand that when he said finely chopped, he didn't mean mostly finely chopped with a few oversized pieces left in.

I escaped the bustling heat of the kitchen to where Mindy was directing the floor with a watchful eye. "How's it going tonight?"

"Busy," she said shortly. "As you well know. But we've got your special table ready, don't worry!"

"I wasn't worried," I answered perfectly honestly. "I know you've got everything under control."

"Then why are you bothering me?" Mindy poked me, but she was smiling. "Go and get your girl; I bet you two could do with a drink before your parents arrive."

"You might be right," I agreed and slipped out the side door.

It was barely a two-minute walk from the restaurant to the house that Abby and I once again shared, but I enjoyed it just the same. The early evening air was fresh and crisp with the smell of salt water, and a gentle breeze ruffled my hair in the way I knew Abby liked. As I walked, I passed a couple I was sure were going to Beach Garage.

"Come on, Marcel!" said one of the men. He was seated in a wheelchair, a gold-topped cane set across his knees. "I don't want to be late for our reservation. Dylan and Tessa have been raving about that lamb shank!"

"We will not be late," Marcel replied. He must be glad of the cool breeze as he pushed the wheelchair because he was wearing a turtleneck which had to be uncomfortably warm even in the evening. "You will have your shank, Alan."

I realised then that this must be Dylan's father and stepfather, and I gave them a smile as they passed. I'd have to thank Tessa and Dylan for recommending Beach Garage to them.

As I fumbled for my keys, the door opened before me, and Abby stepped out. "What do you think? Is this meet the parents appropriate?"

Abby spun in a circle, and I caught her around the waist to kiss her. She was wearing a form-fitting orange dress, cut low in the back and skimming over the curve of her hips and the bottom that I so enjoyed grabbing. "I know the back's a little cheeky, but I'm covered up top. Not that I've got much to cover."

"You've got the perfect amount to cover," I said, pulling back to look at her. "You're beautiful, Abby."

"Mm, I like it when you say that." Abby looked up at me mischievously. "But am I appropriate?"

"You're very appropriate," I said. "I mean, I'm still about to explode with lust, but that's just a given."

"Do we need to make time for a quickie?" Abby arched an eyebrow. "It would be super awkward if you exploded during this dinner."

"Save that thought for later," I told her. "Mindy thought we could do with a drink before they arrive."

"Mindy is a smart woman," Abby said approvingly. "If she ever gets sick of managing your restaurant, I'm totally planning to poach her."

"Now, that would be seriously unprofessional," I said, taking Abby's hand in mine as we began the short walk back to the restaurant. "I'd have no chance of keeping her if you tried to do that. You're way more fun than me."

"Oh, I wouldn't say that." Abby squeezed my hand. She tucked her hair behind one ear, revealing a long, dangly silver earring. "You sure I'm okay for tonight?" she asked again. "I don't like to second guess myself, but..." She shrugged. "I really do want to make a good impression on your parents. I guess I care about you or something."

"Or something?" I teased. "You look perfect, Abby. I promise."

"Perfect sounds just about good enough."

Beach Garage was already beginning to fill up with hungry guests as we took our seats, and Mindy herself brought over two gin and tonics, mine with cucumber and Abby's with lime, as was her preference.

"You ready for the onslaught?" Mindy asked, and Abby grimaced.

"I'll do my best. I mean, I work with fancy rich people all the time. I've got this, right?"

"They'll love you," Mindy said, patting her shoulder. "They'd be stupid not to see how good you've been for this one." She jerked her head at me.

"You have," I said, taking Abby's hand in mine. "The only thing I'm worried about is that they'll like you more than me."

"Oh, is that a challenge?" Abby's eyes lit up.

"It could be," I said, taking a sip of my drink. While my parents and I were once again on good terms, I had never introduced them to a girlfriend before, and I couldn't deny I was nervous. Especially since they had been peppering me with questions about Abby. I just hoped they'd tone down their enthusiastic curiosity when it came to meeting her in person.

"So, did you see that big house on Pine Street is for sale?" I asked. "You know, the one that has all the scaffolding?"

"Oh yeah," Abby nodded. "Tessa told me that Alice – Dylan's best friend's wife, she's a real estate agent – told her that the guy who owned it was renovating and then decided to sell up and move overseas when it was almost done. So, it's super nice inside, but has no functional bathrooms."

"It's a nice-looking property," I said cautiously. "Great location and you'd get nice beach views from the deck."

"Wyatt." Abby gave me a look. "You're going to buy it, aren't you?"

"I was thinking about it," I admitted. "I mean, I've got to live somewhere, and it's an easy walk to the restaurant, so..."

"You don't have to worry that I'll make it weird because you can afford to just buy a house like that outright." Abby placed her hand on mine. "I've made peace with your trust fund status. And hey, I'd be able to visit you super easily if you buy that house!"

"About that," I said, twisting my mouth. "I was thinking I might be lonely without a housemate."

"A housemate, huh?" Abby took a gulp of her drink. "Did you have someone particular in mind?"

"Well, they'd have to be pretty special," I said, taking her hand again. "And I'd need someone very well organised. Because I'm not."

Abby laughed. "Well, that's true." Then she paused. "You're seriously asking me to move in with you? Like, as a couple?"

"Definitely as a couple," I said. "I want you with me all the time. And I know it's a big step, and you value your independence, but..." I let out a breath. "Would you consider it?"

"I don't love the idea of being someone's kept woman." Abby frowned like she was thinking it through. "And I get this feeling you're not going to let me pay rent."

"You'd be right," I said. "Because that would be ridiculous. If we do this, then you'll have to deal with me taking care of you sometimes."

Abby wrinkled her nose. "I'm not great at that," she said slowly. "And it's going to kill me not to pay rent, but..."

"But?"

"I think you might be worth it," she said with a smile. "And hey, it'll give me some material to talk about when I see this psychologist my sisters are forcing me to go to."

"I'm very glad you're doing that. You deserve to deal with all that baggage you're carrying around. Get it sorted out, organised, and stored. That's totally you."

"I suppose it is." Abby squeezed my hand. "So, I think I'm saying yes. Even if it scares me a shit ton. Because being with you is worth facing my fears about losing my independence. You're worth it."

"I don't think anything or anyone, even me, could make you lose your independence," I said. "And if you need any more reasons to say yes, I could tell you that there's a huge storage area under the house. Four-car garage and workshop. All that space just waiting to be used. Maybe by someone who's got an online store."

Abby let out a soft moan of pure need. "You know I'm helpless at the thought of storage space," she complained. "The shelves I could put in! The packing station!"

"Sorry," I said, but I wasn't in the least sorry. I'd do whatever it took to convince Abby to say yes.

"It's just," Abby began, screwing up her face again. "I want you to know, I'd want to live with you even if it was in a horrible studio with a shared laundry and loud neighbours. I need you to know that."

"I think you know how to deal with loud neighbours," I teased. "Something about a disobedient avocado."

"You totally deserved that!"

"And I do know that you'd want to be with me even if I was completely broke," I told her. "So long as I had a plan, of course. Couldn't expect you to want a Wyatt with zero ambition."

"I like this Wyatt," Abby said softly. "Exactly as you are. Actually, I love this Wyatt. Quite a lot, as it turns out."

"Then I think I should make an offer on the house."

I wouldn't tell her, but I'd offer whatever it took to secure the house. Because the thought of having Abby with me, every day and always, was worth any price.

· ♥ · ♥ · ♥ · ♥ · ♥ ·

"And you're from Birmingham, is that right?" My mother asked before attending to her last mouthful of risotto.

"I am," Abby said. "But please don't hold that against me."

That earned a polite chuckle, and I gave her a smile. "I'm a big fan of Birmingham if it made you."

"And you've got a business, organising people's houses?" My father ventured. "Very sound idea; I doubt you'll run out of clients any time soon."

"You're right," Abby said. "I'm actually expanding right now. I've just brought on my first employee, and I've got an online store, too. With organisational products, like shelf dividers and cable concealers. It's doing pretty well." She was being modest, of course.

"Oh yes, Sondra sent me some pictures of what you did for her," Diana said, sounding approving. "You're very talented to get her wardrobe looking like that."

"She was a lot of fun to work with," Abby said, and I winced because I knew that Abby had had the opposite of fun that day.

"If you can handle my sister, you can handle anything," Charles said drily. "Including Wyatt here." He clapped a hand on my shoulder.

I was embarrassed, but Abby just laughed. "Oh, I don't think Wyatt needs me to handle him," she said. "He's doing a pretty great job himself, don't you think?"

There was a pause as my parents digested exactly what she was saying.

"Yes," Charles said finally. "I suppose he is."

"If you'll excuse me for just a moment—" Abby stood. "I'll be right back."

As Abby disappeared to the bathroom, my mother leaned in. "She's a lovely girl, Wyatt."

"And she runs her own business. She's clearly ambitious and a hard worker," my father said approvingly. "And not afraid to say what she thinks."

"No," I said. "She's definitely not afraid of that. It's one the things I like most about her." I paused. "That I love most about her."

"You're serious about her, then?" My mother raised her eyebrows.

"Very."

"Good," my father nodded with satisfaction. "Because I'd be very disappointed if you let her slip through your fingers. You've finally met your match – and now you just need to hold on to her."

"Don't worry," I said. "I've got no intention of letting Abby go."

And that was the truth.

Epilogue: Abby

One year later

The sun was just beginning to sink into the ocean when I joined my sisters at a small outdoor table laden with rosé and glasses. With the smell of salt in my nose and the bright smiles of Tessa and Michelle greeting me, I was once again reminded of how glad I was to have left Birmingham for Brekkie Beach and that my sisters had seen the extreme wisdom of my plan and followed suit.

"There you are!" Michelle pressed a loud kiss to my cheek as I sat down beside her.

"Here I am," I agreed, taking a glass of rosé and enjoying every bit of that first mouthful. "Damn, that tastes good."

"Now that you're here, we can make a toast," Tessa held up her own glass.

"What are we toasting?"

"Uh, you, obviously!" Michelle rolled her eyes like I was being intentionally obtuse just to irritate her. "It's the first anniversary of your online store!"

"Oh, that," I said, shaking my head. Earlier in the day, I had posted on all my social media platforms, thanking my customers for their support and offering a discount code to celebrate. And then I had promptly forgotten all about it.

"Yeah, 'that'," Tessa was shaking her head in dismay. "We're toasting because it's been a big success, and you should be very proud of yourself."

"Oh, well, in that case—" I raised my glass. "I am pretty pleased with myself." I clinked my glass against my sisters' and took another long sip.

"And I'm grateful, too," I added. "For your support. From both of you."

"We didn't do much." Michelle waved away my thanks. "A tiny seed investment from me."

"And a molecule of copywriting from me," Tessa supplied. "But you're the one who did all this. And look at you now! You've got three employees! You're a super boss babe!"

"Actually, I'm thinking of getting someone on board full-time just to process and pack orders," I admitted. "I've been doing most of it myself, but this leadership book I'm reading says I should delegate and outsource stuff like that to devote my time to business development and high-value clients."

Michelle snorted. "I could have told you that."

"I *did* tell you that," Tessa chimed in. "But I guess you had to discover it for yourself, huh?"

"Apparently," I admitted. "But hey, I'm doing it now. That's progress, right?"

"Maybe we need another toast," Michelle suggested. "To celebrate you being a reformed control freak who never relaxes."

I laughed. "We'll have to save that one for when Wyatt's here. He wouldn't want to miss out on the credit for putting me through remedial relaxation tutoring. He made me sit through a whole movie last night without making any labels or checking invoices while we watched! I was ready to jump out of my skin."

"I still can't believe he can make you do anything," Michelle said. "I kind of always thought you'd end up with some dude who you could just order around like a robot."

"I'd hate that." I made a face like my rosé had been replaced with sour milk.

"You would." Tessa was in agreement. "I just never thought you'd meet a guy who could actually, well...you know."

"Handle me?" I suggested wryly. "Because I'm such a pain?"

"No, because you're strong, confident, and independent, and the world is populated by a lot of douchebags who'd feel emasculated by being with a woman as kick-arse as you." Michelle nodded her head. "But not Wyatt."

"No." A warmth rose in my chest as I thought of him. "He's genuinely happy for me when I succeed. And he's as driven as me, in his own way. I think I do a pretty good job of pushing him harder when he needs it, and he definitely steps up to tell me when I need to stop and just take a break."

"Look at you; you're all smiley and cute!" Michelle crowed. "He really is the right guy for you. You've never talked like this about anyone else."

"Whoever would have thought that the first boy you ever kissed would be the right one?" Tessa sighed, finishing her rosé.

"Well, a whole lot of religious people think it works that way," I said, quirking my mouth. "But I definitely don't fit into that category."

"Nope." Michelle pressed another, slightly sloppier kiss to my cheek. "And we wouldn't want you any other way."

"Anyway, how have you two been?" I said, turning slightly to look at my sisters' faces. "This isn't the Abby show; I want to hear about your lives!"

"Well, I did have one meeting this week that had me ready to launch Molotov cocktails," Michelle ventured with a scowl.

"I want to hear all about it," I said, leaning back into the cushions of the shabby wicker bench and enjoying the company of my sisters, the smell of the ocean, and the promise that at the end of the night, I'd be going home to Wyatt. Did life get any better than this?

Except, it didn't quite work out that way. Halfway through Tessa telling us about her serious disagreement with her publisher about the cover of her new children's book, my phone buzzed. At first, I ignored it. And then it buzzed again. And again.

"Are you going to get that?" Tessa paused in her story. "It could be important."

"It's sister time!" But I retrieved my phone just the same. "It's Wyatt."

"Well, answer it!" Michelle sounded oddly insistent.

"Fine," I said, slightly bemused. "Hey, what's up?"

"I'm down at the skate park," Wyatt sounded tense, like he was anxious about something. "And I kind of stacked it."

"Stacked it?" I repeated. "Stacked it how?"

"Stacked it trying to do a kickflip to impress some local kids," Wyatt admitted, the hint of a laugh in his voice. "Which was stupid, I know."

"Are you okay?" A thin line of panic went through me like a wire. "Did you break anything?"

"I don't think so," Wyatt assured me. "Look, I know you're out with your sisters, but do you think you three could just help me back to the house? And then you can go back to the pub, of course. I'll be fine."

"Should I call an ambulance?" I couldn't help feeling worried. "If you can't walk, then—"

"No!" Wyatt sounded alarmed at the idea. "I just need a little help. Is that okay?"

"Of course," I said, downing my rosé. "Give me a few minutes; I'll see you soon."

I ended the call, frowning at my phone.

"What happened?" Michelle asked. "Is he hurt?"

"Apparently, he managed to stack it, trying to do a kick-flip," I explained. My sisters seemed oddly interested, but I couldn't imagine why. "So, I'm just going to go and help him back to the house. You two stay here." I stood, slinging my bag over my shoulder.

"No way!" Michelle was already standing. "We should help you."

"You'll definitely need help." Tessa nodded vigorously. "I mean, he's a big dude. No way could you handle him on your own."

"I don't think I'll be carrying him," I protested. "I don't want to ruin our night."

"Aww, come on," Michelle was already making for the exit. "Don't deny us the chance to laugh at a man over thirty on the wrong side of a skateboarding accident."

"Fine." I was resigned. "Let's all enjoy the spectacle!"

My sisters were quiet as we walked the short distance from the pub to the skate park. Oddly quiet, although Tessa seemed to be texting someone, her eyebrows knitted together as her thumb moved.

"What's up with you two?" I frowned. "I'm not worried; if he's calling me and not an ambulance, he must be fine."

"We just want to make sure everything's okay," Tessa said a little too quickly.

I was starting to get suspicious. Just what was going on? Did Wyatt have some kind of surprise organised to celebrate the one-year anniversary of my online store? If so, I was very touched, but this subterfuge was unnecessary to present me with a cake and party hat. Still, they had gone to some effort, so I pretended not to notice as we turned the corner towards the skate park that looked over Brekkie Beach.

"Wyatt?" I called out, scanning the skate park for signs of a cake or confetti canon. God, I hoped there was no confetti canon. The mess was unbelievable, not to mention bad for the environment. "Where are you?"

And then, with the setting sun behind him, Wyatt appeared, skating towards me. I blinked once and then again because he was wearing…a tuxedo? He looked like something out of a music video.

"What are you…?" I shook my head as the skateboard brought him closer. Suddenly, he dropped to balance on one knee on the board. Well, that was a new trick I hadn't seen—

Tuxedo. One knee. Subterfuge. My sisters acting like they knew something I didn't. My hands flew to my mouth as the realisation hit me, just as Wyatt, tuxedo-clad and shaking slightly, came to a stop in front of me.

"You're not hurt." The words came out in a rush, addressing the least of the situation.

"Nope." Wyatt shook his head. "And I hope you'll forgive me for that little lie, but I…" He paused, looking up at me with hazel eyes. "I needed to get you here tonight. With this perfect sunset."

I could only stare at him as my heart thumped in my chest. Shit, why was I so nervous? I had always scorned those movies where the girl was a quivering mess when the guy proposed. It had always seemed so obvious to me that he was going to do it and that she'd say yes, so what was all that fuss about?

But now that I was the girl, I could see exactly why those heroines got so teary and trembling. It was all I could do to stay upright on my sensibly mid-sized heels.

"Abby Finch," Wyatt began, his voice a little hoarse. "When we first met, you told me you thought my skating was 'okay'. I'm hoping you've got a little bit more enthusiasm for this trick." With a swift movement, he flipped the board from under him so it rested across his hands, and held it up to me like an offering. Then, I saw what was hiding on the underside of the board.

A small, velvet box.

"Abby," Wyatt's voice was low. "It's been seventeen years since we first met at that park. And in all that time, I've never felt like this about anyone else. So, I'm really hoping you'll say yes when I ask you," Wyatt flicked open the box, "if you'll marry me?"

I could only stand there and gape. I was pretty sure I had forgotten how to breathe. I wasn't even looking at the box; I couldn't take my eyes from his face.

Finally, I nodded. A tiny movement. "Yes," I whispered. "Of course, it's a yes!"

"Oh, thank god for that." Wyatt leaned up to kiss me, and I was caught between crying and laughing against his mouth, my arms wrapped tightly around his neck.

"Of course, it's a yes," I said again, trailing my fingers down his cheek over the stubble he knew I liked so much. We stared at each other, smiles wide enough to break our cheeks into pieces, when I realised I had forgotten something.

"Wait, where's the ring?" I looked down at the skateboard on the ground. "Did I drop it?"

"Nope!" Wyatt opened the box again, and I could see a plain band made of clear resin. He retrieved the ring and held it up. "The only person who could choose the right ring for Abby Finch," he said, sliding it onto my finger, "is Abby Finch. So, this is just a placeholder."

I let out a breath. "How did you know I'd want to choose myself?"

"Well, I know you. And I may have had a little help." Wyatt coughed and tilted his head to one side. I followed his gaze, and there were my two sisters, beaming. Tessa was actually crying. Standing beside them was Dylan, who had his full tripod and camera arrangement set up. I hadn't noticed any of that, but I was delighted to have this memory captured forever. "They were in on the whole thing, but not when I was going to do it. Because I knew they'd tell you."

My sisters rushed over to me. "All we knew was that one night, he'd call you and pretend to be hurt," Michelle explained. "I didn't think it would be tonight!"

"And I suggested that Dylan come down to get some photos," Tessa added. "I hope that's okay!"

"More than okay." I hugged my sisters. "I guess there's no way I could have avoided you two getting involved, even in this."

"What are little sisters for?" Michelle hugged me close, ruffling my hair. "Come on, Tessa. Let's leave them to it."

"I can't believe you planned all of this," I said, still hugging the skateboard to me. "It's the cheesiest, coolest thing ever. I'm surprised you didn't have Sk8er Boi playing on a boombox."

"Oh, they tried to convince me." Wyatt shot a final look at my sisters. "But I wasn't sure I'd get a yes out of you if you couldn't stop laughing. Or retching."

"Avril Lavigne's not so bad," I said, leaning up to kiss him again. "And nothing could have stopped me from saying yes."

"Then I'm very lucky." Wyatt's lips brushed over mine. "Can I take you home now? I've got champagne, dessert; the full works for a lazy night in. If you had said no, I'd be eating it all myself."

"That sounds amazing," I said, leaning my head against his shoulder. "You've done the impossible, you know."

"What's that? Convinced you to marry me?"

"No!" I said. "You convinced me to relax. That's much harder."

"Oh, that was a serious challenge." Wyatt's lips curled into a smirk. "A frigging epic quest, with dragons and everything. But..."

"But what?"

"You're absolutely worth it, Abby Finch."

About the Author

Rita Harte is a romantic comedy author who likes to write books with big laughs and big feelings. She firmly believes that characters struggling with mental health, family drama, and painful pasts deserve a fabulous happily ever after.

Living in sometimes sunny Sydney, Rita is powered by caffeine, loud music, and the loving support of her family.

Printed in Great Britain
by Amazon